Thorns
of a
Black Rose

Also by David Craig

<u>Sooty Feathers</u>

1: Resurrection Men

Thorns of a Black Rose

David Craig

Elsewhen Press

Thorns of a Black Rose
First published in Great Britain by Elsewhen Press, 2019
An imprint of Alnpete Limited

Elsewhen Press, PO Box 757, Dartford, Kent DA2 7TQ
www.elsewhen.press
British Library Cataloguing in Publication Data.
A catalogue record for this book is available from the British Library.
ISBN 978-1-911409-45-8 Print edition
ISBN 978-1-911409-55-7 eBook edition

Designed and formatted by Elsewhen Press

To our daughter, Sophie.
Love Mum and Dad

Prologue

Karib cleaned blood from the blade, sweat running freely down his face. He had ignored the cut to his right arm during the fight but now keenly felt the stinging pain, his blood dripping onto the stone cellar floor.

His fellow assassins kept their distance, but he sensed their reserved approval. Verak, Captain of the Royal Guard, had proven himself a worthy foe.

"The girl is dead," Farata reported, walking away from the small body at the end of the cellar. Both the princess and Verak had fled down into the depths of the palace, but the Black Rose had followed.

Karib nodded. "Good." Stalking an eight-year old girl through Mask's Royal Palace was not a task he had relished, but the contract was clear: King Xarius must die, and his queen and children too.

When Verak realised there was no escape for Princess Xaria, he had given her a quick clean death, not that the Black Rose sect had intended any differently. Karib silently thanked the man for doing the deed himself.

His blade still stained with royal blood, Verak had then challenged the assassins to face him man to man, blade to blade.

Karib could have killed Verak in any number of ways, from a throwing knife to a poisoned bolt from his crossbow; duels were anathema to the sect who prized speed and efficiency over pointless contests.

But Karib had felt respect for the grizzled warrior snarling his defiance at them, and so to the surprise of his fellow assassins, he had drawn his blade and agreed.

Verak had fought well, even scoring a hit, but the master assassin had prevailed, gifting the captain with an honourable death. A peace had settled over Verak's face as he died, an odd expression of victory. Karib pulled a black rose from his pouch and left it on Verak's chest. Only those marked for death were due the rose (unless the kill was to remain unclaimed), but Karib had chosen to leave it as a mark of respect.

Farata handed Karib the dead man's sword, a slim curved blade forged from the finest Maskan iron, gold plating its hilt. "A fine trophy," Karib said, cutting free its black-leathered scabbard from Verak's belt and sheathing the sword inside. The sword had been the king's as a prince, gifted by tradition to the captain of his royal guard upon his ascension to the throne.

"Should we return upstairs?" Farata asked, eyeing the dark corridor behind them. She had left a black-petalled rose on the princess' body.

"Yes." But there was no hurry. The king had been betrayed absolutely, Hrekist fanatics and merchant-bought mercenaries were rampaging through the palace with abandon. Karib had hoped that duelling Verak would restore some honour to the contract, but his reservations remained unchanged. And unvoiced, lest they reach the Grandmaster's ears.

Chapter One

Five Years Later

Only the strong endured on Mask's ancient streets. The strong or the fast. People had lived on the banks of the River Tyre for uncounted years, catching fish and baking bricks from the plentiful red mud. Enough bricks to build a city; one that had endured for three millennia. The sun had risen and set over Mask a million times, baking it hard and pitiless.

A scrawny half-starved thirteen-year old, Tamira knew she'd never be strong, so she'd better be fast if she wanted to survive in a city where she had no home, no family.

Scrounging for food occupied most of her time, or stealing goods to sell for coin to buy it. Her usual fence was away from his shop, leaving her with a useless ivory trinket she couldn't eat. She considered finding another fence to sell it to, but decided to wait until tomorrow. Tasim cheated her, but not enough to drive her to a rival, one who might sell *her* to a slaver rather than buy her stolen goods.

Meanwhile, that still left Tamira the problem of breaking her fast while absent the coin to do so. She had found a vendor cooking meat over hot coals, selling it from his stall in a Merchant Quarter souk, but he didn't look the charitable sort.

The meat vendor haggled with every customer but always with one eye on his stall. Tamira too had watched the stall all morning, waiting in vain for the vendor's attention to wander. She'd eaten a scrap of bread the day before and nothing since, hunger cramping her belly and threatening to overcome her reason.

The sight and smell of roasted mutton taunted her, but the streets of Mask were a hard teacher, and she'd had years to learn their lessons. Hunger might goad her to recklessness, but a careless thief was a maimed or dead thief, so she bided her time. She was only thirteen, but that wouldn't save her from losing a hand. If she was lucky. More likely she would be given to the priests of Hrek to be sacrificed on the altar, or sent to the arena. She was too small to give a gladiator any sport, but the crowd would happily watch her being torn apart by wild beasts.

Flies were also drawn to the stall, lured by the smell of roasting meat and from nearby camel dung, ignored by the vendor.

Tamira finally saw her chance and took it. The vendor stood nose to nose with a customer, desperate for one last sale. Already the souks were quietening as the late morning sun drove merchants and citizens indoors. Strips of brightly coloured cloth hung from the buildings to give some shade, but summer wasn't quite done, and few cared to endure a Maskan midday.

Tamira affected a casual demeanour as she approached the stall, her callused bare feet letting her tolerate the sun-baked ground. The strips of meat had been spitted all morning, dried out and congealed with grease. Her mouth watered at the sight of them, and a furtive glance assured her that the haggling continued. The vendor was in his middle years, lean with deep lines creasing his face. Heat from the sun and hot coals had left his face slick with sweat.

Tamira continued her approach, hoping the haggling might turn violent. The other pedestrians would be too distracted by the impromptu entertainment to spot her larceny, and by the time the vendor noticed his meat was gone, Tamira would be too.

Abruptly the would-be customer threw his hands up in disgust and walked off. But Tamira had come too close, was too hungry, to give up now. She snatched a few strips of hot skewered mutton and dropped them into her kalasiris's sewn pocket, ignoring her stinging fingers.

"Thief!"

She flew past the first half-dozen people, relying on them being too surprised to even attempt to catch her. Faces turned, but she passed them before they could decide whether to involve themselves or not. Flight through the narrow souks was always a fraught affair, more than one thief being caught due to congestion.

Being small and lithe, Tamira used the crowd to her advantage. She ducked under arms and wriggled between the bodies around her. A tall man spread his arms and legs in a bid to grab her; she dived between his legs, deftly regained her feet and kept running. Meant for someone younger, Tamira's ragged grey kalasiris – a sheathed linen dress – hugged her tightly and ended just above her knees. She had slit the front and back to ensure it didn't impede her legs when running.

Shouts and curses told her the vendor was trying to bully his way through the crowd. He couldn't catch up, but his repeated appeals for someone to grab her might soon be answered.

She knew the red streets of Mask well, especially the Poor Quarter where she lived, and here in the Merchant Quarter where she usually stole. Every souk in the Merchant Quarter led to Marat Square, the bazaar from where most of Mask's trade was conducted. The market stalls and even most of the shops might close for a few hours around midday, but another form of trade continued inside the surrounding guild and temple banks. Promises scribbled on parchment moved the wealth of kingdoms around the world, and only the sun falling from the sky would halt the merchant princes' pursuit of power and fortune.

Curtained palanquins sat on the ground outside a pillared bank, awaiting the return of their masters. The bearer-slaves were left to endure the sun, but the merchant princes inside would be fanned and refreshed with fruit drinks and teh.

She ran, passing snake charmers and their defanged pets, her flight agitating a troop of leashed baboons who screamed and pointed at her. A Kavari tribesman exited a former temple now owned by the Banking Guild, marked by his distinctive blue djellaba robe and coal-black skin. He watched her run and said something to his entourage. A spike of fear stabbed Tamira as two of his men ran towards her.

Defiance pushed her panic aside. The fierce Kavari might call the desert home, but this city was hers and its heights her domain. She reached a single-floored building and leapt onto its window ledge and jumped, catching hold of the roof.

Years of such desperate escapades had strengthened her muscles and allowed her to pull herself up with little effort.

She rolled onto the flat stone roof and resumed her run, breathing hard but steadily. Millennia of growth had left Mask a crowded city of flat-roofed buildings crammed together and often only separated by narrow, winding streets.

City guards, rival thieves and slaver gangs had chased her across the rooftops of Mask for years, none catching her. She didn't intend for the two Kavari to, either. She crossed from building to building, leaping short gaps and using cracks in the brickwork or mortar to climb whenever the buildings rose higher. Grazed hands, feet and limbs were a small price to pay for freedom.

Her escape route took her east towards the river, a route she had used many times before. She risked a look behind and was relieved to see the two Kavari had given up. Her flight across the rooftops – running, jumping, climbing – beneath the blazing sun had left her drenched in sweat from head to toe, a fact she became aware of as fear and exhilaration drained away.

She stood, trying to catch her breath while watching for any sign of pursuit. No one appeared. Tamira dropped down into an alley and continued at a slower pace, the harbour her destination. There was an anonymity there she liked; a changing sea of people arriving or leaving the city, and hardened dockworkers loading and unloading ships from all over the world. No one paid her any mind. A series of stone quays jutted out from the promenade, worn smooth by the passage of millennia.

Sometimes she thought of sneaking onto a ship, but something always stopped her. Mask was her home, all she knew. She found a shaded spot in the arcade of a derelict building and squatted down. Satisfied that no one was watching her, she pulled out her purloined meat and took a bite, enjoying the luxury of being able to eat slowly without fear of another trying to seize it. In a different life she would have tossed it to a dog; now she savoured the gristly scraps.

Time passed, and Tamira was content to sit in the shade. She watched the dock workers cease their labours, seeking respite from the midday heat. Shouts and laughter drifted across the harbour as the men ate a meal of dates, fetching water from a nearby well. After a while, the sun began its slow decline, and the dock workers resumed unloading cargo from a large galley.

Tamira studied the vessel, its foreign origin obvious. It was built from a wood darker than the cedars used to build ships in most of the continent of Araka, and its timbers were bound together by nails. Arakan ships used shorter planks that were hooked together and bound tight with rope.

She decided to take a closer look and felt her skin prickle as she left the shade. A customs official was inspecting the cargo being offloaded, to determine what tax to levy. A dozen soldiers escorted him, an unusually high number. They wore hardened leather jerkins and linen shendyt skirts, light glinting off their iron pot-helms. Every man carried a spear and shield. Their cold stares were a silent challenge to the sailors, one wisely not accepted.

Closer now, Tamira got a better view of the galley's crew, their pale skins identifying them as men from the northern continent of Keram. That explained the mutual distrust between the Maskan soldiers and the ship's crew. And why so many of the crew looked like mercenaries rather than sailors. Keramese ships sailing the River Tyre were often raided by river pirates and could expect no aid from Mask's navy.

Mask had been ruled by an uneasy alliance of the Cult of Hrek and the Merchant Council for the past five years, ever since they murdered the king. The priests were suspicious of foreign influences, and the merchant princes preferred their own ships to conduct Mask's trade. Tamira suspected they didn't ban foreign traders for fear of their own ships being banned in retaliation, but they did turn a blind eye to river pirates raiding Keramese ships travelling with insufficient protection.

Despite the risks, pale-skinned traders still crossed the narrow Darish sea separating the north and south continents of Keram and Araka, hiring mercenaries to guard their ships as they navigated the River Tyre to the city of Mask. That north-flowing river, stretching from the edge of the Kavari Desert to the Darish Sea, made Mask the trading hub of northern Araka. Vast caravans brought goods from all over Araka – salt, slaves, ivory, gold and gems – wealth enough to tempt merchants from their cold, wet northern lands to risk lives and ships.

Salt water, wild winds and the harsh sun had roughened the sailors, leaving many with skins not much lighter than her own dusky complexion. She was fascinated by the wildly differing colours of hair among them, a mix of browns, blacks, reds and yellows. Her own hair was a rich dark brown that she hacked short with a knife.

The Keramese wore long sleeveless tunics that ran down to their knees; Maskan men typically wore either a shendyt along with a short tunic, or the long, loose djellaba robe favoured by the Kavari.

Tamira loitered around the docks on the lookout for opportunity, but tension between the mercenaries and soldiers convinced her to keep her hands to herself. Instead, she sat on the edge of the promenade and gazed out across the river. Small papyrus boats were visible in the distance, fishermen casting their nets into the river.

Chapter Two

The wind blew the sail taut as the small ship fought against the river's north-flowing current. Reddish-pink towers were visible in the distance as they approached the last bend in the river.

Shukara leaned against the railing, staying out of the way of the sailors as they followed their captain's bellowed instructions. For the past day they had stayed out of her way too, cowed by her response to a crewman's unwanted drunken advances. She was thankful the man had no relatives among the crew, lest family loyalty compel them to suicidal retaliation.

The sun beat down on her, sweat staining the cheap cotton of her robe. Her journey across the continent had been an eventful one, leaving her with little more than the djellaba she wore, four rubies, a little coin, and whatever reagents remained in her pouch. And her wytchwood stave, of course, hidden under her robe.

Shukara had found the voyage a novelty after two years of jungles, deserts, savanna and mountains. Sailing the Darish Sea had been exhilarating, even if the small ship was a coast-hugger. One clear morning she had even spied the southern coast of Keram peeking over the horizon. *I'll visit there, some day. When my business is done.*

Sailing the Tyre, on the other hand, had been two days of tedium. Hard-faced fishermen had watched their passage suspiciously but otherwise ignored them. Other ships had been less lucky. They had sailed past the skeleton of a vessel lying on a mudbank, its carcass picked clean. A crewman identified it as Keramese by its construction, telling her its owner had probably hired too few mercenaries to protect it. But they were safe, he had assured her; the pirates mostly left Arakan vessels alone. That night the crew had learned she was more than capable of ensuring her own safety.

The ship rounded the bend, giving Shukara her first proper

look at the Red City, bloody beating heart of the Maskan Theocracy. Soaring towers and crammed-together flat-roofed buildings rose up from the river bank, almost uniformly the colour of salmon flesh. An exception loomed ominously over the heart of the city; the black-stoned pyramidal High Temple of Hrek.

Slaves had died in uncountable numbers three thousand years earlier quarrying the dense black rock and transporting it here, and yet more in building the temple. Legend whispered that the pyramid was built over the entrance to the Underworld, or that Hrek's immortal body slumbered within the catacombs below. Shukara would be happy to never learn the truth of such legends. The black rock was a jarring reminder of home and happier times.

A small boat carried the harbour pilot to the ship, the captain yielding him the wheel. Shukara returned her attention to Mask as the pilot guided the ship into harbour. Four ships of varying size were currently docked, but there was room for more.

The ship reached the quay and was quickly tied up. A fussy-looking customs official waited to check any cargo being offloaded. There was none – the captain carried only passengers to Mask and would return to Arrioch with salt.

*

Tamira watched a second vessel glide into the harbour and moor at a quay. This one was lithe and delicate, made from cedarwood, and clearly Arakan. The banner flying from its mainmast identified its home port as Arrioch, a coastal town to the west. Arrioch's relations with Mask were cordial, so it had little to fear from the river pirates; the pirates' slim, fast raiding boats could evade Mask's naval triremes, but their villages couldn't, so they rarely risked the Merchant Council's wrath.

A woman walked off the boat with a straight-backed confidence that caught Tamira's eye, standing almost a head taller than most women. Aged maybe twenty-five years, she walked with the regal assuredness of a queen swathed in syek – a rare and costly southern material that breathed like linen and shone like silk – but in truth her brown djellaba was cheap cotton. It hung loose from her slim figure, the torn and ragged hem ending just above her ankles.

Her skin was darkest brown – almost black as ebony – suggesting she came from a land to the south. Tamira had seen many southern travellers in Mask over the years, but few quite as dark. Except the Kavari, of course, and the woman was not of that distinctive tribe. She had angular features, striking rather than pretty, emphasised by a sharp nose and cheekbones, with dark eyes that radiated will and purpose. Long black hair hung loose past her shoulders.

She held herself erect, long legs giving her a fast pace. A pouch hung off her shoulder, made from a tough-looking black leather. Tamira wondered from what beast's hide it had been fashioned, but she was more curious about its contents.

Intrigued, Tamira followed the woman from a distance. The woman's pace slowed, hinting that she was perhaps unsure of her destination. She spoke briefly with a fruit merchant whose hand motions suggested he was giving directions. She bought an orange, the sight of which re-awoke Tamira's hunger. The meat had taken the edge off her appetite, but hadn't sated it. Tamira noted the woman paid with a coin removed from the hood hanging down her back. What then did the pouch contain?

The woman walked further into the Merchant Quarter towards Marat Square, and Tamira followed.

*

Shukara left the ship, ignoring furtive looks from the crew and her fellow passengers. Some might consider reporting her to the customs official, but they would also fear her response. All the same, it would be unwise to linger.

I'm finally here. But what to do first? Turning coin into rubies had been a weight-efficient means of carrying it at the start of the expedition, but now she must sell one. She also needed to replenish her reagents, permit herself the luxury of new clothes, find an inn, visit a bathhouse, and sate her hunger.

The bath and meal tempted her the most, but prudence

prodded her to visit an apothecary first, to gauge how much refilling her pouch would cost her. The commonest reagents in one land might be rare this far north. She likely had enough reagents to last her, but it would be some time before she next visited a city as famed for trade as Mask. *I can stink and starve for a little longer.*

A ragged young girl sat on the quay, probably a beggar. Her brown hair was a mess, dirty and cut short with no regard for appearance. Bare arms and legs protruded from a torn, filthy kalasiris dress so short it was almost a tunic, sleeveless and ending above her knees. Her brown limbs were toned but otherwise thin and dirt-stained, her face gaunt. Her eyes were sharp, focusing on Shukara's distinctive pouch. It often drew eyes, some asking where the leather came from. She knew that most would not have believed the answer.

The city wall separated the harbour from the rest of the Merchant Quarter, likely a long-ago precaution against invasion from the river. Shukara passed through a tall arched gate, seeking the famed bazaar. The wall joined a four-towered kasbah that commanded a clear view of the harbour. It had no doubt garrisoned soldiers in times of war. Now it looked weather-worn and abandoned.

Shukara approached a fruit vendor. "Good day. Where is the main bazaar from here?"

Her height took the vendor by surprise, a common occurrence. Some men shorter than her took it as a slight. "Ah, I can direct you to Marat Square..."

"My thanks," she said as he told her the route. She bought an orange, pulling a coin from her hood in payment.

He nodded. "My honour to help." Her diction and manner were at odds with her dress, likely confusing him as to her status. Like most he erred on the side of caution. Better to treat a beggar like a noble than a noble like a beggar.

Shukara walked to the end of the street and turned into a narrow souk. An unfortunate consequence of so many people crammed together was sanitation, or the lack thereof. There was some provision for the disposal of human waste, but it was insufficient. Smells from piles of shit and pools of stagnant urine dogged her through the souk, the waste running sluggishly down a sewage trench towards the river.

Some women wore a djellaba like her, but most that she saw wore the long, tight linen kalasiris, a garment she had first seen in Arrioch. The richer the garment, the longer its length, she noted. Some of the girls and younger women favoured a shendyt skirt and tunic.

She almost fell to the ground as her pouch strap was yanked from her shoulder, pulled free before she could react. Outrage replaced shock as she saw the girl from the harbour sprint down the street with her pouch in hand.

"Thief! Stop her!" Shukara commanded the startled onlookers as she pursued the wretched girl, confident her longer legs would compensate for the thief's head start.

She briefly considered reaching under her robe for her stave but feared that by the time she did so, the thief would be out of sight. To say nothing of how the crowd might react. Shukara tried to decrease the distance between them, but the girl was fast and nimble, barely slowing to dodge past obstacles. The city guards were annoyingly absent.

Bitter frustration coursed through Shukara on seeing the girl scramble up a wall and resume her flight across the rooftops. She wouldn't catch her. Not giving up, she kicked off her sandals and followed the thief up the wall, scraping her feet and hands as she did so. Shukara reached under her robe and held the stave hidden there, whispering. *Done.*

The girl leapt onto an adjacent roof with a grace Shukara would have applauded in other circumstances, disappearing from sight.

Her rubies were sown into her robe, thankfully, but the pouch contained her reagents, many she would need. Any apothecary worth their salt should stock much of what she had lost, but a few items were rare this far north, and others might be. A bitter laugh bubbled up inside her. Two years of travel, of hardship and loss, and her quest might fail because of a barely adolescent thief.

Less than an hour in this wretched city and already I've been robbed. She stopped, leaning against a wall to catch her breath, the theft a sore blow to her pride. Shukara bit into her orange, eyes narrowed as she considered how to proceed. Any thoughts of visiting an inn for a meal and lodgings were banished, her first thought being to hunt down the thief and recover her pouch. *In a city this size, with more thieves and beggars than rats? At the least I would need to be in the same area, and I don't even know where to begin.*

No. Better to see what reagents might be replaced from the local apothecaries. She recalled the directions given by the fruit-seller and followed them towards Marat Square, juice from the orange slaking her thirst.

Even in distant Tokombu, her home far to the south, Mask was famous as one of the hubs of the world's trade. Marat Square was where most of Mask's trade was conducted, and Shukara was curious to see it.

The bazaar was crowded, mostly native Maskans mingling with dark-skinned merchants from southern Araka, and pale travellers from Keram. It was her first encounter with people from that northern continent, and she studied them curiously. Most were olive-skinned, not much paler than the Maskans, and likely hailing from Daria whose city-states ruled most of southern Keram's coastline on the Darish Sea.

Others were red, their faces and exposed skin cooked crimson by an unforgiving sun. Shukara saw flashes of almost-white skin beneath clothing and guessed them to be from northern Keram. Those near-mythical lands were said to be rain-soaked almost every day and near-sunless for a quarter of every year. Some scrolls in Tokombu claimed those lands were so cold in winter that rivers and lakes turned to ice, and rain fell frozen from the sky.

Judging by the expressions of misery on their roasted, peeling faces, those visitors would be glad to return to their cold, drowned, sunless homeland.

Stalls on the edge of the square relied on the buildings for shade, and strips of red and white cloth mounted on poles provided some respite for the stalls clustered in the centre. The wealthier merchants sold their wares from owned or rented shops in the buildings surrounding the square.

Shukara wandered the bazaar, ignoring hawkers thrusting their wares at her. Goods from all over the world were for sale: salt from Khespha Province a few day's sail to the south; gold, gems and ivory from the southern kingdoms; carpets and blue-dyed djellabas sewn by Kavari tribeswomen; rice, teh, silk and spices from the east; olive oil, pottery and wine from Daria; and small bronze statues and plaques from the Munin Kingdom to the south-west, a land Shukara had passed through on her trek north.

Some merchants had brought no goods, sitting instead in the shade while their clerks took orders for Keramese lumber or Arakan cedar. Others bought or sold quarried stone, wares too large to bring to the bazaar.

Agents bartered with mercenaries to man ships or escort caravans preparing to leave Mask. A deserted slave block lay to the eastern edge of the bazaar, its cages empty today.

Once her curiosity was satisfied, Shukara spent her time searching the shops on the edge of the square, knowing no apothecary would sell from a stall and risk direct sunlight ruining their stock.

Her hopes were initially raised on finding a large apothecary shop that promised quality reagents. Unfortunately, the shop's other chief virtue was quantity rather than variety, with it offering only the commonest reagents.

"Firethorn seeds?" The shopkeeper shook his head. "Not here."

Shukara held up a coin. "Where might I find a shop that does stock them?"

Indecision briefly warred on the man's face, but he decided to take the coin and name a competitor. "Zhalo ban Nyeb has a small shop in a nearby souk. He *may* have what you want."

Shukara listened to his directions and left the shop. Everything was for sale, it seemed. Except what she required.

She entered the narrow souk, finding a small apothecary shop next to an emporium of spices. The proprietor, presumably Zhalo ban Nyeb, shook his head. "I'm afraid I have little of what you seek, mistress."

Frustration nipped Shukara. She was unsurprised at the lack of firethorn seeds, but much of what else she required were not uncommon in this part of Araka. "I've found the apothecaries in this city to be a disappointment."

The merchant glanced around, lowering his voice. "Some of what you seek has only one use, and such ... ability is forbidden by the priests. You know of them, yes, the Cult of Hrek? Only those affiliated with them may practice it, and they provide the reagents." He shrugged. "As such, there is no need for me or my competitors to stock reagents with no other use. No need, but much risk."

Shukara nodded, understanding now that she would find little of what she needed in Mask's apothecaries. She knew of one individual who had exactly what she needed. "I was robbed by a girl near the harbour. Aged between twelve and fifteen, thin, dressed poorly. Nimble. Where can such thieves be found?"

"When they're not plaguing honest citizens? You can find no shortage of them in the Poor Quarter, may Hrek's wrath fall upon it. But don't go there. Thieves and pickpockets are the least of the dangers in there, especially for a woman alone. Cutthroats haunt the alleys, gangs rob anyone foolish enough to enter their territory, and it is not unknown for them to sell their victims to slavers. Those they do not kill."

Shukara accepted his warning without comment. She had faced worse dangers than a city's dregs.

Chapter Three

He had warned them, pointing to the dark brown clouds that heralded its coming. They had squinted up at those distant clouds, small against the endless blue sky, and nodded blithely at him like fools. That blue sky was now gone.

Only when Jassan had pointed to the horizon a short time later, to that approaching mile-high wall of sand and dust had they truly understood. And by then it was almost too late. He had warned them of this back in the Pashbur Caravanserai, and they had laughed as if he had been making a joke. As if he were inventing perils to drive up his price.

No one was laughing now. One of the merchants struggled to wrap the loose end of his shesh around his lower face but succeeded only in unravelling the whole scarf from his head, the wind snatching it away. Jassan shouted for the man to come to him, but his words were lost to the storm. The last he saw of Ferres ban Favel, he was staggering blindly in the wrong direction, towards the desert.

Jassan's own shesh covered his head and lower face, leaving only his eyes partly exposed. The caravan was a small one, numbering only two trains of sixteen camels, owned by three merchants who thought to make their fortune buying goods transported from Mask to Pashbur, and selling them in the outlying towns and villages.

Not a bad notion. Except they had never travelled the desert before. They had hired Jassan to guide them, not being foolish enough to think they could survive even twenty days in the desert without a Kavari ranger. But they hadn't truly heeded his words.

They had thought the hot dry winds that occasionally scoured Pashbur were a storm; now they knew a *true* sandstorm. The sand they had complained of filling their sandals and getting into their clothing and food had now been whipped up into a tempest of countless tiny razors that would flay exposed flesh bloody.

One of the other merchants had taken shelter in his tent, relying on the leather hide to protect him, which it would, but it might also see him buried alive. Jassan was fortunate enough to have experienced few storms as bad as this one. It might last for hours or even days.

The third merchant, Subed ban someone-or-other, was the junior partner in this venture, a former camel puller who had made a living carrying salt from the outlying salt mines to Pashbur, mistaking that arid land as desert. The merchants had decided to cut expenses by hiring only one camel puller and letting Subed handle the second file.

He at least might survive, having copied the camel puller Sulen's actions in using a camel as cover. The storm worsened, the air a choking sea of sand and dust. Their camels had been made for the desert, able to travel for days without water, protected by coarse hair and with nostrils that closed when necessary. Men were not.

Jassan was a Kavari ranger, a son of the desert that had forged and named his exiled people, but he knew who the true desert survivors were. The camels had all fallen to their knees, content to endure the storm. Jassan huddled next to one, letting its bulk shield him from the scouring sand and dust.

The sky was gone. Even the air around him was thick with dust and sand, the land itself being remade by the storm. They were left with no choice but to endure and pray it died before they did. Time passed, and consciousness slipped away.

He was jolted back to wakefulness as the camel shook off a coat of sand and stood on its long bony legs with a deep-throated grumble.

The air was still gritty, and he could see nothing but blackness until he looked up. Stars glittered overhead, an endless sea of them, the storm having endured long past sunset. Jassan pulled off his shesh, shaking free the sand before winding the long blue scarf back around his head once more, the loose end lying on his shoulder.

He got up, or tried to, looking down to find himself buried up to his waist. He tried again, this time freeing himself and shaking off the sand covering his blue djellaba. His throat felt cracked and sore, so he pulled free a water skin and eased his thirst, disciplined enough to take no more than a single mouthful.

His usual expeditions saw him cross the entirety of the desert with caravans numbering camels by the thousand, from Pashbur south to the kingdoms of gold and ivory, of jungles, bush and savannah. Ninety days there and ninety days back. He had not survived those journeys by assuming fresh water was within easy distance. Like all rangers, he knew where the oases and hidden wells were on the Kavari Caravan Route, but they could dry up, be buried by storms or seized by hostile clans.

Subed and Sulen had survived, at least, two silhouettes visible in the light of two moons. "Where are the others?" Subed asked hoarsely.

Dead. Buried with their dreams, ambition and pride. "I'll look for them. Help Sulen with the camels and set up camp." The storm had lasted hours, but Jassan had no idea how far off dawn was. It was too dark to check the camels for wounds or chafing, but they needed to be fed.

"Start a fire," Jassan advised. "If anyone else survived, it will help them find us."

"There's no dung," Sulen complained.

"Find something else or wait until the camels start shitting again," he called back.

The storm had hit shortly after they had stopped for the day and set up camp, burying their tents. Worse, most of their supplies had been unloaded from the camels and were likewise lost.

Jassan looked for any sign of Ahmed, the second merchant. He hoped Ahmed had realised that sand was piling up against the tent, and gotten free, but there was no sign of him. The weight of the falling sand had caused dunes to slide, and he was very likely buried.

Ferres, the merchant Jassan had last seen staggering blindly away from the caravan, was surely lost, unless a kind-hearted god had taken pity on him. Jassan doubted there were many kindly gods, and certainly none to be found in the Kavari Desert.

"Where are the others?" Subed asked as Jassan joined them

by the small fire. Sulen ban Lat gave him a knowing look as he handed him a plate of dates. He was a thin man with a straggly beard, Maskan, but almost as experienced in the desert as anyone Kavari-born.

"I couldn't find them," Jassan said. "Ahmed is buried somewhere beneath us. When I last saw Ferres he was heading in the wrong direction. I'll look again at dawn, but at best we'll find his body."

"You're going to do nothing now?" Subed asked angrily.

"I'll look again at dawn," Jassan repeated, giving Subed a warning look. "If you remember what I told you back in Pashbur, the desert is no place to go out alone in at night." He left it unspoken that had they heeded his words back in Pashbur, the two missing men might be sitting at the fire with them.

Subed lowered his head. Jassan wondered when it would occur to the merchant that the storm had ruined him. Their goods had all been sold, the satchels containing their profits having been left next to the tents. The desert consumed gold as greedily as it did travellers. *There goes the last half of my payment for this trip.* He would get something if the camels were sold back in Pashbur, but he would still need to find another contract quickly upon his return.

Sleep eluded Jassan, so he lay on his back and watched the stars glittering overhead, slowly wheeling around the world. Both moons burned silver, one full, the larger a crescent. The stars faded as the sky lightened, and the moons fled the rising sun.

Dawn brought no better news. Of Ahmed there was no sign, nor even any point of reference as to where they might dig for the tent that was now his tomb. The storm had transformed the land.

Jassan left Sulen and Subed to ready the camels while he searched for any sign of Ferres, the orange glow on the horizon giving him a frame of reference as to the direction Ferres had taken. If there were any bandits in the area, doubtless they were still recovering from the storm. But he still strapped on his sword and secured his recurve bow on his back. A quiver of black-feathered arrows hung from his right hip.

Shifting dunes of sand stretched out before him, utterly changed from the day before. Four curled sticks grew together from the sand ahead, but as he drew closer he realised that they weren't sticks at all.

Jassan knelt, piling sand around the desiccated brown fingers, finishing what the desert had started. He considered leaving a stone as marker but decided otherwise. Even if he found one, the desert would soon consume it.

He rejoined the other two. Subed never asked, and Jassan never said.

"How far are we from Pashbur?" Subed asked.

"Three days, but we've barely enough water for two, even rationing what's left." Sulen said.

A small voice in a dark corner of Jassan's mind whispered that, if Subed were dead, there might just be enough for him and Sulen to reach Pashbur. He ignored it; he killed only when necessary, and cheating the Kavari Desert of victims was a matter of pride with him.

Jassan considered his knowledge of this area. If he died only a day from Pashbur, his ancestors would never let him live it down. "There's an oasis maybe two days to the north," he said slowly. "But going there will delay our return to Pashbur by a day, maybe two."

Sulen managed a smile. "Better an extra day or two than never at all."

Subed just shrugged. He'd lost his partners and his money on this trip, maybe he figured an extra day or two as no great loss.

Sulen and Subed each led a train of sixteen camels northward, following Jassan. Midday was still hours away but already the sun beat fiercely down on them, the air itself rippling in the distance, taunting them with visions of water that wasn't there.

Chapter Four

Tamira snuck over the inner wall separating the Merchant and Poor Quarters. A basalt pyramid towered over all other buildings in the distant Old Quarter, the dread High Temple of Hrek. Smaller temples were scattered across the city, but it was from the pyramid that the priests of the Cult of Hrek ruled. The Cult and the Merchant Council officially co-ruled the city as equal partners, but the Cult dominated, tolerating the Merchant Council only for the wealth it created. One word from the Archpriest would see the merchant princes and their families seized, bodies for the twice-daily sacrifice to Hrek.

The merchants had the money to hire mercenaries to fight, of course, but a bloody civil war would ensue. The priests and their fanatics were willing to die for their dark, bloodthirsty god; the merchants were less willing to die for gold, and so their uneasy alliance had lasted.

Other gods had once been openly worshipped in Mask, but the Cult had bled their influence over the centuries. The fall of the monarchy five years past had seen the few remaining non-Hrek temples conveniently destroyed in the chaos.

Tamira turned, the vast circular Mask Arena rising to the south. Men and women died there, too, sacrifices to gold and entertainment to placate the masses. Most of the year it was gladiators, slaves, criminals and beasts who turned its red sands redder still, but once a year it hosted the Sacrifice, a ten-day long orgy of death devoted to Hrek.

Years of running had strengthened Tamira's lungs, leaving her tired but not overly so. Cognisant of the climb that was still before her, she slowed her pace to give her muscles time to recover. She was pleased that it took little time for her heart and breathing to slow to normal. In years past she would have been near exhaustion after such a run.

Tamira jumped from the wall onto the highest building within reach. Half of the Poor Quarter had spilled over the city walls as the population grew, but this was the oldest part of that quarter, full of crumbling slums packed tightly together.

A tiny stab of guilt pricked her as she remembered the woman who owned the pouch hanging off her shoulder, but guilt was a luxury she rarely indulged. It implied she had choice.

Tamira used the roofs where possible, treating them as a private highway to avoid the myriad dangers waiting below. Shadowy movements registered on her periphery as footpads skulked in dark corners and feral gangs roamed territory paid for in blood.

A scream echoed out, falling abruptly silent. Life expectancy in the Poor Quarter was not high, perhaps two decades. Almost all the street children Tamira had run with in her early days as a thief were gone, most dead, some simply vanished. Others had taken their place, though Tamira knew better than to get too close to them. In time, they too would fall foul of the guards, die from disease, be taken by slavers, or simply be in the wrong place at the wrong time.

She came to a halt atop a house hidden in the shade of a two-storey building, curiosity winning out over prudence. Confident that no one could see her, she sat down and removed the stolen pouch from her shoulder. She ran her hand across it, the leather rough and almost rocky.

A thrill shivered through her as shaking hands fumbled to open the pouch, untying the flap and flipping it open. Her imagination ran riot at the thought of what she might find within – gold, precious stones? Lightheaded at the thought, she carefully emptied the pouch, small pouches, glass vials and tiny clay bottles spilling onto the roof. Those too she examined.

Any dreams she had of the pouch's contents offering an escape from the streets withered as she found herself staring at dried plant leaves, seeds, herbs and other assorted reagents, many desiccated. She picked up some large black seeds that were as hard as stone and stank like bad eggs. Disappointment drove her to hurl them over the side of the roof.

Some of the leaves had the look and scent of lotus, even if

they were green, red and black rather than blue. Perhaps they had the same intoxicating effect? Tamira sorted through the spilled reagents, discarding those that looked worthless. The rest she placed back in the pouch. If they were lotus, she might still make some coin. But selling illicit lotus was a dangerous business and not something to be undertaken lightly. The city levied a heavy tax on lotus, so some smuggled it into Mask. Trying to sell it ran the risk of falling foul of either the guards or the smugglers, the latter dealing savagely with competition.

Sunset was still several hours away, and the pouch's disappointing contents decided Tamira. Had it contained valuables, she would have made straight for her home – if a crumbling ruin could be called such – and hidden it. But she had neither coin nor food and was resolved to find some before dusk. At least the pouch would be useful for holding whatever she could scavenge.

*

Shukara exercised caution as she walked through the Poor Quarter, alert for danger. Like the Merchant Quarter, the demand for space in the cramped city meant that most of the buildings were crammed together and expanded upwards a few storeys. There the similarities ended. The structures had been built in a similar fashion, but where the Merchant Quarter homes and shops were well-maintained, here they had been left to crumble.

She passed a building that looked like a shabbier twin of many she had seen in the wealthier part of the city – flat-roofed and built from bricks of red mud and water – but where such a building would house a single family of moderate wealth in the Merchant Quarter, here whole families occupied a single room.

The riads she had seen earlier – two-to-four storey houses or palaces built around a courtyard that were favoured by Mask's wealthier citizens – were absent this part of the city.

Flies swarmed the ragged collectors who shovelled up dung filling the narrow streets, some carrying wooden buckets, the more fortunate pushing small carts. Despite the coin to be made selling it to farmers for fertiliser, the sheer volume of inhabitants ensured that the streets would never be cleared. The streets nearest the Merchant Quarter had the same sewage trenches dug into the sides of the street, but here they had clogged up long ago. The outlying streets lacked even this token attempt to clear the waste.

An enterprising crowd of children roamed the streets, entreating any who needed to urinate to do so in their buckets. Tanners would buy it to soften hides before tanning them into leather, or dyers to seal colours into fabric. Failing that, it would bleach fabrics and remove stains.

Shukara never slowed her pace, scowling to see off any who thought to accost her. Beggars sat disconsolately, those too feeble to reach the wealthier parts of the city to elicit pity from the rich. Many were children, missing limbs or otherwise deformed. A merchant's child might be apprenticed into a trade or dowered into a good marriage, but a beggar's only means of improving their offspring's prospects was to remove an arm, leg or eye to garner coin through pity.

Thieves, too, lived here, watching for opportunity, one having already taught Shukara a hard lesson near the docks. She hunted that thief, and not only with her eyes. But she couldn't sense the girl or, more accurately, what she had taken.

Other denizens were less industrious, despair having driven them to alcohol or lotus. Those unfortunates lay slumped in the shade, inebriated. Shukara doubted they were concerned about thieves, anything they owned of value having already been traded for intoxicants. If they lingered past dusk, the gangs might seize them and sell them to slavers. The most intoxicated might awaken tomorrow chained to an oar or bound for an outlying quarry. Shukara doubted the army, or gladiator schools would bother with such dregs.

Some of the winding narrow streets boasted souks of their own, ramshackle markets offering scraps of food, lotus and alcohol. Other buildings operated as taverns and brothels, darkened holes she knew better than to venture near.

Shukara felt something, a hint of what she sought. She followed her sense of it, the trail leading deeper into the Poor Quarter.

*

Rat Square was a poor distant cousin to Marat Square. The latter was a conduit for much of the world's trade; the former sold stolen goods, cheap wine and lotus. No one even knew what the ancient market's real name was. 'Rat Square' had just stuck.

Tamira slaked her thirst with water from the well, thereafter joining a small group of street children like herself. Locals visiting the market to buy food or sell their wares gave the crowd of hard-eyed feral youngsters a wide berth. The youngest was aged maybe six, the oldest was a year or two older than Tamira.

She knew most of them by sight and was acquainted with at least half of them. In her early days on the street she had befriended a small gang of child-thieves, clinging to them and learning their ways. That gang was long gone, the few survivors having joined the adult gangs that terrorised the Poor Quarter and turned their knives on any who defied them.

By the time her friends had died or moved on, Tamira had learned enough to survive on her own. She refrained from seeking out another gang, trading companionship for safety. Small gangs that proved too successful soon found themselves crushed by those larger, and if loneliness was the price she must pay to survive, so be it.

But that didn't mean she always worked alone. Her reputation as a runner and climber was hard-earned among the juvenile thieves of the Poor Quarter, and on occasion she joined her peers for jobs too big for a single thief.

"Tamira," Laya said in greeting. She was a couple of years younger than Tamira, a gaunt girl with long, stringy black hair and a bow-legged gait. Her long nimble fingers and steady nerve made her an excellent thief, but a lifetime of poor food had left her legs malformed. One day Laya would be caught cutting a purse or dipping a hood, Tamira knew, and there would be no escape.

Tamira's nod took in all six of the group as she joined them in the shade. "Greetings." Some of them had kicked around a pig's bladder until it finally burst, smearing the ground with blood and piss. The bladder's remains lay in a corner, swarming with flies.

A boy called Mek and aged about fourteen sat on a wall and eyed the group. A dipper for now, he was growing up and broadening out, traits anathema to a thief relying on speed, dexterity and the ability to squeeze past people and into small places to escape. Sooner or later he'd join an adult gang, his days of loitering with this juvenile group nearing an end.

Mek was gauging how restless the group was becoming now that their game with the bladder was done. Tamira knew what he was about – he had a scheme in mind. She would hear him out and if it didn't interest her, she would strike out on her own and with luck find something to eat before nightfall.

"Who's interested in an opportunity?" Mek asked with a sly look in his eye. He remained seated on the wall, forcing the others to come to him.

The younger children walked over, bored and intrigued. Tamira waited, not wanting to be either the first or the last to join him. She had learned quickly that avoiding attention was essential to surviving the Poor Quarter. She leaned against the wall, listening.

Mek ran his eyes over the group, looking pleased that he had their attention. His age and size meant the other child-thieves of Mask deferred to him, but if he joined one of the older gangs he would find himself back at the bottom. Whether he extorted money from businesses, cut throats in alleys or sold lotus on corners, he would either become a cold-eyed killer, or very quickly a corpse. The odds were against him seeing his thirtieth year.

He lowered his voice but assumed the manner of one imparting wisdom. "What do I always tell you, Nio?"

One of the youngest boys squirmed at the attention. His eyes widened. "To always look for opportunity!"

Mek nodded self-importantly. He enjoyed being a king of sorts to the urchins and street-brats. "Yes. Opportunity." He leaned back with an air of feigned nonchalance. "As it happens, me and Naved have found one."

He said nothing more, letting a buzz of excitement build up

from his impressionable young audience.

"What did you find?" Nio asked, bouncing on his toes impatiently. Tamira had to credit Mek with one thing, he had a talent for the theatrical.

Mek frowned at him. "Why should I tell you?"

Nio looked crushed. "We could help you."

"I think this job might be too big for you lot," Mek said, feigning doubt.

Yeris, a boy Tamira had worked with a time or two, gave her a knowing look. Mek was winning over his audience.

"We're fast, we can help," a young girl insisted. Tamira didn't know her name.

"Maybe, Ghamia," Mek said. He made a show of thinking about it.

"Why don't you tell us what the job is, first?" Laya said, perhaps bored of his games.

Mek frowned at her. "I'm getting to it. But you won't be able to take part, not with those legs," he said spitefully.

Laya shrugged, but Tamira suspected she had goaded Mek deliberately. If he forbade her from taking part, she didn't need to lose face by refusing to.

"Me and Naved were watching the rivershore one day a few ten-days ago, eyeing up *opportunities*." He paused, making sure the others noted his initiative. They might be content to spend their days stealing scraps in the Poor Quarter, but *he* had *ambitions*, his expression said. Tamira suspected that the pair had been hiding there getting intoxicated on stolen wine or lotus, but she listened on.

"A dahabiya ran aground, deliberately so. From Pashbur, I reckon." The flat-bottomed barges were a common sight on the river, transporting goods such as salt, gold and ivory north, and returning south with goods brought to Mask from all over the world. If such a boat risked getting stuck on the mud just south of the docks, it was likely a smuggler wanting to avoid paying the customs tax.

Mek continued. "Goods were then moved from the barge onto a waiting wagon. We followed the wagon into the city proper and spied the teamsters pull a roll of syek out the wagon and pass it to the two guards, who let it pass through. Syek!"

A hushed murmur rose up from the listening group. A wagon-full of syek was worth a small fortune. If Mek spoke true, it was being smuggled into the city, the guards bribed with a roll of the costly material.

"What happened to the wagon?" a young boy asked.

"We climbed the wall and stayed on the rooftops, following it. The teamsters left it in a warehouse's walled-in courtyard a short distance from the gates."

"You said this was a few ten-days ago," Ghamia pointed out. "It'll be long gone."

"Yes," Mek agreed. "But Naved and I have watched the same stretch of shore every day since, taking turns. Every ten days, another cargo arrives and is taken by wagon to the same courtyard." Avarice hung heavy in his voice. "Another boat will be arriving today. Soon!"

"What's your plan?" Tamira asked. *Syek*...

Mek's smile betrayed his confidence, knowing he had them. He beckoned them in closer.

Chapter Five

Tamira crouched on the roof, watching the wagon's passage through the Poor Quarter streets. She had positioned herself near the gate allowing passage from the walled majority of Mask to the rest of the Poor Quarter that had spilled beyond the walls. Two scruffy guards sat behind the teamster guiding the mule pulling the wagon, alert for trouble. If Mek was right and rolls of syek lay hidden beneath the blocks of salt, their vigilance was justified.

Transporting their illicit cargo during the day was risky but less so than travelling at night. Given that the city gates shut at dusk, the smugglers would be left with no choice but to try and hide the wagon within the lawless part of the Poor Quarter that had grown outside the city walls. That was unlikely to end well.

The wagon continued at a steady pace, the teamster keeping his nerve. Some would have goaded the mule to move faster and drawn attention to the wagon, but its slow pace and decrepit condition ensured it drew little notice. Tamira had no doubt many thieves and opportunists on the streets eyed it speculatively, but the two guards were sufficient to dissuade anyone from attempting to grab a heavy block of salt.

To her mild surprise, Mek's story was backed up by the wagon's route through the cramped city. She had kept pace with the smugglers easily, traversing the rooftops far quicker than the wagon could press through the congested streets below. The wagon approached a small warehouse, entering the walled-in yard. The guards hopped off and closed the gates behind them.

Tamira leapt from one building to another, butterflies churning in her gut. She peered down into the shadowed alley; satisfied there were no surprises waiting below she scrambled down the wall, using gaps between the bricks as hand and footholds.

Ghamia, Nio and Yeris waited, their rapid breathing and slick brows betraying their nerves. Mek's friend Naved had joined them, though Mek himself was absent. They looked pleased to see Tamira, her (relative) age and growing reputation a comfort to them.

"Did it arrive?" Yeris asked breathlessly.

Tamira nodded. "Yes, it's secured in the yard."

"I told you," Naved said with an air of superiority, though Tamira saw relief loosen his shoulders. The news seemed to both relieve and terrify Nio and Ghamia. The job was on.

"Hey!" Mek entered the alley, his breathing laboured. He had hidden himself by the shore to see if the smugglers continued their habitual delivery.

"Mek," Naved greeted him with a grin. A few years Mek's younger, the pair were often joined at the hip.

Mek spared him a nod, looking at Tamira. "Can you do it?"

She nodded. "Yes, with Yeris's help."

"We could all—" Nio began.

"No," Mek said curtly. "We stick to the plan."

Tamira and Yeris left the alley, circling round to approach the warehouse from a quiet side-street. The sun was already hanging low, but there was still too much daylight for Tamira's liking. But to delay risked the cargo being unloaded.

Casting experienced eyes along the wall, Tamira identified the best spot to climb. Like most of the buildings here, much of the mortar holding the bricks together had crumbled, leaving gaps large enough for fingers and toes.

"Here?" Yeris whispered.

"Yes." Tamira started climbing, moving up several feet before sidling to the right, moving to wherever the wall offered the best holds. Yeris was below, following.

Her arms ached, and she was breathing hard by the time she reached the top of the courtyard wall, her chest easing on seeing no one below. The wagon waited in the yard, the mules already stabled. Faint noises sounded within – the smugglers. *Quick and quiet as a mouse.*

Not waiting to see if Yeris had made it to the top, Tamira crept along the wall a short distance and turned, lowering herself down. After using cracks in the wall to descend several feet, she let go, praying she had judged the distance correctly.

The impact was hard on her bare feet. A pebble jabbed the toughened sole of her right foot, the blend of fear and excitement dulling the pain. She looked around wildly, but she was still alone in the yard.

A hard thump sounded to her left, and she turned in time to see Yeris's face widen in pain. "Are you ok?" she mouthed. He must have let go too soon, too high up, and landed hard.

His face had gone a sickly grey, but he managed a nod.

Like spiders, they scuttled over to the courtyard gate, the heavy bar requiring both to lift. They dropped it to the ground and pulled the gate open.

Mek, Naved and Ghamia stood without, relief washing over their faces on seeing Tamira and Yeris.

Mek managed a manic, terrified grin as he nodded at Tamira and led the others inside. Nio remained outside nearby, acting as lookout.

They reached the wagon, throwing aside blocks of salt covering the more precious cargo below. Any other day, salt would have been considered a fine acquisition by any thief, but today they were after syek, worth a small fortune.

"Here!" Mek rasped as they unloaded enough salt to see the cloth-wrapped cargo below. He seized a block and tugged it loose, letting it fall to the ground.

Assuming the syek lay below, Tamira reached in and grabbed a sack, pulling it free. The rough cloth tore as she did so, spilling out its contents.

Her blood froze as she stared down. Ghamia's indrawn gasp told her she was not alone in realising what truly lay beneath the salt. Powdered lotus, not syek.

"Oh gods," Ghamia whimpered. Mek's mouth opened but no words came out. A fortune in lotus lay before them, but taking it would cost them their lives. Only fools crossed lotus smugglers, fools usually found with their throats cut.

Tamira found her voice. "Let's go!" There was no thought of taking any of the sacks – the smugglers would hunt them down without mercy, inflicting indiscriminate terror on the Poor Quarter denizens until they learned who had stolen their precious cargo. Their only hope was to flee and pray the smugglers were satisfied that none of the contraband was missing, letting the attempted theft end there.

Mek stood frozen, flinching when Tamira struck his arm. "Come on," she insisted.

He started to nod before spinning to his left and collapsing to the ground, Ghamia's shriek breaking the quiet. A crossbow bolt sprouted from Mek's upper chest, his eyes turning glassy.

Two more bolts followed, wood cracking as one struck the wagon. The second threw Ghamia backwards. Tamira turned to see the wagon driver and two guards drop their spent crossbows and run towards the thieves with knives drawn, murder written on hard faces.

On the streets of Mask, only the strong survived. Or the fast. Tamira ran. Yeris ran too, or tried to, slowed by his injured leg, falling behind Tamira as she flew out of the courtyard. Terror drove out any attempt to plan her flight. The last she saw of Naved was him staring down at Mek's body in shock, heartbeats from joining him.

She heard rapid footfalls behind her and Yeris's cry for mercy, followed by a broken-off scream. Her only chance was to lose the smugglers in the maze of alleys, hoping they would cut short their pursuit rather than leave the lucrative contraband unattended for too long.

If she could gain the rooftops she could lose them, but there were no easy routes up. The winding alleys led her into one of the Poor Quarter's main thoroughfares, the pursuit drawing many eyes. But none moved to assist, preferring to mind their own business. Tamira navigated through the knots of pedestrians, grunts of pain and shouts of outrage behind telling her the smugglers preferred brute force.

The internal city wall partitioning the Poor and Merchant Quarters loomed ahead, stirring a desperate hope within her. If she could reach the gate, the smugglers would not dare follow her into the Merchant Quarter where the city guards acted to keep the streets relatively free of violence lest it harm trade.

Left here and through the lane ... the shortest route. A beggar lying on the ground blocked her path, and she leapt over him, entering the shadowed lane, slowing just enough to turn the corner. Too late she realised she should have taken the next left.

The lane ended ahead with nowhere to go, nowhere but up. Tamira increased her pace and jumped, spreading her hands and praying they found a grip.

She slammed into the wall, her fingers and toes skittering over the surface like spiders as she started to slide down. Elation surged through her as she found a purchase on the cracked wall, her left hand shooting up in search of another hold.

She cried out as a hand grabbed her leg and pulled her down, throwing her roughly to the ground. She lay on her back, fear spiking through her as she fumbled for the small knife hidden beneath her kalasiris. The wagon driver and one of the guards stared down at her with dark eyes as hard as iron, their own knives bared and ready, longer and sharper than her own.

"Please, let me go," she pleaded, knowing she might as well beg the sun to cool or stone to soften.

One of the smugglers – the wagon driver – listened pitilessly, his blade red with the blood of her companions. "You tried to steal from us. All in Mask know what happens to those who steal from the Bloody Lotus." His accent was foreign to the city, his twisted vowels marking him as a son of a western province of the theocracy.

Oh gods. The Bloody Lotus were not the largest of the lotus gangs, but they were among the most vicious. The only mercy she might find this day was a quick death.

"We didn't know who you were, we thought you were smuggling syek," she babbled, knowing words would not save her but trying anyway.

"Kill her?" the wagon guard asked.

The other looked her up and down. "Yusef ban Vanno might buy her. If not…" he ran a finger across his throat.

Hrek save me, she prayed. But Hrek had no use for mercy. Yusef ban Vanno was fearfully regarded in the Poor Quarter, his name said in whispers lest he somehow hear it. Those who fell into the hands (and chains) of the slaver gangs haunting Mask's more lawless districts were often bought by that flesh trader, ending up on the Marat Square slave block for auction.

The wooden grip of her knife felt warm and slick with sweat. She considered turning it on herself, counting death a better fate than the brothels that coveted young flesh.

"That girl is mine," a woman said. "Leave her be." She sounded foreign, but fluent in the Traders' Tongue, a language universal to much of the world.

Tamira craned her head around to see who was suicidally stupid enough to challenge lotus smugglers, surprised to see it was the tall black woman she had robbed earlier. A hysterical laugh caught in her throat. *If everyone I've stolen from recently arrives here, this alley will be crowded indeed.*

"Begone, or you're next," one of the smugglers snarled. The Bloody Lotus were not used to being challenged, certainly not by a lone woman armed only with a broken stick maybe a foot long.

Tamira had not survived years alone on the streets of Mask by missing opportunities. She quietly edged towards the wall. Let the woman and the lotus smugglers fight amongst themselves.

"I think not," the woman said, her voice rich and confident. "I am tired, dirty and hungry, my patience very nearly at an end. Leave now." She started walking towards them.

The wagon driver ran at her, drawing his knife back. An invisible force struck his head, felling him. Tamira blinked; it was as if the air itself had come alive and attacked him. *She's a mage ... I've picked my victims poorly today!*

The woman kept walking, not sparing the fallen smuggler a second look. His companion threw himself at her with a cry. He must have realised what the woman was, but the Bloody Lotus were not known for shirking a fight.

Deciding she'd rather not be here to face either mage or smuggler, when only one remained, Tamira flipped up onto her feet. The air seemed to move in front of the remaining smuggler, and something invisible but hard struck his throat. Tamira was already climbing the wall as he clutched his crushed neck, flailing at the mage with his knife-hand in a desperate bid to kill his slayer before succumbing.

*

The sky began to darken and Shukara quickened her pace, irritated at losing the thief again. The Poor Quarter was no place for a stranger to be after nightfall. Dealing with the two thugs had been satisfying but tiring, her abilities hobbled without reagents. Concern tightened her chest. She had not found any trace of the thief again, but the city wall was drawing nearer, and she was running out of city. She should have felt something by now, a hint at least.

The explanation almost made her curse. She reached the city walls and looked through the towering gatehouse. The Poor Quarter did not end at the city wall but stretched beyond it. *I have no choice but to venture on.* If she delayed until tomorrow, the thief might have sold her pouch. She had caught a glimpse of it hanging from the girl's shoulder as she scaled the wall.

A guard watched her approach the gate. "The gates close at sunset," he warned. "If you're not back by then, you're in there until dawn."

"I've business to attend to," she said firmly as she walked beneath the iron portcullis. Gods willing, she would find the thief quickly.

If the Poor Quarter within the city walls was a crumbling, overcrowded shadow of the better parts of Mask; what lay beyond was even less. An attempt had been made to give the buildings more space in the narrow patch of floodplain available, but most of the gaps had been filled with shacks built from rubble, or tents of stretched hide.

This part of the Poor Quarter was little more than a camp, filled with people every bit as desperate as those within the city walls.

She retrieved her stave, gripping it tightly. Guards clearly stayed away from here, so she had little fear of being caught. The denizens watched her pass, and she exuded an air of menace that would dissuade most from accosting her. For now.

Shukara felt something, a hint of what she sought. She followed her sense of it, the trail leading her to a ruined tower squatting in the distance, little more than a pile of broken bricks. Given the thief's unpleasant encounter in the alley, Shukara expected she was lying low somewhere, somewhere very near.

At last. Nightfall was almost upon the city, and without reagents, survival would be unlikely.

*

A red glow on the horizon was all that remained of the sun. Not that the night could be described as cool. Heat still clung to the bricks and stones of Mask.

Tamira sat atop the tower, squatting amidst the rubble at the top, the interior inaccessible. The smugglers might have been dealt with, but she was acutely aware that the dark-skinned woman – a *mage*, no less – hunted her, and she was happy to be off the streets.

The squat, ruined tower was Tamira's sanctuary. Built as an outlying watchtower when Mask had been confined behind its walls, it had since been swallowed by the Poor Quarter's outward expansion. The tower had collapsed in on itself and was thought uninhabitable. Tamira had climbed it two years past and claimed the small unroofed gap at the top as her own.

She bit into a piece of fresh bread stolen earlier from a bakery, feeling safe for the first time since the morning. The bread she scavenged was usually stale, so the texture of soft fresh bread in her mouth was a rare luxury. Guards and outraged merchants were the dangers she usually had to contend with; today she had managed to antagonise lotus smugglers and a mage. Sadness weighed her down as she remembered Ghamia and the others, but Death stalked the Poor Quarter often, so she knew better than to get too attached to people.

She licked the crumbs from her fingers and leaned back, gazing at the river. Mask's squalor was hidden by the dark, made beautiful by the sunset. Red walls and towers glowed a pinkish-red, and the setting sun blazed a trail of crimson gold down the river.

"A truly stunning sight," a woman's voice said.

Tamira snatched up her knife and rolled to her feet, heart pounding. The tall mage from earlier stood on the edge of the tower, her dark skin gleaming in the dying sunlight.

Chapter Six

The climb had left Shukara slightly out of breath, but the gratifying look of startled terror on the girl's face made the exertion worthwhile.

"Get back," the girl-thief snarled, waving her knife. Shukara could see her trying to decide what to do – should she attack, should she flee? The erratic way she waved the knife betrayed her lack of skill with the weapon. Shukara had little doubt she could disarm the girl.

Tamira glanced over her shoulder, betraying her decision to flee.

"I am here to talk," Shukara said, in no mood for another chase. "Return my property and I will not harm you. Try to flee, and…"

She willed a loose stone to fly off the tower.

The thief froze, the stone conveying the warning: if she tried to climb down the side of the tower, she would be flung away from it. "Mage."

Shukara nodded in appreciation. "Indeed." The girl wasn't slow-witted. She considered herself a magicker, but many lands had their own names for those who practiced magick. She exhaled in relief on seeing her pouch lying nearby. "I see you still have it. Good."

The girl looked at her with fearful defiance. "You may have it back," she said as if she had any choice in the matter.

Her imperious manner made Shukara smile. "That's very gracious of you," she said, humouring her. She walked over and picked it up, keeping an eye on the brandished knife.

"What leather is that?" the girl asked.

"Dhaemonhide, and it's not quite leather." Shukara answered as she opened the pouch.

"Ha!" she girl scoffed. "No, really?"

Shukara looked her in the eye. "Really." Dhaemonhide was preciously rare, sought after due to its extreme durability. A dhaemon's body decayed swiftly, but she had succeeded in carving free a slice of hide from one sent against her and her companions a year past. She had fashioned a pouch from the cured hide, the rocky skin enduring once it was cut free from the smouldering corpse. That pouch would be almost as good as new long after Shukara's own hide had rotted to dust.

"How did you find me?" the girl asked, putting the knife down. "Twice."

"I Marked the pouch and was able to find it." A lack of reagents had made tracking it difficult, requiring her to be relatively close to sense it. It was as well that she had; she had little doubt that after dark the Poor Quarter would turn perilous for those without sanctuary or guards. She opened the pouch and looked inside.

Most reagents seemed to be present but not all. Anxiety squeezed her chest. "Where are the firethorn seeds?" She checked again, but they were gone. Others were missing too, but it was those seeds that concerned her the most.

"The what?"

Shukara stared at the girl. "Reddish-black seeds, very hard."

The girl swallowed. "The ones that stank like bad eggs?"

"Yes. Them." Her voice cracked like a whip, turning the girl grey.

Her expression told Shukara the answer before she spoke. "I threw them away," she whispered. Fear had driven the confident façade from the girl. No doubt she was remembering every story describing the fate of those who crossed magi.

Shukara was sorely tempted to punish the wretched girl in a manner sure to inspire more stories, but quashed the impulse.

"There are herbalists and apothecaries in the Merchant Quarter's Marat Square and surrounding souks," the girl said, trying to be helpful.

Shukara just shook her head. Some of what the girl had thoughtlessly thrown away could be replaced, but firethorn seeds only grew in the ash-fields of Karadhur, many months to the south. She had brought as many as she could on coming north, using them only at direst need. Without them, her quest looked doomed to fail.

"You need them for your magick?"

"Yes." The principal component of magick was a piece of

wytchwood, groves of which were rare and scattered, the wood harvested carefully to ensure the grove's survival. Matrices evolved throughout the wood the longer a magicker used it, becoming unique; a mirror of their mind. Some magi could use another's wytchwood if it wasn't too old, too set in its owner's ways, but it would take years for it to truly adjust to another user.

But reagents were also needed for the more powerful or complicated spells, and all the wytchwood in the world would be of little use to her without them, not against what waited at the end of her journey.

A frown touched the girl's face. "Do the Magi of Hrek practice the same magick? If so, they may have some of these seeds."

"Magick requires reagents, and as reagents vary from land to land, so does the magickry," Shukara told her. "But yes, I believe they will possess firethorn seeds. A few spells require them. Where can I find these magi?"

"They live in the Kasbah Arcana, in the Old Quarter. But it is guarded," the girl warned.

Shukara knew that the Cult of Hrek had forbidden magick across the entire theocracy to anyone not aligned with themselves, leaving the Magi her only hope. "Your theft has greatly inconvenienced me. I have killed people for less. But if you get me into the Kasbah Arcana I will overlook your offence."

The girl gave her a derisive look. "Killed by you, killed by the Cult's magi – what difference?"

Shukara maintained a stern expression, privately amused at the thief's insolence. "I have no doubt the kasbah is filled with valuables. All I want are reagents, you can keep whatever else we find." She wagged a finger at her. "But remember, I will Mark you as I Marked my pouch, and will hunt you if you betray me."

The girl shot her a look of sullen defiance. "I'll go up a tower too high for you to climb."

"I'll topple it to the ground and banish you to the deepest pit in the Underworld."

"Your home?" the girl retorted quick as silver. "The Magi of Hrek guard their stronghold well, and are in turn watched by the priests. But there may be another way to find what you need. Whatever I … find, I sell to my fence who boasts he can get almost anything. I suggest we visit him in the morning."

With little choice, Shukara nodded. "Very well. But your debt to me will not be settled until I am in possession of what you lost."

The girl bowed with a mocking courtier's grace. "We have agreement, Great Mistress. You should stay here, it's much too dangerous to risk the streets."

Shukara had no intention of leaving the girl, having spent much of the day hunting her and fighting off two thugs to find her. There was little room amidst the rubble and nothing in the way of comfort in the ruined tower save for a blanket. So much for a bathhouse, a meal, and a room for the night. But at least the tower offered safety. "What's your name, girl?"

"Tamira." She put her palms together.

Shukara did likewise. "I am Shukara." She spied a battered tome sitting in a corner. "What is that?"

"It's a book." Her expression suggested a less courteous answer went unspoken.

"I can see it is a book. Which book, and why do you have it?" Perhaps to burn should the nights ever cool.

Tamira handed it over. "I found it."

You mean stole it. "Kamlo's *Heart of Kavari*, a collection of verse inspired by his time in the desert," Shukara said in recognition. "'*By day cometh an inferno born of its rage, its anger scourging all with wind-hurled sand. Leaving naught but baked brittle bones.*'"

"'*But even Kavari's temper must cool when passeth the sun; but cometh the night cometh its malice, born of a heart colder than Death's. Only one people can endure; the tribe forged in its sands,*'" Tamira shocked her by quoting.

"You can read?"

Tamira shrugged like it was no great thing. "Yes. I've read it many times."

Shukara wondered what to make of her. "When did you learn to read?" she asked carefully. She studied the book. It was a slim volume, the text scribed onto the quality papyrus in a neat hand. A better book than the poor verse deserved.

But the girl refused to answer.

Chapter Seven

A noise snatched Tamira to wakefulness, her disorientation momentary. She rolled to one side, her knife in hand before she was aware of drawing it, and she looked up with bared teeth, heart thudding in her chest.

Shukara looked calmly down at her. "A good morning to you, too."

Tamira recalled her courtesies. "Good morning, Mistress Shukara." She put her knife down and leapt to her feet, making no apology. In the Poor Quarter, one slept lightly or risked not awakening.

Dawn's first light was beginning to brighten the sky, but Tamira knew the city was already awake as its people strove to complete their business before midday forced them to find shade. "I would offer you something to break your fast, but my larder is bare," she said in mock-apology.

"I'll buy us some food," Shukara said as Tamira hoped she would. "Is there a well nearby?" She paused. "And is it drinkable?"

Tamira shook her head. "There is a well, but it's been claimed. The Dead Knives 'tax' all who want to drink from it. Better to wait, there is another well near our destination."

"Very well."

"The two men chasing me in the alley; are they…?"

"Both dead," Shukara said with an air of nonchalance.

Relief loosened Tamira's chest. "Good. With luck the Bloody Lotus will believe their men, chasing me with bloodied knives, ran into a rival gang who thought they were being attacked. Better that than them hunting us." She felt a slight unease on remembering the third smuggler who must have remained to guard the wagon and ensure that her friends were dead, but she hoped he would think his two companions had simply ran into the wrong people while chasing her. Regardless, she couldn't hide atop her tower forever.

"Follow my lead in climbing down," Tamira warned. "If

any see us, I can never return here."

They climbed down without incident, the mage's longer arms and legs making up for her inexperience. Once on the ground, Tamira motioned for Shukara to follow her. "My fence has a shop in the bazaar."

"In Marat Square?"

Tamira laughed. "You jest! No, the Poor Quarter has a bazaar of its own within the walls. Rat Square, we call it."

It was only yesterday that she had met the others there and listened to Mek's plan to get rich. Yesterday seemed like an age ago. If Nio had the brains of a flea, he would stay well away, too; the Bloody Lotus would be implacable in trying to find the would-be thieves.

She led Shukara through the disordered slums and through the re-opened gate into the city proper. Beggars sat forlornly along the narrow streets, guarding their chosen spots. One-armed Hesad smeared dung over his foul rags to present himself as being more pitiable than he already was.

The gangs who ruled the Poor Quarter were mostly absent, resting after last night's depredations. Word would soon spread that someone had killed two Bloody Lotus, and the other gangs would be forced to prepare in case blame fell on them.

A man's body lay naked in the street, stripped clean. No one moved it from fear it had been left as a message. The unspoken consensus seemed to be to let the guards deal with it, should any trouble themselves to enter the Poor Quarter.

Hawkers cried out their wares, and vendors cooked meat over coals on the street, haggling with passers-by. Rat Square was where most trade in the Poor Quarter took place, a sprawling collection of shops and stalls clustered together.

Tamira and Shukara queued at the well. "I'll re-join you soon," Tamira said on spying Laya sitting on a wall by a small courtyard cracked and overgrown with weeds.

Laya's eyes widened on seeing her. "Tami! What happened? Nio said you were all killed."

Tamira looked around to ensure no one else was within earshot. "Apart from Nio, I'm the only one who escaped. That idiot Mek was wrong, it was lotus they were smuggling, not syek."

"Lotus smugglers?" Laya shook her head, doubtless glad she had not joined the ill-fated band of thieves.

"Oh, it gets worse. Bloody Lotus, so tell Nio to keep his mouth shut. Two were killed chasing me, and the rest will be out for blood."

"Bloody Lotus? I'll tell him to forget yesterday every happened. So will I." She knew as well as Tamira that the gang would chase every whispered rumour until they found everyone responsible, not shying from threats and torture to get information. She frowned. "I heard they were out in force last night, hunting for a girl your age, but I never thought … who killed them? Not you, surely?"

"Who killed them doesn't matter," Tamira said, in no mood to discuss Shukara. "Just make sure Nio keeps his mouth shut, or we'll join Mek and the others. With luck, they'll have their hands full fighting the other gangs." It was a vain hope, and she knew it. Two smugglers were dead. The gang wouldn't think a barely adolescent girl had killed them, but the two men had been last seen chasing her. A street-full of people had witnessed the chase, and the best she could hope for was that none of them could name her.

Laya nodded. "You should lie low for a while."

Tamira smiled bitterly. "Where?" For most, death was the only escape from the Poor Quarter. She couldn't hide forever; she had to eat which meant she had to steal.

Laya had no answer. "Watch yourself, Tami."

"You too, Laya."

She re-joined Shukara at the queue for the well.

"What was that about?" Shukara asked, suspicious.

"A friend." She looked Shukara in the eye. "Those two men you killed have friends who will bribe, threaten and torture to find out who was responsible."

Shukara didn't appear unduly troubled. "I don't plan to stay in this city long. If any more cross my path, I'll deal with them."

"You can't kill everyone, and every fight makes it more likely the Cult and their Magi will learn there's a rogue mage in Mask. And that you *really* don't want."

Silence fell after that and they gulped down water when their turn came at the well. Tamira splashed some over her face and hands, washing off most of the grime.

The mage did the same. "Had it not been for you, I would have bathed yesterday, be wearing clean clothes, and have spent the night at an inn," she complained, but with little heat behind her words. She had seen the Poor Quarter and what Tamira endured daily just to survive.

Shukara bought two oranges and some dates, giving half to Tamira who devoured them quickly. Her food was gone before Shukara had finished her orange. It was a novelty to see someone eat slowly in public with no fear of having the food snatched by someone bigger. Shukara caught her gaze and tossed her a date, Tamira snatching it out of the air.

"Where can we find your fence?" Shukara asked.

"His shop is close," Tamira said. "Come."

Tasim's shop was one of several that made up the narrow souk leading into Rat Square. Built centuries before the surrounding streets had fallen into poverty, the buildings were in a poor state. The exteriors had once been covered in clay to preserve the brickwork, but most of it had long since broken off.

Tamira led Shukara into the small shop. Tasim's goods were piled haphazardly or gathered dust on wooden shelves. His inventory always varied, depending on what he could get his hands on, mostly by illicit means. Sometimes he sold Kavari carpets, but none were in evidence today. A few slabs of salt sat on a shelf, hued pink from the blood of the camels whose hides they had chafed at.

Tamira recognised a battered set of goblets on the floor, stolen by her from a merchant eleven days prior and sold for a fraction of their worth to Tasim.

"Mistress, welcome." Tasim bowed obsequiously to Shukara, ignoring Tamira. "You honour my humble shop with your presence."

"She's with me," Tamira said before Tasim tried to sell the mage his wares through colourful and less than accurate appraisals.

Tasim looked between them, his welcoming smile at odds with the hard look in his eyes. He might play the part of the humble shopkeeper, eager to serve, but there was a hard edge to him. Harder than usual. "Are you here to buy or sell?"

Tasim's nephew Nim sat on a stool, a stocky boy on the verge of manhood with slow wits and fast fists. His job was to fetch, carry, and beat any young thief foolish enough to cross Tasim. Judging by the bruises and abrasions, he had recently been on the receiving end of a beating.

As agreed, Tamira did the talking. "My companion seeks … certain items that are hard to come by."

Tamira watched him study Shukara. Fools did not survive long in Tasim's trade, and Tasim had been trading in stolen goods for years. He didn't know she was a mage, but he likely sensed she was not someone to cross. *A pity I did not reach the same judgement before I robbed her.*

"Perhaps I can help you acquire them?" Tasim gestured around the shop, having caught Shukara's sceptical appraisal of the wares on sale. "This is only representative of my stock, as young Tamira can attest."

Shukara looked at Tamira who gave a small nod.

"I seek reagents not for sale by the apothecaries here," Shukara said calmly. "Including firethorn seeds."

Tasim's eyes widened as her words sank in, and he grasped their significance. It wasn't every day a mage entered his shop. Tamira just had to hope he didn't give in to the temptation to sell that information to the Cult. She thought not; he had traded in the Poor Quarter for years and knew the denizens nursed a resentful hatred of the rich and powerful living in splendour while the poor suffered in squalor. The gangs guarded what little they possessed jealously and would reward anyone responsible for bringing the Cult's attention here with a red throat.

"Getting such … items are beyond me," Tasim said, such an admission looking like it troubled his digestion. "But have you heard of the Eye of Mask?"

Tamira had, but Shukara shook her head. "No, what is it?"

"*Who* is it. The Eye of Mask is a broker of secrets and information. It might be an individual or it might be a group." The shopkeeper shrugged. "But little in this city escapes the Eye's notice. Even the Cult and Merchant Council dare not cross the Eye."

More likely the Eye was in their employ, another instrument wielded to maintain control. Or perhaps they found them too useful to hunt down. Tamira hoped the Bloody Lotus didn't turn to the Eye for information on who killed their men, or the girl they had chased moments before. "How do we contact the Eye?" Tamira asked.

"I can assist you," he answered. "But for a price."

"How much?" the mage asked.

Tasim glanced at his bloodied nephew. "The price is not coin." Hard eyes locked with a pair equally resolute. "A merchant called Calan ban Ahmet has been giving me trouble. He has been aggressively expanding his business interests, putting several mutual competitors out of business, and now he has his eye on me."

He pointed to his nephew. "Three of his men visited yesterday and beat poor Nim, to 'encourage' me to surrender my business interests to Calan."

Tamira frowned. "Calan ban Ahmet's never had a large presence here. His main business is selling incense to the priesthood."

"Yes, I've succeeded in keeping him in check for years. However, he recently married a priest's widowed daughter, a priest who happens to be the nephew of High Priest Thukenatap. Calan's ambitions have been emboldened by this new family connection to power, and a substantial dowry is allowing him to fulfil those ambitions."

Tasim looked disgruntled. "He daren't challenge the merchant princes and trading syndicates controlling the bulk of Mask's trade, but he is moving against smaller merchants like myself." Meaning Calan was forcing many of the fences out of business, increasing his illicit activities in the Poor Quarter. His dealings with the slave trader Yusef ban Vanno had dissuaded Tamira from dealing with him.

"He has approached you?" Shukara asked.

"Yes, encouraging me to sell my shop to him. I declined, and yesterday his men paid a visit." He pointed to his nephew. "I was attending to business elsewhere, but they beat Nim as a message: sell, or else."

"An unfortunate circumstance," Shukara said, not sounding particularly interested. The matter was more troubling to Tamira. She had no great fondness for Tasim or his brutish nephew, but he bought whatever she brought him. If Tasim was killed or driven out of business, she would have no choice but to risk dealing with Calan.

"Most unfortunate," Tasim said. "Not so long ago, I would simply have had Calan dealt with, but he has married into a powerful family and can afford guards to escort him wherever he goes."

"You mentioned a price for an introduction to the Eye of Mask," Shukara observed.

Tasim nodded. "Yes. Calan has been boasting of a new lock-safe he has bought, constructed by the Guild of Artificers and believed impregnable. He keeps it within his private office. My price is that you enter his home and gain access to this lock-safe. Your ... special skills will allow you to overcome the lock-safe's locking mechanism?"

"I can overcome the lock. But getting to the lock-safe sounds a daunting task," Shukara observed. "As you said, he has guards."

Tasim glanced down at Tamira. "Young Tamira has a certain reputation on the streets for getting in and out of places. I'm confident she can get you inside Calan's riad unnoticed."

Tamira nodded slightly. The difficulty would be getting Shukara inside. "I'll need a rope."

"I can provide one for a very reasonable price, a discount between friends," Tasim said, his voice like oiled honey.

"You can provide it for no cost," Tamira countered with a hard grin. "Consider it an investment."

Tasim held his hands up in surrender. "As you say."

"Very well," Shukara said. "What do you wish us to take from the lock-safe?"

Tasim's smile bared yellow teeth. "I don't wish anything taken. Your task is to put something inside.

Chapter Eight

They found Calan ban Ahmet's riad on Aneksuno Street. The street had once been a quiet suburb of the Merchant Quarter before Mask's mercantile expansion saw souks and smaller housing fill the gaps. Unimpressed, the nobles had moved to the newer Gold Quarter, a segregated paradise of spacious palaces and riads that overlooked irrigated parks and olive groves instead of busy souks and dung-stained streets.

The merchant class, growing in wealth, power and numbers over the centuries, had at first taken over the riads vacated by the nobles. Now second in power only to the High Priests of Hrek, the wealthiest of Mask's merchant princes lived among the nobles in the Gold Quarter while their lesser fellows in turn occupied the Merchant Quarter riads.

Calan ban Ahmet might never be counted among the merchant princes of Mask or sit on the Merchant Council, but marrying into a prominent Hrekist family was a good start to realising such ambitions. Tamira studied the riad, realising why Calan was expanding his interests so aggressively in the Poor Quarter. Even with the riad's busy location lowering the value, it was still a large building. The dowry received for marrying the priest's daughter doubtless helped Calan buy it, but maintaining it would not be cheap.

Unable to compete yet with the merchant princes whose fortunes poured in from around the world, Calan was seeking to dominate Mask's illegal trade. Seizing control of the Poor Quarter markets and monopolising the fencing of stolen goods was a good first step, perhaps to be followed by lotus smuggling. With a high priest supporting Calan, Tamira had no doubt the Poor Quarter would soon see temple soldiers cracking down on any smugglers not aligned with Calan.

Unless Tasim had his way. His plan was devious, the only risk to himself being if Tamira or Shukara were caught and revealed that they were acting on his behalf. A risk, to be sure, but Tasim was no fool; if Calan wasn't stopped now,

Tasim's days as a merchant were done.

Noon was approaching, the sun still rising. The walls of Calan's four-storey riad needed repair, reddish clay cracked and crumbling in parts, but Tamira knew she could never climb them.

Like most riads in the city, it had few outside-facing windows, the rooms instead facing into an interior courtyard or garden. This riad was a rarity in that it stood detached from any other building, the gaps on either side too narrow to accommodate other buildings.

But too wide for her to leap across. Tamira frowned. Getting inside was going to be a bigger problem than anticipated. She abandoned her reconnaissance and joined Shukara in a small teh-room across from the riad. A few others sat within, mostly shopkeepers and merchants drinking before the midday rest.

The teh-room was exposed at the front save for three pillars supporting the flat roof overhead. Beige tiles covered the floor, many cracked after years of use, and cushions surrounded several low circular tables. Shukara sat alone at the table nearest to the street, enjoying a good view of the riad. "Be seated," she told Tamira.

Tamira sat, nodding her thanks as Shukara slid across a second cup. She took a sip, pleased to find it had been only lightly minted.

"What are your thoughts?" Shukara asked.

Tamira took another sip, trying to quell the slight tremble in her hands. The teh did little to calm the butterflies rioting in her belly. "I can see no obvious way in," she admitted. "There are no windows on the lower two storeys, and the building stands alone."

Shukara digested her report silently. "The door is clearly guarded. The gap from the nearest building is too large to jump?"

"Yes, unless you can give us wings." Tamira said. Maybe there was another way to find the Eye of Mask?

"You mentioned windows three storeys up. Do any face the closest building?"

Tamira recalled the riad and its neighbouring buildings. "Yes, but as I said, the jump would be too great."

Shukara discreetly removed a small tied pouch from the larger one she claimed to be dhaemonhide, pulling out a pinch of powder which she sprinkled into her teh. After that she dropped in a dried leaf and thoroughly stirred the cup. "We'll see."

"Will that help us?" Tamira asked, watching.

"I certainly hope so." The mage made a face. "A shame to ruin such fine teh, otherwise."

"When do we go in?" If they could get in.

"Once we've finished our teh. Master Calan should be attending to his business at this time of day, so his riad's office will be empty. Our biggest challenge will be avoiding his wife, servants and house guards."

"So soon? I thought we would wait until after dark." Tamira's last job before nightfall had not ended well, and she would rather wait until the master, mistress and servants of the house were asleep.

"And be delayed another day in replacing my reagents?" Shukara shook her head. "No, we'll move quickly and quietly." The mage sounded confident for one new to thievery.

Tamira let out a breath, trying to ease the tension gripping her chest, both hating and envying the mage her stoic demeanour. She let her remaining teh go cold while the mage sipped her own.

Shukara drained her cup and stood. "Now, I think. They will not be expecting thieves to strike during the day," she said in a comforting tone.

Now you're an expert in burglary. Tamira held her tongue and hoped the mage was right.

*

"As I told you, the distance is too far." Tamira had led Shukara up to the rooftop of the building closest to the riad. She pointed down. "There's a window there, but I'd likely as not strike the wall and continue falling."

Shukara studied the gap between the two buildings. "I agree. Your best chance is to jump onto the roof and climb down the interior walls."

"I can't jump," Tamira protested. The riad and building they stood on were of a height, but the gap between them was too great. "And neither could you."

Shukara held her stave. "I'll help you."

Tamira grudgingly nodded as the mage outlined her plan. "It could work," she said cautiously.

"Then let us waste no more time."

Easy for you to say. If this doesn't work, I'm the one who ends up broken on the ground below. Tamira walked back to the far end of the roof and took several breaths, eyeing her destination. She took one last breath and sprinted towards the edge, running as fast as she could.

Steeling herself and knowing that to lose her nerve now would see her tumbling over the edge, she fixed her gaze on the edge of the roof. Every inch was needed.

She threw her right foot forwards, drawing up her left and slamming both feet down, squatting as she tilted over the edge, momentum pulling her over the side. Exhaling sharply, she sprang up and forwards, throwing her hands out in front.

The ground below looked frighteningly distant, far enough that a fall would kill or cripple her. She looked ahead to see the riad roof – the distance too great. Her belly fluttered as she started to fall, the riad's roof still out of reach…

Something struck her from below, pushing her up and shoving her forwards. Her fingers caught the wall surrounding the riad's roof, and she struck the wall with bone-jarring force.

Gods… She hung there frozen, tears leaking from her eyes as her heart thundered. After a moment she pulled herself up, her arms shaky. She rolled over the side of the wall, the rooftop three feet below.

Glad to be grounded once more, Tamira looked across to the adjacent rooftop and gave Shukara a small wave. None of Calan's guards were on the roof, not that she expected any to forsake the shade at this sweltering hour.

The riad was focused inwards, built around and looking into a courtyard or garden. Keeping low, Tamira crept to the edge and peered down. A small fountain lay in the centre of a courtyard of white tiles. Arched pillars surrounded the enclosure, permitting entry to every room on the ground floor. Balconies ran along the upper levels, looking down into the courtyard, a sanctuary offering shade from the sun and respite from the bustle of life in the city.

Satisfied that the courtyard was deserted, Tamira slipped over the edge and lowered herself down, clinging to the nearest pillar. She swung herself forwards, landing on the fourth storey's interior balcony. With luck, the house slaves and servants were attending to their chores on lower levels or visiting the market.

Her next task was to find Calan's office and bring Shukara inside.

*

Shukara leaned over the edge, watching the third storey window for any sign of Tamira. The time it was taking the thief to appear made Shukara anxious, but she consoled herself that had Tamira been discovered, she would have heard the outcry.

Finally, the window shutter opened and Tamira's head emerged, looking upwards. She held out her hands and Shukara threw her one end of the rope. The girl caught it after which Shukara threw the other end and watched Tamira disappear back inside. The middle of the rope was wrapped around the bars of a window on the building Shukara stood on.

The rope went taut and Tamira re-appeared, giving her a wave.

"I'm not looking forward to this," Shukara whispered to herself as she lowered herself over the building and took hold of the rope. Holding the rope with both hands and wrapping her legs around it, she slowly moved diagonally down towards the window, controlling her descent.

A hand took hold of her wrist. "Let go," Tamira said.

Shukara forced herself to do so, and her feet touched the floor as Tamira pulled her inside. Her arm muscles ached and friction burned her hands.

"Enjoy that?" Tamira was grinning.

"You took your time," Shukara said, ignoring the question. The room was unfurnished, perhaps awaiting the eventual birth of Calan's progeny.

"I decided to find the office first." She closed the window's shutters.

"Did you?"

Tamira smiled. "Yes. Remove your sandals and follow me … *quietly*."

Both ends of the rope were tied around one of the pillars that ran around the edge of the riad facing into the courtyard. While Shukara removed her sandals, Tamira untied both ends of the rope, pulled it inside the riad, and left it in a corner of the room.

Shukara followed Tamira out onto the balcony that ran around the riad, connecting every room on the third storey. Muffled noises could be heard from below as the house slaves and servants attended to their duties.

"The office is one level below," Tamira whispered as she glanced down into the courtyard. A slave or servant was on his hands and knees scrubbing tiles. Not visibly alarmed, Tamira climbed over the cedarwood railing and lowered herself onto the level below.

Shukara followed her, lacking the thief's easy grace and dexterity. Clinging hard to the pillar and hoping the man cleaning the tiles didn't choose that moment to look up, she dropped onto the railing of the level below.

She lost her balance, almost crying out as she felt herself fall. Tamira grabbed her djellaba and pulled her back.

"My thanks," Shukara managed as she tried to regain her breath and dignity.

Tamira never responded, too busy looking around, face screwed up in concentration. "I thought I heard … never mind."

She led Shukara past a room, bare feet padding silently against the tiles. "That's Calan's bedchamber. His office is nearby."

They entered a small room on the far side of the riad, the door thankfully unlocked. Perhaps Calan felt no need to lock doors within his own home.

A cedarwood desk stood at the end of the room, an extinguished oil lamp lying on top next to a pile of papyrus documents and an ink well. Aside from a wooden chair behind the desk, the office was sparsely furnished. An ivory plaque inlaid with a golden pyramid hung on the wall, the symbol of Hrek. Expensive; probably a wedding gift from Calan's High Priest step-relation in law. And a reminder to Calan of where the power truly lay in Mask.

A solid black iron lock-safe sat against the wall, the one Tasim had told them of. "Keep watch," Shukara whispered, her eyes fixed on it. According to Tasim, Calan had boasted of the lock-safe's impregnability. Was it simply protected by a robust mechanism, or had the would-be merchant prince arranged for a magicker to further protect it by arcane means?

The only magi allowed within Mask were the Magi of Hrek, controlled by the Cult. But given Calan's family connection to the Cult, Shukara decided to exercise caution.

She held her stave and focused on the lock-safe. Her initial impression revealed nothing but metal, so she gingerly rested her left hand on top. Nothing. If a magicker had added an arcane layer of protection, he or she was a subtle one. More likely Calan was relying on the workmanship of the city's Artificer Guild.

That made her job a little easier. She rested one finger on the locking mechanism and concentrated. Delving it was not easy, slowed by the dense iron, but she soon *felt* the complicated locking system. One by one she manipulated the tumblers securing the lock, releasing them.

The last tumbler clicked, and she pulled the lock-safe door open with a satisfied smile.

"You done?" Tamira asked.

"Almost," Shukara murmured. She reached into her pouch and retrieved the small idol Tasim had given her. To her, the delicate ivory man holding a spear was inoffensive, but Tamira assured her the Cult of Hrek would regard the image of Niash, God of Hunters, poorly. Very poorly indeed.

She placed the idol inside the lock-safe and closed the door. One turn of the handle reset the lock, freeing her from having to manipulate the tumblers again.

"Done," she announced, standing.

"Good, let's go." Tamira seemed agitated, and Shukara knew better than to doubt the thief's instincts. This was her domain, and Tasim's scheme relied on them entering and exiting the riad undetected.

The pair slipped out of the office, and Tamira froze. "Someone's coming." Shukara heard it too, the sound of sandals scuffing against the stone steps leading up from the level below. The stairs leading up to the second level were in the same room, meaning they would be seen if they tried to climb them. *No time...*

Shukara considered her stave. She could deal with any guard but to do so would betray their intrusion and compromise Tasim's scheme. Should they hide in a room and hope that whoever approached would not enter it?

"Come," Tamira whispered harshly, darting out onto the terrace. Shukara followed, hoping the thief knew what she was doing.

Tamira reached the terrace railing and turned, pointing upwards. "Climb." Her tone brooked no argument.

Shukara climbed up onto the railing, helped by Tamira. Fuelled by urgency, Shukara pulled herself up, reaching for the terrace above while Tamira held her feet and pushed.

She hauled herself up onto the third storey terrace, climbing over the railing and rolling over it, muscles burning from the sudden exertion.

Tamira joined her moments later, lying still. There were no cries of alarm, no shouts for the guards to come.

"That was close," Tamira breathed.

"Let's get out of here and inform Tasim of our success," Shukara said. The novelty of sneaking into the home of another was fast wearing off, and she was impatient to continue her quest.

"Yes," Tamira said, but not without some ambivalence. Shukara caught her looking around the riad and guessed her thoughts.

"Our success depends on no one knowing we were ever in here," she reminded Tamira. "Which means we take nothing." The thief could return to the riad in her own time and empty the place, for all Shukara cared.

Tamira rolled nimbly to her feet and hunched low as she returned to the room where they had left the rope. Shukara slipped into the room and opened the window shutters while

Tamira wrapped the rope around one of the pillars.

Holding both lengths of the rope, Shukara climbed out of the window, a quick glance assuring her that no witnesses stood in the small lane. She lowered herself down, using her feet to push herself away from the building while gripping both lengths of the rope.

Shukara let go the rope two feet up from the ground, looking up to see Tamira was already halfway down. The thief landed nimbly beside her and pulled one end of the rope, bringing the whole length down.

"Forget something?" Tamira asked as she wound the rope into a neat coil.

Holding her stave and willing the shutters to close, Shukara frowned. "Not that I can think of."

"Your sandals?"

Damnation! She stared up at the window, cursing her carelessness. "Maybe they'll be overlooked?" Otherwise Calan would know someone had intruded in his home.

Something landed on the ground. "Or maybe you can thank me with some food?" Tamira suggested, pointing to the two sandals she had just dropped.

"I'll consider it," Shukara said in relief as she put her sandals on and re-tied them, silently blessing the thief's attention to detail. "But first we'll visit Tasim. I want to meet this 'Eye of Mask' before nightfall."

Chapter Nine

Tasim looked surprised as Tamira and Shukara entered his shop. "I had not expected to see you again until tomorrow. I do hope you've not reconsidered our arrangement?"

Tamira heard the veiled threat in his voice, but recognised too the reigned-in panic. The beasts were baying at his door, herself and Shukara his best hope at fending them off.

"I keep my word, Master Tasim, and expect others to do likewise," Shukara said, the threat in *her* voice plain. "We have fulfilled our end of the bargain, kindly fulfil yours."

Tamira hid her smile at Shukara's affected casual tone, as if the task had required little effort. She wondered if all magi played such games, leaving others off-balance. Tasim's eyes had widened in surprise and he regarded her with a mix of respect and awe, doubtless wondering the limits of her magick.

"You left the idol in his lock-safe?" he asked cautiously, wanting confirmation while taking care not to offend the mage.

"That was the task, was it not?" Shukara sounded bored.

"Yes … yes." Tasim struggled to regain his composure. "I had not expected you to act today, I must speak with someone."

"After you've told us how we might contact the Eye of Mask." Shukara watched the merchant coolly.

He forced a smile. "Of course. I keep my word also, Mistress Shukara."

Tasim told them where to find an agent of the Eye's and hurriedly started to close his shop despite dusk still being some hours away.

"Why did you want us to put the idol in Calan's lock-safe?" Tamira asked, curiosity getting the better of her.

"Calan is not the only one with friends in the Cult. I too am on good terms with a priest, even if one far less regarded than Calan's father in law's uncle. Acting on 'rumours' that Calan ban Ahmet is secretly a worshipper of Niash, this priest will visit Calan's riad with a troop of soldiers and search it."

Tasim smiled, not a pleasant sight. "And when Calan opens his lock-safe – a lock-safe only he can open – the idol will be found within, seeing him disgraced and very likely executed."

*

Shukara followed Tamira into the Merchant Quarter and onwards to the harbour, a welcome respite from the unremitting poverty she had witnessed earlier. Tasim had admitted to having never dealt with the Eye of Mask himself, but he knew where to find one of their agents. He directed them to a small house near the harbour, an unremarkable building in the shadow of larger structures.

The house had a sturdy brown door at the top of six worn steps, and Shukara knocked on it.

Three bolts clanked back in succession and a boy answered the door, letting them inside. The tattoo on his arm marked him as a slave, though he looked well-fed and healthy. There was a sharpness to him as he appraised the two visitors without apparent fear of being accused of insolence. Most slaves kept their eyes down.

"We require an audience," Shukara told him as he led them into a modest parlour. They sat and waited, Tamira studying the plain room with a thief's eye for items of value. There was nothing: Chairs made of cedar, red tiles covering the floor. Such ready access to the Eye struck Shukara as odd; while an information broker needed to be approachable, anyone who took umbrage knew where to find him or her.

The slave returned. "My mistress will see you now."

Shukara and Tamira followed him down the narrow corridor and into a room where a woman waited, seated on a cushion behind a low table. She looked to be perhaps thirty, Maskan, with short dark hair that flared out to cover her ears, and wearing a yellow kalasiris.

"Welcome, be seated. I am Erasi." A fresh pot of teh smelling of mint stood on the table, two clean cups positioned at the vacant cushion.

Shukara sat on the cushion while the slave left. Tamira stood near the door, failing to hide her anxiety. Erasi poured them all teh.

Shukara passed a cup back to Tamira and sipped from her own, nodding her approval at the taste, not unduly bitter. "My thanks. I am Shukara, this is Tamira."

"What brings you to my home this day?" Erasi asked.

"Firstly, I am curious about the Eye of Mask. Will you humour me?"

Erasi smiled. "All are curious about the Eye. Suffice to say, we are a group who value information. We buy and sell it, sometimes for coin, other times for services or information of equal value. We take no sides in Mask's politics."

"Are you not concerned about your safety? Dissatisfied clients know where to find you."

Erasi's smile hardened. "I have nothing to fear, I assure you. One does not kill sheep for mutton today if one wishes wool tomorrow. And we pay some tough rams handsomely for protection."

Shukara's left hand rested on her hidden wytchwood stave, sharpening her senses and questing outwards.

Five sets of heartbeats. Five drawing breath. There were a further two persons very close by, likely concealed within the walls. And no doubt armed with crossbows or similar should any threaten Erasi. Shukara nodded. "To business, then?"

Erasi clasped her fingers. "To business. How can the Eye assist you?"

There was no way to proceed without letting Erasi know what she was. "I require certain reagents that are proving hard to find in this city. Specifically, firethorn seeds."

Erasi blinked and edged back slightly. Shukara supressed a smile. The woman was a sharp one, she knew now that Shukara was a magicker, and was probably wondering if her hidden guards were sufficient. *Even without my reagents, I think not.*

"Few if any places in Mask will have such items," Erasi said slowly. "But the Eye may be able to provide what you need. Go to the Red Serpent Tavern near the docks, you'll be contacted there." She handed Shukara a wooden token with an eye carved thereon. "Show this to the bartender, he will ensure you are undisturbed."

Shukara stood. "What will the price be?"

"That's still to be decided." Erasi rang a bell and smiled.

"A pleasure meeting you."

The slave entered the room and silently led them out.

*

The Red Serpent had looked disreputable from the outside, and as Shukara's eyes adjusted to the darkness inside she saw nothing to contradict this impression. Old straw lay strewn over the dirt floor, and the clay walls were cracked and crumbling. Pungent smells of stale urine and unwashed bodies soured the air. The narrow windows were shuttered, and the candle sconces nailed into the walls were too few to light up the common room.

Maybe that was intentional. Rough-faced sailors and scarred mercenaries sat on crudely mended stools around gouged wooden tables. Some gambled while others drank in sullen silence. Shukara was surprised to find the tavern half-full, given that dusk was still some hours away. *What must it be like in here after sunset?*

Brawls aplenty, she suspected. That explained the sparse furniture and the broken state of what there was. "Sit there," Shukara said quietly to Tamira, pointing to a quiet corner away from the other patrons. She approached the bar, nothing more than a piece of driftwood sitting atop a barricade of large red bricks. Cover for the bartender should the patrons grow rowdy, no doubt.

"Two cups of teh," she requested, surreptitiously passing him the token along with two coins.

Time passed, Shukara and Tamira sitting quietly in the corner. Tamira had taken one sniff of the teh and surreptitiously emptied both cups in the corner, already damp from less pleasant deposits. The locale and the teh may have disappointed, but the rest was welcome after their eventful day.

Shukara suspected the Eye owned the tavern, or at least paid the owner for their use of it. Given its proximity to the docks, she had little doubt the Eye's agents worked the tavern to overhear gossip from visitors hailing from all over the world.

The bartender attended their table and lifted the empty cups. "Go to the room upstairs, second on the left," he said in a low voice.

"A trap?" Tamira asked when he left.

A fair concern, Shukara conceded. "I doubt the Eye would betray its clients, that would be bad for business." All the same, she ensured her stave was within reach.

They ascended the creaking wooden steps to the upper level and entered the second room on the left. It was empty save for Erasi, a table and two chairs. Shukara sat across from the Eye's emissary while Tamira stood at the entrance.

"Shut the door," Erasi said to Tamira. Perspiration ran down her face, and she looked less confident away from the safety of her house.

"Should we be honoured you're meeting us absent your two guards?" Shukara asked.

Erasi didn't bother to ask how Shukara knew about her guards who had been concealed during their first meeting. "You should be honoured I'm meeting you here myself. Normally I would send someone else, but this is a delicate matter."

"Could you have picked a worse tavern?" Tamira asked.

Erasi smiled a little. "We've only recently acquired it, and plan to improve it to encourage more trade. It is on a prime spot, but the previous owner was his own best customer."

"Are you able to assist me?" Shukara asked, impatient for news. She hadn't travelled a continent to discuss the merits of a flea-pit tavern. Tension eased in her chest as Erasi nodded, a tension she hadn't realised was there.

"Yes, the Eye can supply what you need."

Tamira blew out a breath; Shukara kept her own relief hidden. "And what is the price?" Gods willing, her remaining rubies would be enough. Funding her long return journey home was a concern for later.

"The price is why I attended personally," Erasi said. "Someone is willing to provide what you require – including firethorn seeds – in exchange for information that the Eye possesses. In return we require a service from you, with little time for you to complete it."

Must everyone demand a service of me today? Shukara leaned back, knowing she was not going to like this. Erasi did not prove her wrong.

Chapter Ten

The crowds parted for the merchant prince and his escort, three of his personal guard marching ahead to ensure he was not delayed, shouting, "Make way for Master Wakib ban Hikeem!" There was little need for them to use force against any save the slow, most of the pedestrians hastily moving to one side of the cramped streets with no voiced complaints and few risking even a vexed look.

And with good reason. Wakib, son of Hikeem had been a prosperous merchant in the days before the last king's fall, and his wealth and power had waxed greatly in the years since. Aged maybe forty, he was a tall vigorous man who rode the streets on a magnificent black horse, disdaining the palanquins favoured by many of his august fellows.

Tamira peered over the rooftop, taking care not to be seen by Wakib's escort. A further three flanked him with the last two forming a rear guard. The guards – all on foot – each wore a leather kilt, ring mail tunic and conical helm, their limbs protected by metal vambraces and greaves. A slightly curved sword hung from each man's side, a round iron buckler strapped to his left arm.

Tamira gave silent thanks that she was just required to follow Wakib rather than accost him. She had questioned why Shukara could not just use the same spell on him that she had used on her pouch after Tamira had snatched it, but apparently such a spell could be detected by another mage if they studied him closely. Too risky, given that they knew nothing of who Wakib was on his way to meet.

Instead Shukara had cast the spell on a pebble carried by Tamira, allowing the mage to follow her from a distance. Shukara lacked Tamira's skill on the rooftops and was too distinctive to chance following Wakib on the streets.

Almost as distinctive as Wakib, sitting regally atop his horse and dressed in a crimson syek robe, wearing a turban made from the same material. A sapphire-crowned pin held it in place, the gem catching both the last rays of sunlight and Tamira's breath.

Only a fool would risk trying to snatch it, a thief sure to be cut down by the guards. A beggar shuffled towards Wakib, entreating the merchant prince for just a few coins.

He never got close, a guard striking him to the head with his shield and kicking him several times to ensure he stayed down. No emotion registered on the guard's face, he might as well have been kicking a dog. Wakib never so much as looked at the broken, bleeding man. The merchant prince was not known for his charity.

Dung from his horse littered the street as the procession continued, Wakib's only contribution to the commoners of Mask. Tamira clambered up the side of a building, her small fingers squeezing into the cracked clay façade.

Shadows lengthened across the street, the city bathing in reddish-gold as dusk fell once more. Shops were closing, though food vendors would persist throughout the evening. Watchmen from the City Guard maintained a respectful distance as Wakib and his escort passed. The streets thronged as people returned home while Tamira watched unnoticed from the roofs above.

Most of Mask's prosperous citizens lived in the Merchant Quarter, but the truly rich lived in decadent splendour elsewhere in the city, in a world apart from the desperate poverty endured by many; the Gold Quarter. Wakib lived there, but if Tamira recalled the city layout correctly, he was taking a detour.

She moved from rooftop to rooftop, following Wakib across the city. Erasi's information was clear; Wakib was meeting someone tonight. What was not known was the identity of the other party, and that was Erasi's price for Shukara's reagents. Part of the price.

Wakib stopped his horse in front of a four-storey building in a small street, the first and tallest of a series of houses and shops. The building was cloaked in darkness save for one window three storeys up at the end, where candlelight danced within. Two red-cloaked soldiers stood at the entrance. Wakib was helped down from the saddle by one of his guards with whom he conferred briefly. The two soldiers guarding the entrance stepped aside to allow Wakib and his guard inside, the others remaining outside.

Tamira watched from across the street, considering. Unlike Wakib's escort, the men already guarding the building were actual soldiers. *Red-cloaks wouldn't be escorting a merchant no matter how rich. Wakib's meeting an officer, a high-ranking one.*

She hissed out a breath. Clandestine meetings between merchant princes and army officers suggested a conspiracy, and there was no way for her to avoid it if she was to repay her debt to Shukara. *And I thought sneaking into Calan's riad was as dangerous as today was going to get.*

But first she must learn who Wakib was meeting. Waiting until he left the building was the safest course, but one with no guarantee that she would see his face. No, she had to be sure.

Tamira crawled away from the edge of the building to the other side and clambered down to the street. A peek around the corner satisfied her that the guards weren't looking in her direction, and she slipped across the street under cover of night.

Cracks in the brickwork let her climb a single-storied shop, from where she scampered lightly across the roof towards the building Wakib had entered. That building was three storeys higher, not a problem for her well-practiced hands and feet. *Thank the gods for old buildings no one cares to maintain.*

She peered over the edge, a not-unpleasant thrill shivering through her as she looked down on the soldiers and guards who were ensuring that their masters met undisturbed, ignorant of her presence above.

The lit window was at the far end, a soldier and guard standing below, studiously ignoring one another. Tamira lowered herself over the edge until her feet found the topmost window-ledge, her fingers digging into cracks in the mortar. She moved as slowly as she could, wary of betraying her presence with dislodged debris.

Balanced on the ledge, she chanced a look down, relieved to see the two men still unaware that she perched above them. She peered through the narrow window but knew better than to slip inside. Doubtless Wakib's guard – and a soldier – guarded the door to the meeting room.

Tamira stepped to the left and felt for toeholds as she began her careful descent. Sweat pooled on her brow, an unwelcome distraction. Even less welcome if a drop landed on one of the two men below and caused him to look up.

Inch after inch she descended, probing with fingers and toes for gaps sufficient to hold her as she approached the lit window, close enough to hear voices.

"–loyal?"

"The officers are loyal to me, their soldiers will do as commanded, Wakib," a deeper voice said. "I've two regiments of conscripts dredged from the southern provinces, none of whom will cause problems, and the third regiment are slave-soldiers, blindly obedient."

"But three regiments, will they be enough?" Wakib fretted.

"Three regiments of infantry, reinforced with two of chariot," the other said. "And your money has already paid for three mercenary companies until winter."

"Mercenaries," Wakib spat. "Loyal only so long as victory is certain, and no one makes them a better offer."

"Victory will be certain, I'll make sure of it." The officer sounded confident.

Tamira listened, the conversation tightening her chest. Did they plot a coup to overthrow the Cult's rule of Mask?

"Admiral Hessian is with us?"

"Yes, he is with us," the other said in a tone of weary impatience. "Enough doubts, Wakib. We are committed. The orders are in my office, signed and awaiting dispatch. In three ten-days the 5th Regiment will march to the harbour and board Hessian's troop ships. The 13th Regiment will be recalled from Pashbur, sailing north on barges. Ships will meet them just to the south and carry them north. The 9th Regiment is already on the Egarian border with both regiments of chariot."

"The mercenaries?" Wakib asked.

"They'll escort our supplies by caravan piecemeal into Egaria. So far as the Egarians will know, they're merely caravan guards escorting merchants east."

A brief silence fell. Egaria. Tamira clung to the wall as disappointment weighed her gut. Not a coup but a foreign adventure by a soldier and merchant craving wealth and conquest.

"I've invested most of my fortune in this endeavour," Wakib said.

"You'll get your gold back, and much more … *Padshah*."

Wakib snorted. "Don't take me for a fool, General. You know as well as I that the Cult will send a high priest to 'advise'. He will rule Egaria no matter who is appointed Padshah."

"The high priest will be too busy crushing heretics and rivals to be troubled with actually governing. And if he proves overly meddlesome, send him a black rose."

"I've promised the Black Rose enough of my coin," Wakib grumbled. "This has done nothing but cost me. Money to provision our expeditionary force, money to hire mercenaries, to bribe that Border Captain, to buy Egaria's naval patrol schedule. And not least, a small fortune sent south to those damned assassins. I've bought a garden-full of black bloody roses!"

"A necessary expense, Wakib. They'll deal with most of Egaria's generals, paralysing their army. They're reliable."

"They're fanatics. By the time they've finished in Egaria, black roses will be more common than red."

The General chuckled at the grim jest. Black roses were a rarity, cultivated in Rhemi by the sect of assassins who left one with the body of every contracted kill. Tamira realised she was tensing her fingers and forced them to relax slightly, lest she dislodge a piece of brick or mortar.

"When will you dispatch the orders?" Wakib asked.

"Soon. What of those in Mask to be given black roses?"

There was a rustle of papyrus. "I have the list here." Tamira heard nervousness in Wakib's voice. "Killing Egarians is one thing, but to have our own murdered is…"

"Another necessity. Councillor Rehman enjoys too close a relationship with Egaria's merchants. Silence him, and the rest of the Merchant Council will accept the conquest of Egaria without protest."

"So long as it succeeds, and so long as they receive a share of the spoils," Wakib said. "High Priest Yusef is another 'necessary' death, but if the Cult suspect we ordered…"

"They won't. The sect will agree not to leave their habitual roses in Mask – for a quarter over the usual fee."

"Assassins who pout at being unable to claim credit," Wakib muttered. "You'll get the list to their agent here?"

"Yes, I am to meet him in two days. The gold is ready?"

Tamira heard a heavy sigh. "Yes, send word when it is to be paid. Keep that list safe, or we'll die screaming on the altar."

"I will. Our business is done?"

"For now, General. I'll leave first. Hrek watch you."

"Hrek watch you."

Tamira chanced a peek through the window, just long enough to see the General. A tall, muscular man clasped Wakib's forearm, a thick black beard growing below an angular, lined face. The General wore a red cloak and shendyt like his men, albeit his shendyt was lionskin rather than linen, a sign of his rank. A red turban was wrapped around his head, threaded with gold, and a curved sword hung from his waist.

The room was bare except for a table near the window, a chair on either side. A leather satchel lay open on the table, scrolls of papyrus peeking out. Neither the General nor Wakib were looking towards the window, and Tamira saw her chance…

Afterwards, she climbed back up to the roof, her limbs cramped after being stationary for so long, heart hammering in her chest. What she had done was reckless, but she had not been caught. Less risky than entering the room to snatch the scrolls. Wakib was mounting his horse by the time she had reached the roof and peered over, his face hidden in shadow.

Her interest in him had passed, however, to the General and the documents he possessed.

Chapter Eleven

Tamira was moving again, Shukara knew, sensing the distance increase between herself and the Marked pebble Tamira carried. Worry had begun to gnaw at her when the pebble was stationary for so long.

She walked briskly through the winding streets, a massive wall looming ahead. Her knowledge of Mask's labyrinthine streets was still scant, but the black pyramid visible over the inner-city wall ahead confirmed that she was heading towards the Old Quarter, not the Gold.

The Old Quarter was the original city and forbidden to foreigners. Knowing the guards stationed at the gate would never let her pass, Shukara slowed her pace. Frustration nipped her as she considered her choices. She could easily overcome the guards but that would draw attention. Follow Tamira's example and use the rooftops?

That would be foolish. She lacked the thief's experience, and it was dark besides. She had the means to overcome the latter but spending hours trying to find a route that would take her over the walls did not appeal. Meanwhile, Tamira was getting further ahead.

Something dropped down behind her, and Shukara spun, stave gripped in readiness to defend herself with the limited spells at her disposal.

"Enjoying the night air?" Shukara sensed Tamira's grin in the dark.

"What are you doing here? Where is Wakib?" Shukara asked in irritation.

"Riding home, I would assume," Tamira said carelessly. "We're following the man he met, a general escorted by soldiers of the 5th Regiment."

"Following him how?" Shukara frowned. "He has the pebble?"

"I tossed it through a window into his satchel." Tamira sounded pleased with herself. "But if we're to get you into the Old Quarter, we'll need to go up." A doubting tone entered her voice. "If you can manage?"

"I can manage," Shukara snapped. *Insolent brat.* "Why are we following this general?"

"He and Wakib are planning to invade Egaria, a small principality to the north-east."

Shukara frowned. "And?" Surely the Eye of Mask knew of it already.

"And they've not troubled themselves to get permission from the Cult or Merchant Council. The General is providing the soldiers and transport, Wakib is funding the invasion."

"Won't they be executed?" Shukara asked.

"If they fail, yes. If they succeed, the Cult and the Merchant Council will pretend they knew about it all along."

"Then why not just get their blessing now?" Shukara asked. These Maskans were a strange people.

"Because the Spice Route east passes through Egaria. If Wakib, the General and their fellow conspirators get there first, they'll have first pick of the spoils and take over the trading routes east. The General will have wealth enough to live like a king, and Wakib gets to rule Egaria as padshah. They'll need to pay a fortune to placate Mask's ruling priests and merchants, but it's still a fine prize."

Shukara was surprised and not a little impressed at Tamira's grasp of the politics involved. "And the Eye of Mask has gotten wind of their plan?"

Tamira nodded. "Enough to know Wakib is up to something."

"Will this information be enough to exchange for reagents? Erasi wants proof, remember."

"The proof is in the General's possession; names of Maskans to be assassinated by the Black Rose to ensure their invasion is blessed after the fact. If he is returning to his office, we may even find orders written up to set the invasion in motion. More than enough for your reagents. More than enough to see Wakib and the General executed." There was a savage satisfaction in Tamira's voice. Pleasure at the thought of the rich and powerful suffering like the poor, or something personal?

*

Her companion sucked in deep breaths, sinking down onto the roof. The General – or rather the pebble he unknowingly carried – had stopped moving, leading them to a kasbah lying in the heart of the Old Quarter. Tamira was unsurprised. A few crumbling kasbahs – four-towered fortresses – remained in the Old Quarter, legacies from a time when the Kingdom of Mask had extended not much further than the city walls. The pebble had led them to the Kasbah Baraq, used as a barracks for the 5th Regiment. Another nearby kasbah was known now as the Kasbah Arcana, home and school to the Hrek-sworn magi.

"Stay here," Tamira said. "I'll look for the best way in. In any case, we'll wait before entering." A few hours before dawn was the best time for thievery, when most slept deeply and sentries relaxed their guard.

Shukara nodded, looking grateful for the rest.

"You did well, I hope I'm still as able when I'm as old as you," Tamira couldn't resist saying. Shukara gasped out a profanity between breaths.

The Old Quarter was the oldest in Mask, home mostly to those unable to afford houses in the Merchant and Gold Quarters, but prosperous enough to avoid a squalid existence in the Poor Quarter. A few ancient riads remained from the long-ago days when Mask's rich had lived here too, but most had crumbled over the centuries and been replaced with smaller buildings.

Houses and souks shared this part of the city with the decaying symbols of Mask's millennia-old splendour, growing like weeds amidst the Royal Palace, High Temple, and the three crumbling kasbahs.

The Kasbah Baraq loomed ahead, an imposing square fortress cornered by four towers rising slightly above the main building. From her rooftop perch three streets away, Tamira had a good view of the kasbah, close enough to consider their entry. She suspected it would be harder than getting into Calan's riad.

Home to the feared red-cloaked soldiers of the 5th Regiment, Tamira was unsurprised to find the kasbah guarded, silhouettes visible on the battlements. Probably more from soldierly habit than any need for protection. Mask the city hadn't been threatened in centuries, a legacy of aggressive outward expansion.

Climbing the kasbah directly was almost impossible, she decided. Even if she could, there were no reachable windows and most of the gaps looked too small even for her to enter, never mind Shukara. The prospect of failure loomed like a spectre, the prospect of angering Shukara. She liked something about the tall woman, her independence perhaps. Tamira doubted she would really kill her, but stories of those who crossed magi rarely ended well for anyone except magi.

She decided to view the kasbah from a different angle, the closeness of the buildings allowing her to circle round with relative ease. From the north she identified a possibility. With the threat of invasion a distant memory, and the kasbah no longer part of Mask's defences, other buildings had crept closer. An extension had even been added to the kasbah, a single storey barracks.

The extension had no doors or windows wide enough to squeeze through, but the original kasbah had a window high above the extension's flat, crenelated roof. Maybe too high to reach even from the roof, but Tamira could see no better way in.

She returned to Shukara, pleased to see that the mage had recovered. Entering the kasbah would be a job for two.

"Follow me," Tamira said quietly. Voices carried in the night. The mage rose and followed her down onto the street. The kasbah loomed over them as they circled round to its extension.

Tamira looked around quickly and gestured for the coil of thin rope she had asked the mage to carry. Satisfied they were alone, she nodded at Shukara. "Help me up."

Shukara crouched and cupped her hands, accepting Tamira's left foot. She lifted while Tamira steadied herself against the wall with her left hand, reaching up with her right. Her hand cleared the roof and found a hold. She reached up with her left hand, pulling herself up onto the roof.

Tamira uncoiled the thin rope and wrapped it around a crenelation. She dropped the other end over the side and saw it go taut as Shukara started her ascent.

"That was the easy part," Tamira whispered as she gathered the rope. There were no shouts of alarm, so she assumed none of the guards up above had noticed them.

They crept over to the kasbah wall, the narrow window high above them. "Now what?" Shukara asked.

"You magick us into birds and we fly up to the window," Tamira deadpanned.

Shukara frowned at her.

"Or we repeat what we did to get up this far," Tamira said beneath the mage's penetrating glare. She wrapped the rope around herself.

Shukara crouched again, and Tamira stepped onto her cupped hands, bracing herself against the wall as the mage lifted her up. She felt Shukara's arms tremble slightly as they stretched up to their limit. Tamira reached up too, taking care not to overbalance and fall.

Her fingers brushed the edge of the window, her reach too short to get a grip. She raised herself up on her toes. Still too short. She took a breath and slowly bent her knees, and after letting out half her breath, sprang up.

Her hands snatched at the window's edge and for an instant she thought she would fall. But her hands caught stone and found purchase. She hung there, feeling her heart pound in her chest. After allowing herself a few seconds pause, she began to pull herself up, her bare toes feeling for purchase on the mostly smooth clay wall.

Tamira ignored her straining muscles and the grazes on her arms and legs as she fought to pull herself through the window. Her feet scraped against the wall in vain, and when her burning arms started to tremble, she knew she was in trouble.

Something shoved her up, and after a heartbeat's surprise she hauled herself through the window. She tumbled to the floor, her arms shaky as she forced herself to her feet. The room was dark and Tamira went still, listening for breathing not her own. Nothing.

She unwrapped the rope and felt around for something to tie it to. The force that pushed her up must have been Shukara's magick, she decided, like earlier. Had the mage not helped her, she'd be lying broken on the roof.

Tamira's hands brushed against a wooden surface and she knew she'd found a door. She ran her hands down until she found the metal hoop handle. Gently pulling the door to no avail, she was satisfied it was shut securely and tied the rope to the hoop.

Confident that the rope was tight, she leaned out of the narrow window and threw the other end down to Shukara. Tamira kept watch as the mage started to climb.

She helped Shukara inside, her skin tingling as it always did when she was somewhere she shouldn't be. "Thank you for the push."

"Welcome," Shukara gasped. The silhouette of a hand went up to the mage's face, and Tamira heard her swallow something. A slim glass bottle was pushed into her hand. "Drink."

Tamira obeyed, the taste unpleasantly bitter. "What is it?"

"You'll see."

Her eyes started to water and sting but as she blinked away the tears, she found that she *could* see. Enough to discern the contents of the room if she squinted. "Useful, but can you not make it stronger?"

"A concentrated dose would make our eyes sensitive enough to see almost perfectly in the dark, but we would be blinded the moment we encountered light. Expect some discomfort from torch or candlelight until the potion wears off."

Tamira looked around, identifying a desk at one end of the room and stools at the other. She felt smooth tiles beneath her feet.

"A teaching room for officers," Shukara guessed.

They couldn't just wander around aimlessly until they found the General's rooms. "Where is the pebble now?"

Shukara froze in concentration. "On the other side of the kasbah ... and up."

"A tower," Tamira guessed.

"Then let us waste no more time."

"Leave your sandals here. Follow my lead," Tamira whispered as she turned the door handle, the rope still tied to it. Given the late hour, most of the soldiers would be asleep, but she knew the kasbah was still guarded. "And remember them when we leave." *If we leave.*

The corridor was in darkness and they crept along it, treading softly on the tiled floor. Tamira motioned for Shukara to stop as they reached a corner. She peered round, her potion-aided vision showing one soldier guarding the tower entrance at the end of the corridor. Bile pricked Tamira's throat.

"I'll deal with him," Shukara whispered, stave clenched in her right hand. The guard looked suddenly discomfited, then seemed to be trying to gasp for air for several very long moments. He fell to his knees, clutching his throat in a futile bid for air before finally collapsing to the ground.

"You killed him?" Tamira asked, left timid by the mage's apparent ruthlessness.

"He's alive. I thickened the air in his lungs until he passed out," Shukara said as if that were perfectly natural.

They hurried down the corridor, Tamira listening for the sound of anyone approaching. Her jaw clenched as the door creaked on opening, but they slipped into the tower without incident.

They padded up the worn brick stairs, finding a door one level below the top of the tower. The door looked old but sturdy, secured by a padlock.

"The pebble is within this room. Can you pick the padlock?" Shukara asked.

Tamira made a face. "No. Can't you just...?" She waggled her fingers.

Shukara looked down at her, the dark masking her expression. "Not without certain reagents." Opening Calan ban Ahmet's lock-safe must have exhausted her capability in that regard, at least until she replaced the necessary reagents.

Tamira studied the padlock. Even had they a tool to smash it, the noise would attract attention. "It's beyond us." To have come so far...

Shukara cocked her head. "We don't need to defeat the lock. It is the door we must overcome. Hand me your knife."

"If you plan to saw through that door, you're on your own," she said as she handed the knife over.

The mage ignored her, jamming the knife blade into the top

hinge of the door. Tamira kept watch while Shukara struggled to prise off the hinge. Sure enough, the padlock was formidable, but the brickwork holding the hinges was ancient and crumbling.

Shukara worked quickly, first jemmying off the top hinge and then the bottom. Tamira sensed her amused satisfaction when she forced open the door, only the padlock holding it up.

Moonlight poured through a narrow window into the small room beyond the door, leaving it brightly lit to Tamira's potion-enhanced eyes. It was clearly the General's office, a cedar desk and chair occupying most of the space. Tamira felt a thrill on seeing the satchel lying on top of the desk, but it was empty. Shukara's pebble had fallen onto the stone floor.

A coat of polished ring mail hung from an armour stand, a gold-banded helm sitting on top. Next to it lay a large wooden chest.

Tamira gently lifted the chest lid, disappointed but unsurprised to find it contained only a red cloak and scabbarded sword along with iron greaves and bracers: the General's war gear, which might soon see action in Egaria. No documents.

"Here," Shukara said softly, drawing Tamira to the desk. An ink pot and grey-feathered quill lay on the desk next to the empty satchel, but a heavy iron chest sat beneath the desk. Locked.

"We won't force that with a knife," Tamira said. It was also too heavy to carry.

"No. We need the key."

"The General still has it," Tamira said with certainty. Given the chest's suspected incriminating contents, he wouldn't risk anyone else opening it. "Shall we go ask him for it?" she asked sarcastically.

Shukara smiled. "Let's." The mage turned before Tamira could reply.

Gods, you'll get us hung! Tamira followed, not daring to voice her protest. She found Shukara climbing up to the top of the tower where another room awaited, this one unlocked. The General's bedchamber.

They found him inside, thankfully asleep. 'Watch him,' Tamira mouthed as she explored the table across from the bed. The room was small and held only the bed, a table and a clothing trunk. And a sleeping general who would not be pleased to find intruders within his bedchamber.

Her hand brushed against cold iron and she lifted a linen cloth, revealing two black keys. A relieved smile crossed her lips as she picked them up, goosebumps running down her arm. She hated being a thief, sickened by the desperation and constant fear.

But she loved it too.

Shukara's eyes were fixed on the sleeping general, the linen sheet rising and falling with every breath. Tamira scented the sweetly-sick smell of burned lotus, an explanation for his deep slumber. She tapped the mage on the shoulder and showed her the keys. Shukara's smile mirrored her own.

The first key looked too small for the iron chest, no doubt the key for the padlocked door they had forced off its hinges. Shukara shrugged at Tamira's wry grin; had they visited the bedchamber first, they could have saved themselves the effort of forcing the door.

They crept back to the office, where the second key unlocked the chest with a heavy click, a weight leaving Tamira's chest as it did so. She opened the chest and found scrolls of tied papyrus within.

"Just take them all," Shukara suggested, handing her the satchel.

"If this is the proof we seek, that guard you knocked out may wish you had killed him," Tamira remarked as she filled the satchel with scrolls. Depending on what the Eye of Mask did with the evidence, so might the General.

*

"Come, it is time we were leaving." Shukara led Tamira out of the room and back down the winding staircase. The corridors were still deserted, the guard still unconscious, and they returned safely to the room through which they had entered.

Tamira untied the rope from the hooped handle.

"What are you doing?" Shukara asked. At least the thief had the sense not to want to linger in search of valuables.

Tamira managed a grin. "I might want to sneak in here again. Never let them know how you entered." She pulled the rope through the hoop until two equal lengths remained free. "You first."

Shukara held both lengths of the rope and squeezed through the narrow window, lowering herself down onto the flat roof below. There was no raised alarm, no sign of pursuit.

Tamira followed, and on reaching the bottom she released one end of the rope and pulled the other. The rope came free and fell next to them. "Good rope is precious," she said as she gathered it up and coiled it around herself. "Follow me."

They lowered themselves down onto the ground and made off, losing themselves in the maze of streets.

"I think we're safe," Tamira said, halting in a dark alley.

"I agree." An oddly exhilarating experience, thievery. So long as one wasn't caught.

"Now what?" Tamira watched her warily, perhaps fearing Shukara would dispose of her now the heist was done.

"We agreed to meet Erasi at dawn; we shall do so."

Tamira nodded. A grin slashed her mouth. "I wouldn't want to be that guard when the General awakens."

"I wouldn't want to be the General or the merchant if the Eye of Mask decide to pass those scrolls to the Cult of Hrek and Merchant Council." Or maybe the Eye would ransom them back, demanding a heavy price. Shukara cared not.

Chapter Twelve

Gravel crunched underfoot as Jassan led the file of camels onwards, guessing they would reach the oasis before dusk. They had left the shifting sand dunes to the south as the desert landscape became hamada – a barren plateau of bare rock, gravel and boulders. Many believed the Kavari Desert was a near-endless sea of shifting sand, but in truth most of it was like this. Rocky hills rose to his left that delayed their journey, lying between the small caravan and the oasis.

A furnace scorched the sky overhead, so hot it consumed Jassan's sweat as fast as he perspired, leaving his skin dry. Desert novices often believed they weren't sweating at all as their body's water was stolen away, just one of the desert's fatal little tricks. Even the air itself writhed beneath the merciless sun.

Jassan kept up a brisk steady pace, balancing speed with strength conservation. The desert was a patient killer, and moving too fast would see him die of exhaustion.

He had planned to scout ahead to see if the oasis they aimed for was occupied, and if so by whom, but Subed had collapsed before midday. The heat, the rationed water and the loss of his friends had sapped the man's spirit. He was bound to one of the camels, and Jassan now led his file.

Sulen kept up, suffering in silence as he led the second file of camels, a reliable man. A share of the cargo sold had been his, but he hadn't said a word of complaint about the lost money. Not yet, anyway. Doubtless he would weary Jassan's ears over wine and lotus back in the Pashbur Caravanserai. If they made it back.

Loose scree rattled down the slope and Jassan's sharp eyes snapped up, running across the hilltops. *There...*

"Sulen," he said quietly, not looking at the man. "'Ware left, we're not alone."

"Bandits or Kavari?" Sulen asked.

"I cannot say. Scouts from whoever holds the oasis." Not

that it mattered much; without the oasis they were dead. Jassan turned to face the camels he pulled, hoping that whoever watched would see his black-feathered arrows and know him for a ranger.

Five men in sandy-brown djellabas appeared atop the hill, whooping and hollering, bows and swords raised in the air. Jassan cursed at the sight of them. They were Kavari like himself, but little more than youths. *Strutting young fools, looking to prove themselves.* The caravan had too few men with too many camels, too tempting a sight for any to ignore.

Jassan passed the rope controlling his file to a fearful Sulen and unslung his recurved bow, notching an arrow from the quiver on his right hip. He raised his bow high and pulled the string back, muscles straining with the effort. The arrow whistled as it sprang up in the direction of the hills.

The scouts fell silent as the arrow passed beyond them, recognising Jassan's intent: a warning. *Heed it.*

One young man resumed the hollering, no doubt the leader. Some of the scouts had bows of their own, and one sent an arrow towards the caravan, an arrow that fell short. Sulen skipped back with a curse, but Jassan had no time to calm the man's fears.

He watched as they began to descend the slope, weapons drawn. *Sands take them!* He pulled out a fowling blunt, one of two arrows he had with a blunt iron tip instead of the usual pointed broadhead, intended for stunning birds and small animals.

He aimed at the leader and loosed, gratified to see him double over as the blunt arrow hammered into his gut. His fellows slowed, perhaps thinking him dead. *Show some wits and retreat.*

Instead, the leader struggled back to his feet, bent slightly over. He held Jassan's arrow high before snapping it in two. His men raised their weapons and roared insults at Jassan and Sulen as they resumed their charge down the slope.

Irritation wore at Jassan, not helped by the heat and his thirst. *If you dung-eaters want to play, I'll play.* He pulled out another arrow, notching and loosing.

A cry rang out as the leader tumbled to the ground, rolling down the slope a few feet before stopping. Jassan smiled in vicious satisfaction as his target screamed in pain, clutching his left thigh, the arrow sticking out from it.

Again, the others stopped, two of them attending to their leader while the other three continued their howling, outrage replacing their earlier excitement. Jassan knew they wanted to charge, but he stood firm, another arrow notched to his bow. His meaning was clear; the first to resume the charge would die. They were on the cusp of manhood, likely untried in true battle, and before them stood a desert-forged ranger.

No one charged.

Instead they carried their wounded leader back up the hill, disappearing out of sight.

"A wise choice," Sulen said, his voice a little shaky. "Could you have killed them?"

"Probably," Jassan said, though one of the bowmen might have managed a lucky shot. "But their kin at the oasis would take it ill."

Sulen grimaced. "Wounding that one won't help, then."

"He left me no choice," Jassan said with a shrug as he took back his file of camels.

*

Plants and palm trees grew around the pool of water, a welcome sight to Jassan. Less welcome were the tents and camels of the Kavari occupying the oasis, crossed spear sigils identifying them as Clan Pelhou.

He was not surprised to see hostile expressions on the faces of the waiting warriors, sunlight glinting off bared blades and spear-tips. Arrows were notched to bows, which Jassan was relieved to see were undrawn. Even had he not shot one of their kin in the leg, his arrival would have been met with wary suspicion.

The only men and women he saw were warriors and rangers like himself, enough for the clan to hold the oasis and demand tribute for access to its water. Rangers scouted the trails for approaching caravans or rival clans, or escorted the clan's own caravans to their villages with the goods and coin exchanged for water, returning to the oasis with fresh supplies.

A scowling warrior pointed her spear at Jassan. "Put down your weapons. You're to stand before Chief Mehkou."

Hearing that the Pelhou Chief himself was at the oasis was less than cheering. Mehkou might desire to make an example of any who had defied his warriors. Nonetheless, Jassan had no choice but to comply, handing over his bow, sword, dagger and arrows.

He pointed to Subed, still bound to the back of one of his camels. "My employer needs water urgently."

The warrior regarded him impassively. "That will be for the chief to decide." Meaning, 'why waste water on men who may be ordered killed'. Sulen waited with the camels, giving Jassan an entreating look. Someone cried out in pain. The overconfident scout having his wound treated, he suspected.

Jassan was led into the chief's tent, a large square pavilion of stretched hide. Two stern-faced warriors wearing the traditional djellaba and shesh stood behind Chief Mehkou, a gaunt man whose hair and beard were flecked with grey, lines on his black face mapping a life hard lived. Cushions lay on either side of a small table, but he remained standing. His djellaba was as plain as those worn by his people, a thick gold broach pinned to its front the only badge of his rank.

"Welcome, ranger." The chief's voice was deep and assured. "What brings you here?" He made no mention of Jassan's encounter with his clan's youngsters, but neither did he offer teh and dates to confirm guest-right.

"Greetings, Chief Mehkou," Jassan said with a deferential nod.

"Do you have a name?"

"Jassan Idus-Anir Kavari." Jassan, son of Idus, of the Anir Clan of the Kavari Tribe.

Mehkou nodded slightly. His clan, the Pelhou, were not enemies of the Anir, but neither were relations particularly cordial. "You have already met some of my people. What brings you to our humble camp?"

Jassan decided to try and brazen the meeting out. "My arrow. I misplaced it in one of your scouts. Can I have it back?"

Mehkou studied him for a moment, then barked out a laugh. "His arrow, he says. Can he have it back," he said with a backwards look to his men. The warriors smiled dutifully, but their eyes never left Jassan.

"Of course, if you wish to keep it, I would be willing to trade it for water," Jassan offered in the tone of one offering another a rare bargain, relieved by Mehkou's apparent good humour. The Pelhou Chief was said to appreciate wit. Except when he didn't.

"Perhaps it can be returned, if Wiwul is finished with it."

"Wiwul?"

Another scream warbled across the camp. Mehkou nodded in the direction of the scream. "Wiwul. My son."

The revelation that he'd wounded the chief's son was not a welcome one, but Jassan knew better than to show fear. "A brave warrior."

Mehkou snorted. "A brave fool. Who else would test a ranger's bowmanship?" Amusement glinted in the older man's eyes. "Maybe he *would* be willing to return it?"

Yes, by the same method I gave it to him. "The young are often foolish, and we were all young once," Jassan said with a wave of his hand. "That's why I aimed for his leg." *Your son's life was in my hands.*

Mehkou nodded slightly and sat on the cushions, gesturing for Jassan to sit across from him. He poured teh into both cups and snapped his fingers. "Perhaps he will heed the lesson and choose his fights more wisely in future. Apart from your arrow, can we offer you anything else?" He knew very well why the caravan had come to his oasis.

Jassan sat, sipping the teh in relief, knowing he was now a guest and protected as such. "Water. We suffered in the recent sandstorm and lost many of our provisions. My surviving employer is currently in the care of your people."

Another flicker of amusement crossed Mehkou's dark eyes. One of his men placed a bowl of dates on the table. "I am surprised to see a ranger-led caravan brought so low by a little sand and wind. Do the Anir train their rangers so poorly?"

"My employers failed to heed my advice," Jassan said with a shrug. "A final mistake for two of them."

"Quite so." Mehkou leaned back. "I understand your camels are unburdened with goods, and you have thirty-two of them requiring watering. What, then, do you offer in trade for my water?"

Jassan knew where this was leading. All that remained as to haggle out the number. "I would trade you four camels for water. After all, this oasis is only two days from Pashbur."

"Without my water, two days will kill you as surely as two hundred. Four is an offensively low number. Twenty-eight camels will buy you water and allow me to forgive the insult."

The counter-offer was outrageous. Unfortunately, the extra day lost in getting to the oasis meant the camels also needed watering if they were to reach Pashbur. "Twenty-eight camels are too great a price for water enough for three men and only four camels. Sixteen camels would be a fairer price."

"Twenty camels," Mehkou said flatly. "And my man picks them." Wiwul chose that moment to scream again.

"Agreed," Jassan said quickly, offering his hand to seal the agreement. Both men shook, Mehkou's hand rough and callused.

"My healer will attend to your employer." The Chief of the Pelhou smiled. "And I'll see if your arrow can be returned."

Jassan bowed. "May your days be filled with bounty and honour." *You robbing old goat.* Twenty camels were an outrageous price, but Jassan knew as well as Mehkou that the clan could just as easily have killed the three travellers and kept all thirty-two. Wounding the chief's son had not helped the negotiation.

"You must accept the hospitality of my tents tonight," Mehkou said, "and leave refreshed in the morning."

"We will be honoured to, Chief Mehkou." The only problem remaining was that the camels weren't Jassan's to trade, but he hoped Subed would prove reasonable.

The setting sun scorched the distant horizon red and orange, the oasis spring turning crimson. Palm trees swayed slightly as a light breeze caressed them, the water rippling like molten gold. The angry wind from days before had quietened, leaving the evening pleasantly cool as if making amends for its earlier murderous rampage.

Jassan smelled the distinct odour of burning dung as

Mehkou's people lit several fires, surrounding the largest, where the chief would host his guests. Acutely aware that the sandstorm and days of travel had left them dirty and stinking, Jassan and Sulen had made use of the sweat tent. Hot coals had left their skins slick with sweat, and wooden sticks were used to scrape off the dirt before rinsing off with a jug of water.

Sweat tents were a rare luxury in the desert, only permitted here thanks to the oasis. Dry sand and camel urine were the usual means of keeping clean in the desert, the latter used to wash hair. A razor kept Jassan's scalp bald, allowing him to avoid that necessity.

Mehkou proved a good host, feasting Jassan and Sulen with dried mutton, rice, and red wine originating from across the Darish Sea. Subed was to spend the night resting in a tent, the healer confident that he would be fit to walk in the morning.

"What is it?" Sulen asked.

Jassan glanced at him, his reverie broken. "Nothing, Sulen. I was just thinking."

"Is it like this among your own clan?"

"Yes." Sitting around a large fire in the desert among fellow Kavari had reminded Jassan of similar times with his kin, an unexpected pang of homesickness catching him by surprise. He knew few of the songs sung by the Pelhou, songs that told the history and legends of that clan, but some he recognised, the older common to all Kavari.

As the night drew on and the fires started to die, the songs grew somber. Tears pricked Jassan's eyes as he recognised *Long Walk*, a slow melancholic melody. Perhaps the oldest song of the Kavari, *Long Walk* was ancient and shared by every clan, binding them together as one people. It told of the sorrows and losses suffered as the tribe fled north into the desert in exile, of the time before they splintered into many clans.

Every Pelhou man and woman present sang those ancient words, a slow beat echoing from softly beaten drums. Sulen alone sat in a respectful silence as Jassan joined in. The song drifted across the desert, and Jassan knew the night hid many tears.

*

"Twenty camels," Sulen said with a wry chuckle as they led the much-diminished caravan away from the oasis at dawn. "It is well you are a good ranger, Jassan, for you would starve as a merchant.

He wished Sulen would let the matter rest. Subed had taken the loss of his beasts better than Jassan had feared, but he suspected the merchant's mood would change on returning to Pashbur. Jassan knew he could expect no payment beyond the half already paid.

For now, at least, the merchant seemed grateful just to be alive.

A whistle shrieked out behind them, and Jassan turned to see the youth he had wounded at the edge of the camp, attended by a score of kin. Wiwul.

With a bow in hand, the young man raised a black-feathered arrow in his other hand before notching it to the bow and releasing it in the direction of the caravan. Jassan forced himself to stand straight, praying that Wiwul wasn't aiming at him. Or was a poor shot if he was.

He flinched as the arrow thumped near his right foot, quivering where it landed. Jassan pulled it free from the ground, held it up, and bowed deeply at the gathered Pelhou. "My thanks," he shouted over. "It is a good arrow!"

Laughter echoed across the oasis, Wiwul and the others waving off the caravan as it departed for Pashbur. Jassan checked the arrowhead was free of blood and returned it to his quiver.

Chapter Thirteen

Fatigue tugged at Shukara's eyes as she again sat before Erasi in the upstairs room in the Red Serpent Tavern. She took another sip of teh.

Erasi watched her. "You have met your end of the bargain?"

"I have," Shukara confirmed. "And you yours?"

Erasi nodded, patting a wooden chest on the table between them. "So, who did Wakib meet?"

"General Sulliemon ban Marouk," Shukara said, the General's name having been signed on his orders. "Tamira?"

Tamira told Erasi of all she had overheard.

Erasi leaned back, not bothering to hide her surprise. "We had heard whispers Wakib was plotting *something*, liquidating many of his holdings for gold, and our agent in his household had learned from a guard about a meeting last night. But an invasion of Egaria? You have proof?"

Shukara placed the satchel down on the table. "Orders signed by the General, and a list of Maskan citizens to be killed by the Black Rose." Her throat constricted slightly on mentioning the assassins.

Erasi unrolled one of the scrolls and read it. Evidently satisfied, she opened the small wooden box. "Your reagents, as promised. Including four firethorn seeds," she said with a raised eyebrow. "I've since learned what they allow magi to do. I trust you'll forego that particular spell while within the city walls?"

"The seeds will be used elsewhere," Shukara assured her, placing the reagents carefully into her pouch, well-satisfied. Her pouch now contained enough reagents to enhance spells already within her grasp or cast those beyond it.

"They were surprisingly hard to acquire," Erasi said, her demeanour less stiff now their business was done.

"Not as hard as those scrolls," Tamira piped up, waggling grazed fingers.

Erasi shrugged slightly. "Impressive, I do not doubt. But I had to offer much to the Magi to get them. My contact in the Kasbah Arcana did not lightly agree to turn a blind eye to an illegal mage, nor cheaply."

"Those scrolls should more than compensate," Tamira said.

Something nagged at Shukara. "You got these from the Magi of Hrek?"

Erasi nodded. "Who else would have firethorn seeds in Mask?"

No. Shukara rested a hand on the chest previously containing the reagents, sensing the residue of the same spell she had used to follow the pebble. *As I feared.* "A trap!"

Erasi blanched. "No, I assure you—"

"Not you: them," Shukara snapped, as she stood and turned, pulling free her stave. "This way they get their reagents back, capture a rogue magicker, and keep whatever you gave them." If she had time to consume some of the reagents…

She didn't. The door battered open, two men and a woman already entering.

Tamira stumbled backwards and Erasi squawked in outrage.

"Don't move, any of you," one of the men commanded.

Shukara ran her eyes over the three newcomers. The foremost had a greying mane of hair and a neatly trimmed beard stretching from ear to ear. Triumph gleamed in his dark eyes. He wore a rich, red linen robe and held an ornately carved staff of wytchwood. A badge of high office, Shukara guessed, but it served as a spell matrix like all wytchwood. A magicker.

The other man and woman flanking him also carried staffs, less ornate than his, marking them as magi of lesser station. They were younger, with stony expressions. The woman had light brown skin like their leader, the other man almost as dark as Shukara. The two younger magi wore identical grey robes trimmed with yellow.

"Clever of you to Mark the box," she said. Careless of her not to probe it for spells as soon as she saw it.

The leader nodded. "Only magi sworn to Hrek are permitted in Mask." His gaze flickered between Shukara and

Tamira. "A southern mage and…?"

"We had a deal," Erasi said angrily. "The Eye of–"

"Silence. The Eye of Mask is tolerated, and barely so. Besides, we kept our word; we gave you the chest. Nothing else was promised."

Shukara kept fear at bay, knowing that their survival depended on clear thinking. She had reagents enough to cast any spell she wished. Unfortunately, she needed to mix them with water and consume them. Facing three magi – one a master – with the few spells at her disposal did not offer a good chance of survival. Tamira and Erasi would be of little help, the former reminding Shukara of a cat cornered by three dogs. A small cat. The girl stared at the leader with hate-filled eyes.

"I am Magister Cirimon," the leader said. He frowned at Tamira. "There is something familiar about you, girl…" His eyes widened as if he had seen a spirit. "You!"

Tamira ran at him with a yell, flinging her teh into his face before he could cast a spell. She stabbed at him wildly with her knife time and again, screaming incoherently.

One of the other magi hurled her back with a blast of air. Shukara wove her thoughts through the matrices intertwining her wytchwood stave and condensed air together into two solid balls, hurling them against the remaining magi. With a potion of certain reagents, she could have hurled both against the wall; without, her spell lacked such power. She assumed both would have some measure of protection woven around them but wagered they would neglect to protect every angle.

Her air bursts struck both to the rear of their heads, one felling the woman. The other burst struck a shield protecting the man, doing no harm.

Shukara faced the last magicker, knowing he readied a counter-spell. With no wards protecting her and few offensive spells available, little time remained to act.

Most believed air was … nothing. Emptiness. Magickal study was an immersion in the rules and laws of the universe, and she knew there was more to air than nothingness. By drawing it together, she could make it into a liquid that slowed, or solid enough to strike as a weapon.

Her first foe had neglected to protect her rear from such a

spell. Unfortunately, the second had completely enveloped himself in a protective ward that would block air sent against him from every side.

Every side? Yes. But maybe not from every direction. Moments before her opponent released his own spell against her, Shukara willed the air between his knees to compress solid and shot the burst up into his groin. His eyes widened in shock as he sank to the ground, clutching his abdomen.

Shukara disarmed the two stunned magi of their staffs, adrenalin still coursing through her body. She hadn't faced another magicker in combat since that lotus-addled coven of wytches and warlocks in the jungles of Kengu.

Confident the lesser two magi were no threat for the moment, Shukara walked over to the wounded Cirimon and ripped open the slashed robe. Most of his wounds were superficial, the knife having been deflected by bone, but by chance rather than skill Tamira had cut an artery on his thigh. His face was grey, and his eyes had lost focus.

"You recognise the girl. Who is she?" Shukara asked, kneeling next to the dying magicker.

Cirimon gasped out a name. It sounded like Sari, or maybe Zari. When she asked again, he failed to respond.

Shukara cut the throats of the two stunned magi and checked on Tamira. The spell had knocked the wind from her, but she appeared otherwise unharmed. She got back to her feet, awareness returning. *A small cat, yes, but one with sharp claws.*

"Is he dead?" Tamira asked, staring down at Cirimon bleeding out on the ground.

"He's getting there. If you're going to kill with a knife, learn where to strike," Shukara advised.

"I've still killed him," she retorted.

"By chance. Most of his wounds would only have killed him had they become infected." Still, flinging teh in his face had been a good move, distracting him from casting a spell before she struck. Had someone taught her how to face a magicker or had it just been luck? And what had she done, to provoke such a reaction from one of the magisters of the city's magi?

All of which could be mulled over later. "Stand outside and keep watch."

Tamira gave a ragged nod and fled the room.

Erasi stared grey-faced at the bodies. "You killed three magi."

Shukara stood inches from her, hardening her face. "You almost got *us* killed. The Eye now owes *me*."

If Erasi disagreed, the three corpses convinced her to keep any disagreement unspoken. She swallowed, looking Shukara in the eye. "What do you require?"

Shukara was impressed by her composure. "The Black Rose. What do you know of them."

"The assassins?" Erasi gathered her thoughts and told her a few scraps, most of which Shukara already knew or suspected.

"Where can I find their stronghold? I understand it is south of here in Khespha Province, near Pashbur and the Kavarai Caravan Route."

Erasi nodded. "Follow the caravan route for several days to the Black Trail, which will take you to the Oasis of Rhemi. You'll find the Black Citadel there."

"Useful. My thanks." Erasi's information saved her asking in Pashbur and risking word reaching agents of the Black Rose.

"Why do you want to know about *them*? Most try to avoid them."

Shukara said nothing, and after a fleeting glance at her reagent pouch, realisation dawned on Erasi. "You're insane!"

Perhaps. Shukara left the bloodied room without another word, motioning for Tamira to follow. They left Erasi with the unenviable task of dealing with the three dead magi and explaining matters to their colleagues.

Tamira broke the silence once they were out in the street. "You have your reagents. Are we done?" They walked quickly, distancing themselves from the tavern.

Shukara considered the young thief. "Your debt with me is settled. What will you do now?"

She shrugged. "Survive."

For how long? The girl was a mystery, and Shukara could rarely resist those. A street-girl who could read, who was recognised by a magister of Mask's magi. A good mind, quick on her feet, and with the skill to infiltrate a kasbah garrisoned by soldiers. "You've been of great assistance to me. I may have a job for you. Interested?"

Tamira nodded warily. "Perhaps. Not as dangerous as the past day, I hope?"

Shukara smiled. "More so, I fear. But we can discuss it at an inn. I insist you accept my hospitality."

"For a meal, I'll hear you out," the girl promised.

Shukara sniffed and wrinkled her nose. "Baths too, I think."

Chapter Fourteen

A Merchant Quarter jeweller bought one of Shukara's rubies, giving her more than enough gold to get to Pashbur and beyond. She disliked carrying so much coin. They were harder to conceal than stones, but she planned to spend much of it before the day's end.

Curiosity led Shukara and Tamira back to Aneksuno Street, re-visiting the teh-room across from Calan ban Ahmet's riad. Two soldiers bearing the pyramid sigil of Hrek stood outside the riad, gripping spears and standing rock-still.

"Is all well here?" Shukara asked the proprietor casually as he poured her teh.

"What do you mean, mistress?"

"The soldiers guarding the riad across the street. Unusual, no?"

"The merchant who owns it was arrested last night. The Cult have seized his property meantime." The man avoided naming Calan, as if fearing to be tainted by even saying his name.

Shukara nodded. "Ahh. Thank you for the teh. From the east, yes?"

The proprieter nodded, clearly happier to discuss teh than the Cult or those who had fallen afoul of it. "Indeed, mistress, brought to Mask from Jianapp."

"Tasim will be happy," Tamira said quietly once the man had left.

"I wonder if General Sulliemon and Master Wakib will be next to find the Cult's fanatics knocking at their doors," Shukara said.

Tamira smiled. "Since you arrived, no one can accuse the Hrekist soldiery of not having to earn their pay. They've not been so busy since…" Her smile faded, and she raised her cup to her mouth, pretending to drink. Shukara wondered what had upset her.

They next visited a souk near Marat Square where a tailor

sold Shukara two djellaba and a white kalasiris. Reminded of the grass skirts she had worn as a child, she also bought a brown shendyt and two loose-sleeved tunics, both beige. She insisted on buying Tamira new clothing too, not that the girl argued. She chose a white-and-blue striped kalasiris, a blue djellaba, and a charcoal-grey shendyt and tunic. She tried to refuse sandals, but Shukara insisted.

"If you dress like a beggar, you will be treated like one," she had told the street-girl. "Dress like a queen, and you will be treated like—"

"—a queen," Tamira had finished, acquiescing with a strange expression. They had then visited a bathhouse.

The bathhouse was a treat long overdue in Shukara's eyes. That she would have enjoyed it two days earlier had Tamira not robbed her was a fact she charitably chose not to mention. The building was divided into two, segregating men and women. The walls were naked red brick, unadorned by decoration. Salmon-hued tiles covered the floor. The water was heated elsewhere in the building and piped into two of the three rooms, a luxury Shukara had long anticipated. Each segregated area was further divided into three: a tepid room, hot room and cold room.

Shukara and Tamira stripped off their ragged clothes, instructing the attendant to throw them out. A second attendant led them into the tepid room where a pool waited. Tamira seemed self-conscious at being naked, perhaps due to her adolescence.

"The baths are generally divided into three," Shukara explained to Tamira. "The tepid room prepares us for the hot room where the heat lets us sweat off most of our dirt." She paused, noting Tamira's distracted nod. Either she was uninterested, or she already knew how the baths worked. Unlikely, as swimming in the filthy harbour was as close as most Poor Quarter denizens came to bathing.

They walked into the hot room, veiled by a haze of steam. Water heated in a furnace filled the large pool, which was already occupied by several other women. Additional heat was generated by pouring water onto hot coals lying in an iron pail. The coals were replaced periodically with others fresh from a brazier.

The hot room was inspired by the sweat-houses and tents popular in the dryer regions of Araka where the inhabitants lacked sufficient water to waste it in bathing. Shukara poured a ladle of water over the hot coals, sweat escaping her pores, and both she and Tamira scraped themselves clean with sticks.

Three attendants stood by, waiting to tend to their needs. Shukara waded into the pool, gasping in pained pleasure as almost unbearably hot water touched her skin. Tamira followed her in and reacted similarly.

They both sat gingerly until the water was just below their shoulders. One attendant lowered herself into the bath and massaged Shukara's shoulders, another attending to Tamira. Months of tension were soothed away by the attendants' practiced fingers. The hot water relaxed Shukara's muscles, and she arched her head back as oils were caressed into her hair and scalp. *Gods, this feels good.*

Shukara opened her eyes and looked at Tamira. She had expected the thief to be overwhelmed by this luxury, but she seemed to be taking it in her stride, even instructing the attendant where to go harder or softer.

"The table?" her own attendant asked.

"What?" Shukara asked.

"She's asking if you wish a massage on the table," Tamira explained sleepily, her accent more refined than before. *Interesting...*

"That sounds wonderful."

Shukara left the pool, water dripping onto the tiles as she was led to a waiting stone table. She lay face down and shut her eyes as the attendant began to rub oils into her skin, permitting herself a sigh of pleasure.

A contented haze drifted over as the attendant massaged her scalp, neck, shoulders, back, hips and legs. She opened her eyes and saw Tamira lying on a table across from her. This should have been an alien experience for the street-girl, but she seemed implausibly familiar with it.

Once the massage was done, Shukara rose regretfully from the table, her muscles loose and relaxed. Oil and sweat glistened on her skin, blessedly clean for the first time since leaving Arrioch. Steam wafted across the room.

Shukara eyed Tamira. "Lead on," she said innocently. A novice to the bathhouse would have walked into the cold room, but Tamira led them back into the tepid room to cool down gradually. Shukara looked the naked girl up and down. She was understandably thin, but her bone structure and teeth were too good for one supposedly on the streets since birth. Many children born to poverty suffered rickets and other deformities, but Tamira had been spared.

They soaked in the tepid room's lukewarm water for a while.

The tepid room was almost cold compared to the hot room, letting their bodies cool down before moving on to the final stage of bathing. Shukara could grow accustomed to such amenities. Back home everyone bathed in Lake Toko, mindful of predators.

She followed Tamira into the cold room, the last stop before they returned to the changing room.

Shukara walked into the pool, shivering as the cold water chilled her skin. She took a breath and dropped to her knees, letting the cold water envelope her all at once. Her head emerged from the water, shaking it free. "Gods!" She shivered uncontrollably.

Tamira grinned down at her, showing no surprise at what had awaited Shukara. She made a gesture and an attendant poured a jug of water over her. "It contains water cooler than the tepid room, but warmer than the cold pool," Tamira explained smugly.

Shukara splashed her with cold water in response, smiling as the girl leapt back with an outraged squeal.

Tamira joined her in the cold pool with an accepting grimace. They bathed alone, Shukara swimming languidly from one end to the other.

"A glorious experience," she said.

"Yes," Tamira lazily agreed.

Shukara sat in the cold water, considering. The girl was … wrong. What name was it Cirimon had whispered: Sari … Zari…?

A shiver rippled through her and not just from the cold water. The kings of Mask had always been called Xarius by tradition. Their eldest son took the name, and if he died, the next male in line assumed it. The eldest daughter of the king was always called...

"Xaria," Shukara said.

There was a panicked splash as Tamira tried to climb out of the pool. Shukara grabbed her foot and yanked her back.

"Be calm, girl. I mean you no harm."

Tamira – Xaria? – emerged spluttering and stared at her, eyes wide with fear.

"Sit down and relax. Your true name means little to me. But you are Xaria, yes?"

The girl nodded reluctantly. "Yes," she whispered. "I was."

"Eldest daughter of King Xarius?"

She nodded.

Shukara studied the girl. "I heard all the king's children died with him."

"Captain Verak of my father's guards dressed a slave-girl near my age in my clothing while I escaped the palace through a secret passage. He closed it behind me and killed the girl to make the asasassins think I was dead." The girl stared down at the water. "Her name was Tamira."

"And the magicker, Cirimon?"

"An advisor to my father. A traitor, one of many who betrayed my family for greed and power."

Shukara nodded. The priests of Hrek and the Merchant Council had supported King Xarius despite his tyranny, only turning on him when he levied new taxes on *them*. She was unclear on the details, knowing only that the Kingdom of Mask had become a theocracy overnight. "You were fortunate to escape, Xaria."

"Tamira," the vagabond princess corrected. "Xaria is dead."

"Wise," Shukara said. "What happened?"

"There was unrest in the city and outlying provinces. My father stamped down hard on the dissenters, but that only spurred further rebellion. I know now that the Cult of Hrek and the Merchant Council secretly encouraged much of it. With the army dealing with the rebels, the Royal Guard was reinforced with mercenaries hired by the Merchant Council and fanatic-soldiers from the Cult. Not content with placing their men in the palace, the traitors also hired the Black Rose and hid them among the soldiers. The assassins poisoned many of my father's loyal men, opened the gates to let in the traitors, and murdered my family. The loyal guardsmen were slain."

The Black Rose have a talent for making enemies. "So now you live on the streets," Shukara said, impressed that a young girl of perhaps eight or nine years pampered in a palace had survived five years on the merciless streets of a city like Mask.

Tamira opened her mouth but shut it again as two women entered the cold room. Prudent; if word reached the priests or merchant princes that an heir of the Xarian Dynasty still lived, they would scour Mask for her, perhaps going so far as to slay every girl of a certain age within the city. By herself she was no threat and her father's heavy-handed rule made it unlikely the populace would rise for her, but there were powerful nobles and rival rulers out there who might marry her by force, and seek to claim the throne in her name.

"I'm hungry," Shukara said, rising from the water. "Let us find a respectable inn with a good kitchen."

"Yes," Tamira said in fervent agreement. They left the pool and dried themselves before returning to the changing room where their new clothes waited.

Chapter Fifteen

The Laughing Camel Inn was known to Tamira, its kitchen the victim of her foraging a time or two. She recognised the innkeeper, a heavy, balding man with a thick beard. Tamira had no fear that he would associate her with the dirty waif he had chased off, not dressed, as she was now, in a long, well-tailored kalasiris. She hadn't felt so clean in five years, bathing in the river no comparison to a proper bathhouse with steam, hot water and oils. Clean clothes that fitted her were a luxury, too, a reminder of a life taken from her.

The innkeeper, Torro ban Mahmet, responded to Shukara's imperious manner subserviently, taking care not to offend the outlander. Tamira smiled inwardly at Torro's likely reaction had he seen the mage before dawn, dressed raggedly and sneaking into the Kasbah Baraq.

The Laughing Camel was far enough from the harbour that it attracted visiting merchants rather than rowdy sailors, and its room and drink prices were high enough to discourage caravan guards and mercenaries. Patterned tapestries woven of threads dyed in colours ranging from red to indigo-blue, covered many of the walls, and the brick pillars supporting the upper floor glowed an earthy-pink in the candlelight.

Carpets covered most of the red-tiled floor of the inn's spacious ground floor. Low round tables were spread throughout the room, surrounded by thick, embroidered cushions of every colour and pattern. Wooden panels partitioned off several tables near the wall to give privacy to those patrons desiring it. Those wishing to smoke lotus were welcome to partake in a separate lounge at the far end of the inn.

"Where do you wish to sit, mistress?" the innkeeper asked after they had discarded their sandals and washed their hands in a bowl of petalled rose water.

The inn was quiet, with less than a dozen other patrons within. Tamira knew the hour was still early and that the evening would bring in a crowd.

Shukara nodded at a partitioned area across the room. "My companion and I will sit there."

Toro bowed his head, clasping his hands. "Of course, mistress." He led them over, promising a serving girl would attend them presently.

Tamira sank into one of the cushions, leaning back into those piled behind her. "You mentioned a job?" *A job more dangerous than sneaking into a riad, infiltrating a kasbah full of soldiers, stealing documents from a general, and facing a trio of magi.*

"Let us discuss it on a full stomach."

Tamira smiled, her belly aching at the thought of food. Returning to the streets would be painful after this brief taste of comfort, but she would enjoy tonight while it lasted.

A serving girl called Rina took their order. Tamira asked for beef tagine and couscous; Shukara ordered skewered lamb and peppers.

Shukara questioned Tamira about the city while they waited, asking nothing of consequence. A jug of water and a small bottle of red wine arrived, Rina diluting Tamira's cup on Shukara's instructions.

Rina returned a short time later. "Apologies for disturbing you, mistress, but a messenger requested this be passed to you." On Shukara's nod she handed the mage a tied scroll.

"My thanks, Rina," Shukara said, handing her two copper coins. "Give one to the messenger and keep the second for yourself."

"Thank you," Rina said gratefully, backing away with a bow.

After Rina had left, Shukara untied the scroll and unrolled it, reading the message without comment.

"Is there anything we should be concerned about?" Tamira asked carefully, curious about its contents but wary of offending the mage.

"A message from Erasi, nothing for you to worry about," Shukara said firmly, her manner indicating she considered it unworthy of further discussion. She held the scroll over a small candle and held the burning papyrus until it was nothing more than ash. Her fingers were untouched by the flame.

The food finally arrived, its rich aroma almost leading Tamira to forget etiquette. Lessons impressed on a princess came back to her despite five years spent scavenging on the streets. Both she and Shukara raised themselves up from their cushions to sit cross-legged on the carpeted floor. Rina removed the lid from Tamira's tagine pot, tormenting her with fresh smells of peppers and cinnamon.

She forced herself to sit still, waiting until Shukara began to eat. The mage was the elder and, as she was paying, also the host. Tamira dipped her wooden spoon into the pot and took her first mouthful of beef.

Gods ... The beef was tender, the sauce spicy and tasting strongly of cinnamon. Her mouth burned from peppers in the second spoonful, driving her to quench the fire with water.

"Well?" Shukara asked.

"Delicious, mistress," Tamira reassured her, and not just because it was polite to say as much to the host paying for the meal. Despite normally favouring her left hand, etiquette required she hold the spoon in her right, keeping her left below the table.

"Call me Shukara," the mage said, picking up a sliver of lamb with her fingers. She drank some wine. Observing Shukara's cup to be less than half-full, Tamira refilled it from the bottle, noting her curious expression. Maybe they filled their own cups in the south.

Unused to eating food in such quantities, Tamira's belly soon ached under the strain. Etiquette dictated that she leave some food in the glazed clay pot, but she hadn't intended to leave quite so much. She stared down wistfully at the remaining third, knowing she might never eat so well again.

The plates were cleared away, Tamira and Shukara returning to the comfort of the cushions. Tamira sipped from her wine, finding it fruity but strong against her throat, tasting of berries and softened slightly by a lingering hint of vanilla. Despite being watered it still left her a bit dizzy, but she felt content for the first time in five years.

Shukara handed Rina some coins, more than the meal cost. "I would appreciate being undisturbed," she told the girl.

"Yes, mistress," the girl promised.

Tamira ran a finger over the once-thick wool of the carpet,

now worn after years of use, and let herself sink into the cushions. There had been a time when she had taken such comfort for granted, a time when she hadn't known hunger or fear (other than those rare times she had angered her father). *Savour every moment now.*

She became aware of Shukara studying her, the mage's thoughts opaque.

Shukara smiled wryly. "Princess Xaria ... who would believe it? Or *Queen* Xaria, I should say."

Heart leaping in fear as the mage said a name even Tamira dared not, she gave the thin cedar walls separating the alcoves a panicked look.

"Calm yourself, I've warded the walls. No one will hear our words unless they stand directly before us." She nodded at the open space looking out into the common room.

Tamira furled her brow, unconvinced. "How?"

"Sound travels in waves through the air, like water. I've made the air layering the walls more ... turbulent. Sound hitting that air is like water hitting off a cliff."

"...How?"

Shukara chuckled. "To study magick is to study the laws of nature, of what holds everything together, and to train our minds to see the mechanics of the world. Spells are what we use to bend those rules – where we can."

"I thought reagents were what made your spells possible?"

"Reagents make certain spells possible and others more potent, but they do nothing for one not trained and in possession of wytchwood."

"I don't really understand," Tamira confessed.

"Most don't. That's why we just call it magick." Shukara held out her hand, and the air on her palm seemed to grow thicker. She reached over, and Tamira felt *something* touch her hand.

"Air, water and solids all contain the ... materials of the world, called atoms by some. Solids the most, liquids less, and air little at all. This is how you can walk easily through air, less easily through water, and not at all through solids. But when I draw enough of these atoms together, I can make even air solid. With the right reagents ingested, I can wield a blade of air so sharp it can cut through almost anything."

Tamira nodded, understanding what she was saying; almost. "I remember Cirimon making fire from air to entertain the court. He always seemed more … animated when performing magick for the amusement of my father's court."

"Lotus of varying colours is an ingredient of many spells. We magi must discipline our minds to fend off the intoxicating side-effects, but it can be difficult."

Tamira recalled how dilated Cirimon's eyes had appeared that morning and nodded.

Shukara's expression turned pensive. "There are some magi who theorise that with the right reagents, a magicker of sufficient ability could fashion a spell that would draw atoms densely together and then manipulate them to produce a destructive force sufficient to destroy a city."

Tamira tried to imagine such a spell unleashed in Mask and failed. "Could … could you do it?" she asked on finding her voice.

"No." She shook her head with a reassuring smile. "We magi might like to pretend we have unlocked all the secrets of the world, but in truth there are so many, and we have barely scratched the surface. There is too much for any one magicker to learn in a lifetime, so most concentrate on one or two areas. Some study to extend life or even avoid death altogether, so great is their hunger for knowledge."

A chill took Tamira. "Like the Bone King."

Shukara nodded. "You've heard of him, I see."

Few hadn't. He was the stuff of dark legend, a necromancer regarded with fear and awe in equal measure. Reputed to dwell far to the south, many were the tales of him told by storytellers around Arakan campfires. Some regarded him as *the* Necromancer, that the same man was behind every dark legend involving death magick, that he simply hid for a time before returning under a different name. Most liked to believe him dead. If such a term were applicable.

A thought struck Tamira. "What area of magick do you concentrate on?"

Shukara ignored the question. "Royalty usually rely on tax collectors and customs officials to take money from those entering their domains. I suppose I should be honoured that the Queen of Mask 'taxed' me in person."

"Don't call me a queen. I'll never sit on the Red Throne. For most, nothing changed after the priests and merchants took over. The poor are still poor, and the rich get richer. Even if I somehow claimed my inheritance, that still wouldn't change, no matter how much I would will it otherwise. Let Xaria remain in the Book of the Dead; Tamira at least can live." She looked at Shukara. "You mentioned a job?"

Shukara nodded. "Yes. You are not the only one who owes the Black Rose a debt of blood. Your recent actions have impressed me, and your skills would be useful where I am going."

The Black Rose. Gold dictated whom they would kill, and their loyalty ended with each transaction. Tamira's father had often used them to dispose of those he found inconvenient but, despite his regular patronage, the assassins of the Black Rose still turned their blades on him when paid to by Mask's merchant princes. "Their assassins are here?"

"Perhaps a few, but I did not travel a continent to prune a few thorns. I came to tear the rose up by the roots."

Tamira's eyes widened at the mage's mad audacity. "You mean to go to…"

Shukara nodded. "Yes. The Black Citadel is my destination."

The Black Citadel. Guarding the Oasis of Rhemi, the Black Rose stronghold was held in fearful regard. "They say the Grandmaster need only say a name and that person's death is assured," Tamira said quietly.

Shukara smiled down at her. "He once named Princess Xaria. Yet she sits alive before me." She topped up Tamira's cup with wine, not bothering to water it down.

"Tamira the thief sits before you." The Black Citadel lay on the edge of the vast Kavari Desert to the south. Her elder brother had once told her that the Black Rose lived next to the desert so that they might learn from a killer more merciless than themselves. He had voiced his hope of meeting the assassins one day. *He got his wish.*

"How did Tamira the thief feel on killing Cirimon, a man who betrayed her family?" Shukara asked.

"I felt good," she admitted. "For five years I have lived without home or family, stealing to survive and forever afraid. To bring justice to one of those responsible made me feel … good. Strong. No longer afraid, no longer a victim." She flashed the mage a bitter smile. "Like a queen. For a moment, anyway."

"I can help you feel that way again. Bring revenge … justice … to those who killed your family and took your home," Shukara urged. "Bring it to the Black Citadel."

Chapter Sixteen

The Bloody Lotus stronghold stood deep in the Poor Quarter, once a cluster of houses that Calak and his smugglers had seized from a rival gang almost ten years past. Dark legends had been born that night, whispered stories passing from tavern to tavern about the blood spilled when the Bloody Lotus visited the River Kings.

The largest gang of lotus smugglers at that time, the River Kings had become complacent. They had ruled the streets, their competition small and of scant account, and bribes had kept the city guards away. So complacent had they become that lookouts posted in the streets leading to their stronghold were few and mostly drunk the night the Bloody Lotus came.

Those drunken River Kings were the lucky ones, slain quickly and quietly as Calak led his gang from street to street, roof to roof, cutting throat after throat. There was nothing quiet after that. The Bloody Lotus struck with a ruthless brutality, killing every man, woman and child found within the stronghold. The unarmed died the hardest, tortured for hours, dismembered and disembowelled, the walls, ceilings and floors painted red. The River Kings had sung their death-song for hours, screams that didn't end until dawn.

When Mask awoke, the River Kings had been replaced by the Bloody Lotus. The void they left in the lotus smuggling trade was too large for the smaller Bloody Lotus to fill, so other gangs seized territory, but the manner of the River Kings' fall sent a clear message to all; don't cross the Bloody Lotus.

Calak leaned back in his chair, remembering. A few had failed to heed that message over the years, requiring further examples. Calak's philosophy in this regard was simple: Overreaction. Every slight was met with a disproportionate response, and the lesson had been learned.

But not by all. A band of child-thieves had tried to rob one of his wagons, and two of his men had been killed in the streets of Mask chasing one of them. Such an insult could not go unanswered, not with rival gangs watching. The Poor Quarter knew that the Bloody Lotus would keep killing until those responsible were dealt with, and information was hastily passed to the Bloody Lotus that a boy called Nio had been seen fleeing the scene.

Nio had been found, tortured until he spoke, and then tortured until he died, his flayed corpse dumped in the street, another lesson for the Poor Quarter of Mask. He had identified Tamira as the last survivor and named Laya as a friend of hers who may know where the thief was hiding.

Laya had been found near Rat Square and was now locked in a room, soon to be questioned about Tamira. A shame that Lame Laya would die regardless. She had not been involved in the attempted theft of the lotus, but Calak and his people were not known for fairness. Laya's dismembered corpse would be another example of what to expect when those who wronged the Bloody Lotus were not handed over timeously.

It was the deaths of Khulen and Elim that troubled Calak mostly. The third man, Caris, had glimpsed the fleeing Tamira and doubted her capable of killing the other two. Calak had examined their bodies personally, noting that one had died from a cracked skull, the other from a crushed throat. A scrawny street-rat had not done it, meaning that someone else had.

Calak entered the common room, noting that it was half-full of people. Determined to avoid the fate of the River Kings, he had forbidden the lookouts and stronghold guards alcohol or lotus while at their posts on pain of death, but the common room was usually boisterous as the rest of the Bloody Lotus entertained themselves.

But not the past two nights. They could indulge themselves after the last of those who had crossed the Bloody Lotus was dead, he had decreed, and the gang feared him sufficiently that those present in the common room stepped quietly and drank nothing but teh or water. Calak glanced at the barred door beyond which Laya doubtlessly sat in terror. The quiet would not last long.

A runner burst into the common room, breathing hard.

"Lookout's signalled someone coming!"

"Arm yourselves," Calak growled. There were maybe twenty men and women loitering about, and all jumped to obey him. He was feared by his own people even on the best days, and it would not be a *good* day until Mask learned once again that no one crossed him and lived.

The quickest Bloody Lotus armed themselves with rusty swords and old spears from the armoury, the rest making do with knives and clubs. No alarm had been raised, which told Calak that his lookouts perceived little threat from whoever dared approach.

Caris, Sem, Benn and Jala escorted a lone woman into the common room. She was tall, dark-skinned and dressed in a white kalasiris, a stave of silvery wood bound to her right forearm like a splint. "Is she alone?" Calak asked.

"Yes, and armed only with a knife," Sem said, holding a small blade up. "We caught her drawing on the ground with a piece of charcoal."

"Drawing?" Calak asked.

Sem shrugged. "Odd symbols in a circle."

The Bloody Lotus watched the stranger, their silence more ominous than shouts. Calak sat in a chair positioned in the centre of the floor. No one brought before him could miss the broken tables and stools, the crates used as seats, the cracked walls and floors, but nor would they miss seeing Calak of the Bloody Lotus seated like a king. A king of killers, smugglers and street-rats, but a king nonetheless.

"What brings you here?" Calak asked.

"Two of your men were killed recently," the woman said finally. There was a confidence about her that Calak respected despite himself. Few dared walk the Poor Quarter at night, especially not a woman alone. And fewer still dared come here unbidden.

"You have information on those responsible? I already know of the one called Tamira. She will be found soon," Calak said. His gang had wearied themselves scouring the Poor Quarter to no avail, but she would be found.

The woman nodded, her accent odd. "I do. But first, are you the leader of the Bloody Lotus?"

Calak felt the scar running across his face tighten as he

smiled. "I am Calak. I'm also not known for my patience. If you waste my time, you'll regret it."

"First, I wish to barter this information for Tamira's life. She did not harm your men, nor steal your property. On learning the contents of the wagon, she fled empty-handed," the woman said.

Calak sensed grim amusement from his people, though none made a sound. People passed information to the Bloody Lotus from fear, not reward. And any victim bound to the altar in Hrek's Temple would sooner find mercy from the priest wielding the sacrificial knife than from the Bloody Lotus.

"Tamira will die," Calak said flatly. "You will tell me who killed my men. You will tell me where Tamira is. Or *you* will die."

The woman must be foreign. Any Maskan would have fouled themselves after such a pronouncement delivered personally by the Bloody Lotus leader. This woman merely nodded. "I suspected that would be your response. A pity."

Rage brought Calak to his feet, tipping the chair backwards. "Who killed my men?" Fear and anticipation warred on the faces of his people, fear of his rage and anticipation of the awful fate about to be visited on this arrogant woman.

"I did."

Sharply indrawn breaths whispered across the common room at that admission. Even Calak found himself at a loss of words. The woman would have been wiser entering the High Temple and pissing on the symbol of Hrek. She would still die, but the priests would give her a kinder death than the one she would find here tonight.

"Who are you?" Calak managed, anger clenching his throat. Red blurred his vision, and he felt his heart thumping in his chest.

"I am Shukara."

"Shukara, you will find only death here," Calak promised.

She smiled. "No, Calak. I *brought* death here." The guards escorting her were hurled back by an unseen force, and a harsh keening sound issued from her throat.

*

Shukara untied the girl she found in the small room and helped her up, recognising her as the one Tamira had talked briefly with in Rat Square. "You're safe now."

The girl stood slowly, her legs deformed, her eyes wide and red from crying. "I heard screams," she whispered.

"Don't worry about that." The buildings had been smashed apart, red bricks shattered like clay. Using a firethorn seed had perhaps been excessive, but better that than to risk being overpowered and captured by the notorious gang. The screams from outside where she had quickly drawn the glyph before being captured had distracted those surrounding her, enough to create a barrier of flame. And then she became the least of the gang's problems.

"The Bloody Lotus–"

"Are done." Shukara led the girl out into the common room. Erasi of the Eye of Mask had sent her a message at the Laughing Camel, warning her that the Bloody Lotus were tearing the Poor Quarter apart searching for Tamira. Shukara had been tempted to let it lie, knowing they were leaving the city in the morning, but what when Tamira returned to the city after their business with the Black Rose was done? Suspecting that the Bloody Lotus would have long memories, Shukara had resolved to settle the issue tonight, while Tamira slept in the inn.

The girl took one look at the carnage and bent over, vomiting. Calak lay in the centre of the room. Most of him, anyway. Bits and pieces were spread around, mingling with what remained of his followers. The Bloody Lotus were settled.

"What's your name?" Shukara asked to distract the girl from the mess.

"Laya." The girl wiped her mouth.

"Flee and say nothing of this, Laya. You were never here," Shukara said, deciding to keep her own name to herself. The Bloody Lotus were done as a group, but tonight's mess would draw the attention of the Magi of Hrek, and Shukara had already crossed paths with them once.

Though the guards and lookouts stationed outside had

either fled or died, Shukara nevertheless used her magick to spy out any signs of ambush. There were none.

*

She stood in the blackness, wondering if her contact had arrived.

"I'm here."

To preserve its secrecy, the Eye of Mask formed a two-tier structure. There was the council who catalogued the information gathered and made the decisions, whose identities were known only among themselves; and there were the brokers, like Erasi. The brokers met potential clients; agents paid to prowl the streets, souks and taverns for information; and rumour-mongers who sold gossip.

But that left the brokers exposed, each a link who could potentially lead to the discovery of those behind the Eye. So, each broker dealt only with a single council-member, and only in absolute darkness. Even then, further precautions were taken. Erasi maintained the pretence of living in the house near the harbour where she met her clients, using an underground tunnel to come and go, without being observed.

She had little doubt that she was often followed when she left the house openly, and sometimes amused herself by acting furtively, loitering in markets or in bath-houses, visiting teh-rooms and inns as if meeting contacts.

Tonight, she met her council contact, a woman whose name she didn't know and whose face she had never seen. The two guards who protected Erasi from anyone offering violence in truth worked for her contact, and when the Eye wanted a meeting, it was they who took her down, blindfolded, into the cellar and extinguished all lights before leaving.

Only then would her contact enter the cellar. Erasi harboured no illusions about the ultimate loyalty of her guards. If she attempted to learn the identity of her contact by any means, they would kill her unhesitatingly. If the Eye decided she was compromised, they would kill her, and the small house near the docks would be closed.

"Greetings, Erasi," the voice said. Erasi wondered who she

was. A noblewoman, a merchant, a mage, perhaps? She might even be the woman who owned the small shop at the bottom of the road selling tehs from Jianapp. But tonight, there was a tension in her voice.

Erasi cleared her throat, keen to make amends after recent events. "One of our agents in the Regal Lion Inn overheard a Keramese ship captain talking about fresh skirmishes in eastern Keram," she said. "The agent plied him with wine, and the captain revealed the Kingdom of Kern is on the brink of civil war. He was bringing an agent of Baron Gevan's here to hire mercenaries." Gevan's barony in Kern was on the Darish Sea coast, so hiring soldiers from across the sea removed the risk of them being ambushed crossing rival lands.

That information was worth a lot to the Eye. Merchants selling weapons and armour would have a new market. War meant dead farmers and burned fields, so grain would command a high price. Those merchants or nobles with investments in or near Kern would welcome a warning to sell or remove their assets before the kingdom fell into chaos.

"I arranged to meet you for another purpose," the voice said. "The Magi of Hrek are again demanding to know who killed High Magister Cirimon."

"I thought it was agreed that the Eye would not provide this to the magi," Erasi said slowly. "Punishment for their duplicity."

"We agreed that at the time. The magi were reluctant to let it be known that a rogue mage had killed three of their own, and we made it clear to them that if they pressed the matter, the Cult would learn they supplied this southern mage with reagents and failed to catch her. But the situation has changed."

"How so?" Erasi asked quietly. Were there others present in the cellar? Officially she only ever 'met' with her contact, but there were times she fancied she heard others breathing quietly in the darkness. Did other members of the council stand silently by the voice's side?

"Your mage's handiwork against the Bloody Lotus has drawn attention. Had she been subtle, the Cult may not have noticed the destruction of a smuggler gang, but..."

But she was anything but subtle. Shukara had assured Erasi she would not use *that* spell in Mask but did so anyway. Sweat soaked Erasi's kalasiris, the cellar hot and airless. "The Cult are aware?"

"Aware and displeased, to say the least. An apprentice mage was selected as last night's sacrifice to Hrek. This morning, a *ranking* mage was bound to the altar and sacrificed. The magi are angry and afraid. If they don't find this rogue mage soon, the Cult may move against *all* magi in Mask."

Gods above and below. "A war between the magi and priests could destroy Mask." No wonder the voice was uninterested in a civil war across the sea.

"That war has been won by the Cult before it could start. Their soldiers seized the Kasbah Arcana and secured the reagent stores. The magi could put up a fight of sorts without, but they would be destroyed. They've chosen to placate the priests by finding your mage instead."

"Selling out our clients is not something we do," Erasi said. She hadn't liked Shukara threatening her for information about the Black Rose, but nor could she blame the mage, given Erasi had unwittingly led Cirimon straight to her. On learning that the Bloody Lotus had themselves learned Tamira's name and were actively hunting the girl, Erasi had sent a message to Shukara warning her by way of making amends. She had thought the mage would hasten her departure from Mask, taking the girl with her. She had not imagined the mage would choose to *confront* the lotus smugglers.

"We have made our decision, Erasi. Did you hear about the bakery burning down near Marat Square?"

Erasi frowned. "Yes. An oven not properly extinguished?"

"The baker who owned it was one of our brokers, like yourself. His shop served the same purpose as the house above us. The Magi of Hrek burned the shop as a message. The Cult are pressuring them, so they are pressuring us."

Erasi closed her eyes. She had no idea how many brokers like herself were used by the Eye, but there was now one fewer. The Magi were forcing their hands. "Shukara has left Mask, an agent I assigned to follow her confirms she boarded a dahabiya yesterday morning."

"Do you know where she is going?" There was a barely controlled panic in her voice. The priests and magi wanted Shukara's head, but she had already left the city.

I may have brought ruin to the Eye of Mask, Erasi thought, appalled. One small mercy was that no one knew she had sent the message to Shukara triggering the slaughter. "She is going to the Black Citadel." Erasi made no mention of Tamira.

"She seeks an audience with the Black Rose?"

"I don't think so. She didn't say, but I believe she has some grievance with the assassins. That's why she wanted the reagents, particularly the firethorn seeds."

"It was a firethorn seed that allowed her to, to…"

"Yes," Erasi said. No one spoke for a time.

"I'll send an artist to you at dawn. You will describe this mage to him, and he will sketch her. We will pass this sketch to the Magi along with her destination."

"You think the Magi will pursue her?" Erasi asked.

"This mage is heading straight to a den of vipers. Why send hunters when a message will suffice?"

Erasi nodded. She would pass an accurate description of Shukara, having no choice in the matter. There was nothing she could do for the mage, but her silence regarding Tamira might at least save the girl.

Chapter Seventeen

The towers of Mask had fallen below the horizon three days earlier, revealing the world beyond to Tamira for the first time. She had never left the Red City before; she had rarely even left the palace until events exiled her from it forever.

The Black Citadel and its infamous killers loomed ahead in her thoughts like a distant thunderstorm on the horizon, but for now she drank in the new sights that unfolded as they sailed the river.

Caravans travelling from Mask or the north-eastern coastal cities to southern Araka via the Kavari Caravan Route had no choice but to go south across the Dhaemon's Fangs, a perilous range of mountains separating Mask from the Khespha Province. Tamira and Shukara had a faster alternative, a four-day voyage south on the River Tyre by dahabiya, a twin-sailed, shallow-bottomed barge.

Some caravans bringing gold, slaves and other goods from the far south braved the mountains to travel directly to Mask, but many preferred to stop in the village of Pashbur and pay the river-folk to transport their goods by boat, accompanying them to negotiate their sale. No few of them had lost goods and coin thanks to Tamira's quick fingers and quicker feet.

The dahabiyas also transported salt drawn from Khespha Province's salt mines to Mask in the north, from where it was sent to the coastal towns of northern Araka, or across the Darish Sea to Keram. The caravan owners hiring boats in Pashbur sacrificed a little profit to avoid travelling the mountains, also gaining extra days for their vast camel herds to recover in the grazing fields (a two-month period), before returning south with salt and other goods. A ninety-day journey, mostly spent enduring the great Kavari Desert.

Tamira was glad Shukara had chosen to travel by boat. It was by no means comfortable, but more so than breathing in the dust kicked up by a thousands-strong caravan of camels during a weeks-long arduous mountain-crossing.

The crew were a rough lot, skin ravaged by exposure to sun, rope and wood. None gave her a second look, their eyes drawn to the taller, foreign Shukara, but they had the sense to do naught but look. The passengers were a mixed group, mostly salt merchants returning to Pashbur with their profits.

There was also Master Koyo, a trader accompanied by a guard. The desert might have consumed everything soft about him, but he spoke warmly and often about his wives and children, living in a town south of the Kavari Desert. His skin was almost as dark as Shukara's, and his grey-streaked beard had been left to grow wild. His djellaba was travel-stained, and his skin aged by years of desert-crossings, but Tamira suspected he was no less wealthy than the pampered merchant princes occupying Mask's palaces and riads.

The dahabiya was laden with cloth and silk bought by Koyo for transportation south. Koyo's Maskan cotton had been sent south by boat the day before, but he had stayed in the city to see what goods a Keramese trading galley offered.

If a ship from that northern continent crossed the Darish Sea and risked the Tyre's river pirates, he told Tamira, it usually had a cargo worth delaying his departure for. The ship had carried Darish cloth and Cuvan silk, sure to fetch a fine price in the markets beyond the desert. Koyo claimed to own twelve hundred camels, maybe a thousand of them ready for travel, and would need to hire perhaps a thousand more for his caravan south. Mask's merchant princes who operated similar caravans rarely travelled with them, entrusting a caravan master to oversee everything.

That turned her thoughts to one Maskan merchant prince in particular. The Eye of Mask had not been slow to act on the documents stolen from Kasbah Baraq, and the city's heralds had announced the arrests of Wakib and General Sulliemon the morning Tamira and Shukara had departed Mask. A thousand rumours roamed the streets as to why they had been arrested, but all agreed that the General's officers were seized too, and their soldiers confined to the kasbah. The Magi of Hrek were said to have been involved, quelling any thoughts of resistance from the kasbah garrison. Shukara opined that the Eye of Mask had given the magi all the incriminating documents to avoid reprisal for Cirimon's death.

Tamira suspected Wakib and Sulliemon would not be long for this world. The Cult and Merchant Council might have forgiven the plot to invade Egaria without their permission, but not the planned assassinations of their own. Given their involvement in uncovering the plot, and the deaths of three magi at their hands, Tamira was relieved to be away from Mask.

Though at least she was free to return. The morning they sailed, the streets were also crowded with rumours that the Bloody Lotus gang had been destroyed. Had their brutal ways finally pushed their rivals too far, or was someone else behind it? Shukara had been oddly tired that last morning in Mask, and Tamira had consumed enough wine after dinner to ensure a heavy sleep. She kept such speculation to herself, just grateful she could return home one day without fear of the lotus smugglers.

Shukara leaned on the railing, watching a salt-laden dahabiya sail north. "Those bound for Mask seem to carry little but salt," she commented. "I thought this river carried the wealth of kingdoms?"

"The last of the caravans arrived in Pashbur a month or two ago," Tamira said, pleased to know something the worldly mage didn't. "Few travel the desert at the height of summer, preferring to use that time to let their camels rest and fatten up. Their cargos would have been sent downriver to Mask weeks ago."

Shukara nodded. "That makes sense." Their dahabiya turned a bend, a second vessel drawing closer. The current favoured those sailing north, but Dashi ban Savar, captain of the boat, had assured them the wind would pick up and they would lose no more than half a day.

Shukara sniffed and wrinkled her nose. A moment later Tamira too caught the rank smell of filth and unwashed bodies. The approaching dahabiya was the source of the stench, and Tamira's gorge rose on seeing the cause.

Perhaps twenty naked dark-skinned slaves sat crammed together in an iron cage large enough for barely half that number. Their faces were a picture of misery, bereft of hope. Life in the Poor Quarter had exposed Tamira to the depths of human despair, but the casual cruelty shown by the crew towards their human cargo took even her breath away.

Slavery was common in Mask – many had served in the Royal Palace – and since the death of her family she'd seen slaves auctioned off on the slave block. But the crew had crammed into the cage as many as they could, providing not so much as a bucket or loincloth for even a token of dignity. As the boats passed, she observed gaunt faces, protruding ribs and stick-thin limbs. Children were caged too, pressed hard against the bars, too weak to swat away the flies that crawled over their faces and bodies to feed from untreated wounds.

Shukara scowled across the water. "What reason can there be to transport people in such conditions?" she spat. The slaves originated from the southern half of Araka, likely seized in raids between warring tribes and thereafter sold to slavers bound for the insatiable slave markets of northern Araka and beyond.

Master Koyo overheard. "Those slaves who survive the desert journey–" his tone suggested many didn't "–are kept in Pashbur for a month to rest and be fattened up before being sold on."

"You call those poor souls 'fattened up'?" Shukara interrupted, glaring at Koyo.

"Those who recover are sold to work in the mines and fields, some sent to brothels. Others become gladiators or are conscripted into slave-armies. Several kingdoms in Keram, across the sea, import a lot of Arakan slaves. But some – like those passing us – are too sick or weak to recover in Pashbur," he explained mildly. "Most are killed outright, but some slavers send them north to Mask to sell in bulk to the Xarian Arena. They're worth little, hence why so many are crammed into a single cage."

"The arena?" Tamira asked. She knew gladiators fought for the entertainment of Mask's citizens but couldn't imagine those wretches offering any fight.

Koyo shrugged. "The lions must eat."

The slave-carrying dahabiya turned the bend and vanished from view. For a moment Tamira feared – and wished – that Shukara would wreak some terrible judgement on the boat's crew, but the mage merely walked away.

Tamira wondered if Koyo brought slaves from the south but liked the bluff trader too much to ask. She thought of Tamira, the slave whose name she took and who died in her place, and felt a weight in her stomach. The palm trees lining the river banks and the grey mountains looming in the distance no longer pleased her as they had earlier.

She joined Shukara, ensuring they were out of earshot of the crew and other passengers. "What is your grievance with the Black Rose?"

For a moment, she thought the mage wouldn't answer, but perhaps Shukara too wanted a distraction. "I was born into the Kinyet Tribe in the Koumou region of southern Araka, raised in the vast savanna there.

"The village shaman sensed my affinity to magick and instructed my parents to send me to Tokombu, the City of Magi. It is very old, very insular. A village, really, but 'city' sounds grander, and we magi do enjoy our trappings. The Bone King is rumoured to have studied there, but then many places of learning are credited – or blamed – for teaching him."

"Did you like it?" Tamira had not enjoyed leaving her own home but conceded that their circumstances differed.

"At first I hated it. I hated the village, the aloof magi, their arrogant apprentices, and my fellow initiates. Even my parents for sending me there. After two months I ran away, but they found me and dragged me back. I learned later they Mark all initiates, allowing them to track runaways."

Tamira watched the mage's eyes, lost in the past.

"I settled down eventually and my old life faded into irrelevancy. Living in a village, marrying a herder and raising his children?" She shook her head. "What was that compared to unlocking the secrets of the world, of the universe itself?"

Tamira had no idea what a 'universe' was, but chose not to interrupt.

"Tokombu hoards many magickal relics, a staff reputed to have been fashioned by the Bone King among them." She held up her silver-wooded stave. "Wytchwood acts as a matrix for magick, most magi carrying staffs carved from it."

Her mouth twitched. "A woman carrying a staff draws attention, so I broke mine in two before reaching Arrioch and adjusted to its reduced size. The stave works just as well now." She slipped the stave back under her robe.

"You spoke of the Bone King's staff?" Tamira pressed, impatient to hear how Shukara's tale ended.

"Yes. Attempts to use it ended badly. Perhaps the Bone King attuned it to work only for himself, or perhaps it was designed to injure all who used it – the stories often depict the Bone King as a trickster, after all."

Tamira nodded, familiar with several legends.

"Regardless, the staff was hung up on the High Magister's wall, a trophy of sorts. And left to gather dust." She looked at Tamira. "Two years ago, a band of travellers arrived in Tokombu. They had nothing to trade but information from northern Araka and even the continent of Keram, but we were always eager for news from the outside world and welcomed them."

Shukara looked away. "It was a ruse. Shortly before dawn they left the caravanserai just outside the village, sneaking in and killing the guards at the collegiate entrance. They had earlier infiltrated the kitchens, poisoning much of the food and drink. Many of us never awoke, and when the alarm was finally raised, they had already reached the High Magister's quarters and killed him, taking his head. They also stole the Bone King's staff and fled before we fully knew what was happening. All but three escaped into the night, two killed, the third caught.

"Many of the magi of Tokombu died that night, including the High Magister. Under duress ... *extreme* duress ... the captured killer admitted being a Black Rose assassin, sent by their Grandmaster to steal the staff. Our survivors were divided; some wanted to visit retribution on the assassins, others cared little for the staff and argued the Collegiate had lost enough magi already."

"What happened?"

"Twenty of us left Tokombu, vowing to avenge our losses. If we could recover the staff too, all well and good." She shifted, shaking her long black hair behind her. "We tried to follow directly, but the assassins had bribed bandits to attack us, and tribal chiefs to deny us entry to their lands. After losing half our number we returned south and travelled the long route, through the western kingdoms and northwards."

Tamira whistled, trying to imagine the will required to travel an entire continent.

The sun was setting, dusk settling over the mage. "Three of us survived to see the Darish Sea, one thereafter dying of a snake bite. My last companion's heart failed in Arrioch while we waited for a ship to carry us to Mask." Shukara stood, stretching out the cramp from her long legs. "And I am the last."

"We're the last," Tamira corrected. Although, given what had befallen Shukara's previous companions, maybe she should have stayed in Mask.

A black silhouette stood over her. "Get some sleep, child. We reach Pashbur tomorrow."

Tamira looked west, the setting sun burning the horizon orange. Stars twinkled above, both moons casting a silvery soft light over the boat and river. Nights on the river were cooler than in the city, and Tamira fetched her blanket before lying on the deck.

Shukara lay beside her, the warmth of her body a comfort. The rocking of the boat and the gentle lapping of water against the hull soothed her, and she stared up at the blackening sky until sleep took her.

Chapter Eighteen

The wind had strengthened, helping them reach Pashbur shortly after midday. Once the dahabiya was tied up to the rickety wooden jetty, Shukara disembarked with Tamira. She noted the girl's disappointed expression. "Something wrong?"

"No, but is this," she waved at the jetty jutting out from the river bank, "it?"

Shukara smiled. The girl was used to Mask's ancient stone quays, built to host up to ten galleys. "No ships sail south of Mask, only boats and barges. In places the river is too narrow, too twisted, or too shallow for anything larger than a dahabiya. Besides, I doubt your ancestors would have tolerated a rival port on the river, even after Pashbur fell under their rule."

Tamira shrugged, her eyes drinking in the fresh sights before her. Shukara reminded herself that while she had travelled the length of Araka, Tamira had never before left the city of Mask. The land was arid, coated in a sandy layer carried by the wind, mountains rising to the north. Thick, lush vegetation sprouted up along the riverbank, brief islands of greenery in a dusty dry land. Palm trees lined the river too, providing welcome shade.

Tamira turned, gazing out across the river to the distant shore. Shukara was more interested in threats to their safety, distant tell-tale ripples in the river betraying the presence of crocodiles.

They walked down the narrow jetty, meeting a bored official taking shade under palm trees while asking peremptory questions, his indifference obvious.

A market traded along the river's bank, a row of stalls shaded by white cloth. Shukara paid little attention to the goods on offer or the gaggle of vendors and customers gathered round.

The clay-built village of Pashbur was the same colour as

the arid land surrounding it, blending into it, from a distance. The village had the same flat-roofed buildings as Mask, albeit built from brown earthen clay rather than red-mud bricks, protected by three kasbahs. Half of the village spread up a hill, a watchtower at its peak. A protective wall joined the foremost buildings, the rearmost rising above the rest of the village beneath a clear blue sky.

They passed through the main gate, flanked by two sand-coloured towers. Clay had crumbled from both, no efforts made to repair them. Bandits and rogue Kavari clans still raided caravans and outlying villages, but none had dared attack Pashbur itself in many years. The last band to do so had been hunted down, dragged to the outskirts of Pashbur, and impaled. Their bodies were left to rot, a warning to others. Tamira had told Shukara the tale, the retribution ordered by her grandfather.

"An inn," Tamira said, pointing to a sign above a red-painted door, depicting a faded lion beneath a carved cup.

A bald man greeted them inside, his head and chin completely shaved. Like many in Pashbur, his ancestry was a mix of north Arakan and Kavari, his colour darker than Tamira's. His djellaba was stretched over a protruding belly, his portliness a sign that the inn did well. "Welcome to the Black Lion Inn. I am Massan ban Kur, the proprietor." Wind and sand had faded the painted lion to a pale grey, but the innkeeper seemed neither inclined to repaint the sign nor rename his inn.

Shafts of light entered through narrow windows cut into the walls, but the common room was otherwise dark. The walls were bare clay, adorned only by an occasional spear, three curved swords and one battered shield. Tapestries would have benefited the room's aesthetics. The ground was hardened earth and a musty smell lingered.

"I am Shukara, looking for a room for two." She didn't introduce Tamira.

Massan licked his lips, a calculating expression flitting across his face as he regarded the woman and the girl. "That will be ten sols per night, each."

"Perhaps another inn will prove less outrageous," Shukara said, turning to leave.

"Apologies, good mistress. I meant, it is ten sols per night for you both."

Shukara faced him, disliking his oily smile. "Five sols per night."

Beads of sweat rolled down his bald pate. "You jest, mistress. Such generosity would beggar me. Eight sols."

"Seven sols. And I expect the rooms to be clean and our beds free from pests." As an afterthought she added, "And our meals are included, two per day."

Massan shook his head and sighed. "Very well, but I do not know how you will sleep tonight, having robbed an honest innkeeper."

"I will sleep very well, so long as I do not share my blankets with fleas."

"Be seated, and I will bring you both teh."

She nodded. "We thank you."

The tables were square and taller than usual, with wooden stools rather than cushions provided for patrons. Tamira looked at them uncertainly.

They sat at a table on its own. "Comfortable?" Shukara asked, noting Tamira's fidgeting.

"The stools are hard." Maskans favoured the custom of sitting on a carpet or cushions around low tables.

Amusement creased Shukara's eyes. "Humble apologies for the poor accommodation, Highness."

Tamira flushed. Not so long ago any chair would have been a luxury to her. "There are a lot of Kavari here," she said, changing the subject.

"Yes." From what Shukara recalled, the Kavari were native to lands in central Araka. War had driven them north thousands of years before, and those who survived the pitiless desert-crossing had not been welcomed by those living on the other side. Having lost their homeland to the south and finding no welcome in the north, they had adopted a nomadic life on the fringes of the desert, raiding to survive. Kavari clans could be found on the edges and inhabitable regions of the desert from Khespha Province to mid-Araka.

Some northern clans had made themselves useful to the Maskan rulers and been given land and position in reward. According to Tamira, the current padshah of Khespha

Province, Thekti Thami-Bhuul, was the descendant of one such tribesman. He ruled both the province and the Bhuul Clan of the Kavari. A son, Gheran Thekti-Bhuul, was the Quaid of Pashbur. Other holdings in Khespha Province were ruled by quaids whose relation to Thekti went back generations, but Pashbur was too important for the padshahs to allow it to become the fiefdom of a distant branch of the family. As such, the quaidship of the village stayed in the main line of the family rather than becoming an hereditary position. When Gheran succeeded Thekti as padshah, a younger brother or son would rule Pashbur as quaid.

Massan brought them two glazed clay cups and a pot of teh that smelled of mint. Shukara handed him a coin after he had filled their cups. "Thank you, Master Massan. You honour us with your hospitality."

He bowed his head. "You are welcomed guests." They might haggle over the prices, but hospitality was held sacred. A host was expected to offer teh, and to refuse it was to offer insult.

"What now?" the girl asked, stifling a yawn.

"You can rest in our room. I will find us a suitable guide to take us to Rhemi." She lifted her cup. "After I've finished my teh."

Shukara left the inn after ensuring Tamira was locked in their room, for the girl's own safety. She warded the door as a further precaution, ensuring that should anyone force entry, she would know.

*

"Don't laugh," Jassan chided as Adjatay listened to his recent misadventure.

"Sorry, my friend," Adjatay said, sounding not very apologetic. "I know all too well what it's like to suffer in the desert. Will the merchant make any trouble for you?"

"He's grumbled to his friends, mostly to save face and to make sure his partners' kin don't blame him for their deaths," Jassan said with a disgruntled shrug.

He didn't expect Subed's quiet complaints to damage his reputation any; those who travelled the desert knew its perils and that there were no guarantees. He had heard that Subed had sold eight of his remaining twelve camels and given the coin to the families of Ahmed and Ferres. A poor return for the loss of two men, twenty camels and coin from the goods sold on their ill-fated venture. Subed himself planned to return to the desert, this time travelling with one of the larger caravans with his four remaining camels.

"Why did you take the job?" Adjatay asked.

Jassan sipped teh and stretched his legs. "I thought to make some coin before signing on to one of the larger caravans. And you know how bored I get in Pashbur."

"You could visit your home village."

Jassan laughed. "Not that bored. My mother keeps trying to marry me off."

Adjatay's remaining eye watched him shrewdly. "Still thinking of joining a caravan bound for the Spice Route?"

"Yes," he admitted. The problem was, the eastern Spice Route left the Kavari Desert behind after a score of days, so the rangers only signed on for that long, returning west upon reaching Egaria. Jassan wanted to travel the whole route but to do so meant hiring on as a common scout, guard or camel puller for far less money. He still planned to do so one day, taking on smaller jobs to save up what he could.

Adjatay gripped the table as he got to his feet, grimacing in pain. "Be grateful you can travel anywhere. I can barely reach the souk on a good day, and only with the help of my stick."

"You travelled a lot before," Jassan reminded him.

"Yes," Adjatay said. A trace of envy entered his voice. "But I never travelled just for the pleasure of seeing somewhere new."

Jassan smiled. "I will travel east, some day." He stood. "But first, I must take your carvings down to the souk." What his cousin Jeka didn't sell there would be taken south by her brother Afetey.

"My thanks, friend," Adjatay said.

Jassan bowed his head. "My thanks for your hospitality."

"It is your family's house," Adjatay said with a shrug.

"It's Afetey's, and better for you to rent it than for it to lie empty." Afetey was a ranger, like himself, and stayed with

Jeka during his rare visits to Pashbur.

Jassan picked up a heavy pack filled with stone carvings, his back protesting under the weight. At least the souk was downhill. He called out a farewell to Adjatay and set off through the narrow streets, the clay houses around him providing welcome shade.

The four-towered Kasbah Bhuul stood out prominently among the flat-roofed buildings at the foot of the hill. This kasbah was the oldest and smallest of Pashbur's three strongholds, the quaid residing in the larger and more comfortable Kasbah Tahmour. With the threat of raids now a distant memory, Quaid Gheran had allowed the merchants into Kasbah Bhuul to encourage more trade within the city, the other souks already at capacity.

Narrow streets were threaded between the buildings, the village hemmed in within the defensive walls. Many of the villagers recognised him and exchanged greetings as he struggled past with his heavy burden. He wondered cynically if Adjatay's injured leg conveniently worsened whenever Jassan was around to carry his stone carvings down to the souk, but dismissed the thought as petty. Adjatay had been hours from Death's embrace when chance led Jassan and his fellow rangers to him, crippled and dying in the desert those few years past.

Jassan passed through the kasbah entrance and followed the narrow corridor out into the courtyard where the merchants plied their trade. His cousin Jeka owned a large stall within the shaded courtyard from where she sold carpets sewn by their kin, as well as Adjatay's carvings.

"Careful, Jassan!" Jeka exclaimed as he put the pack down with a relieved grunt.

"Sorry, Jeka," he said with an insincere grin.

She threw him an exasperated look, followed by a green apple.

"How are the children?" he asked before crunching his teeth down into the fruit, savouring the sweet juice.

"A trial inflicted on me by the gods, as ever." But her tone was affectionate. "There's a rumour going around that you led a caravan to their deaths."

Irritation nipped at Jassan, and he related the misadventure.

"I then had to trade most of the camels to the Pelhou Clan for water to get us back here."

Jeka nodded. "As long as you made it back." Her husband had been a ranger, last seen with a caravan of a thousand camels heading south four years before. None had ever returned, swallowed whole by the desert. "Where are you off to now?"

"The caravanserai."

Jeka nodded. "Take care, Jassan."

He smiled. "Always." Jassan left the kasbah and followed the short narrow streets that led him to the gate built into the village wall. He walked south towards the caravanserai, the River Tyre to his right.

The land was dry and dusty, the desert proper waiting a short distance to the south. Carefully irrigated grazing fields lay to the north, hosting thousands of camels left to fatten up after their months-long trek. Some caravan masters owned houses in the village or rented rooms in its inns, waiting until their camels were fit enough to make the daunting cross-desert journey. Kavari like himself were common among the travellers, some owning their own camels, most hiring themselves out as camel pullers, rangers and guards.

He reached the caravanserai, an inn for passing caravaners and a home of sorts to nomadic rangers such as himself, a place to trade stories and find work with caravan masters.

A large, square, stone building, the caravanserai's portal was wide enough to allow visiting travellers to bring their beasts inside to stalls built in the courtyard. The stalls were favoured by those owning only a handful of beasts. Camel herds numbering in the hundreds or thousands were led to the northern pastures.

He entered the common room and jostled through the crowd to the bar where he waited for service. A third of the patrons were non-Kavari but almost all wore a djellaba, the robe well-suited for the climate.

A Kavari rose, unsteady from wine. "I'm heading to the village," he announced to no one in particular.

"Need help?" someone asked, prompting a smattering of laughter.

"Just don't ask Jassan or you'll never make it," another

called out to the mirth of (almost) all.

Jassan accepted the mockery in good humour, knowing no offence was intended. Almost everyone there knew how fickle the desert could be. The bartender brought him a cup of teh and he found a small table in the corner, sinking into one of the beige cushions on the floor next to it.

He sat alone, allowing the din of chatter and second-hand lotus smoke to wash over him. He caught the sound of his name being mentioned and looked up to see a grizzled caravan guard direct a tall dark woman in his direction.

Chapter Nineteen

Shukara's enquiries in the market for a dependable guide sent her to Jassan, a well-regarded ranger. She was assured that he could be found in the caravanserai outside the village. Many people and beasts milled around the caravanserai, built next to the start of the caravan route. Pashbur was known as the Gateway to the Desert.

She found Jassan sitting inside, sipping teh amidst the crowded bustle. He was maybe a few years older than her, wearing a blue djellaba and sturdy brown sandals. The ranger had the coal-black skin of the Kavari, a legacy of generations spent in the desert. Only Kavari could find water in the deep desert that named them, or negotiate passage with their territorial brethren therein, and so rangers accompanied every caravan.

He looked at her quizzically, motioning for her to join him. "Help you, mistress?"

"I need a guide, Master Jassan," she said, sitting on a cushion across from him. "I'm told you're a fine ranger."

He laughed, his manner easy. "I pay all my friends to tell people that." He was shorter than her and slender, his head and face shaved smooth. "Where are you wanting to go?" He gestured around. "A big caravan leaves in three days and these fellows hope to come along." If the fiercely independent clans and raiders inhabiting the desert failed to kill small groups trying cross the deep Kavari, the desert would.

"How big?"

He considered it. "Maybe fifteen hundred, two thousand camels? Master Koyo's been resting his beasts for two months, and he plans to carry salt and cloth to the kingdoms south of the desert. I hear his men have been hiring more camels and pullers." He sipped some teh. "No doubt he'll bring back gold, spices, ivory, kola nuts and slaves."

"Have you hired on with him?" she asked.

"No. I might, or I might sign up with Gannen ban Ahmed who plans to carry salt east and north along the Spice Route." He shrugged. "I'll get better paid going south across the whole desert, but I've never been east, and it does a man good to see new places." He regarded her. "Where are you looking to go? South or east?"

Shukara took a breath. "South for a bit. And then west along the Black Trail." So-named because it led to the Black Citadel, guarding the Rhemi Oasis.

Jassan regarded her, mirth draining from his dark eyes. He got to his feet and led her out of the common room into the courtyard. "Too many ears in there," he said. "Tell me more."

*

Tamira followed Shukara through the crumbling, narrow paths separating Pashbur's buildings, blocky clay structures rising with the hill. She had refreshed herself in the inn's bathhouse – built as little more than an afterthought, a cramped room with a hole in the ground, lined with bricks and tiles. The tiles were mouldy and cracking, and the water tepid.

I'm getting spoiled, she thought, half-amused, half-alarmed. Not so many days past she had made do with a dunk in the river, with the same filthy kalasiris awaiting her afterwards. Now she dressed in her clean shendyt and tunic, keeping her djellaba fresh for the desert crossing.

A Kavari tribesman waited for them. "Mistress Shukara, greetings again." He looked at Tamira curiously.

"Greetings, Jassan. Shukara will suffice. This is Tamira. Tamira, this is Jassan, a Kavari ranger."

Jassan bowed his head, placing his right hand over his heart. "Honoured."

Tamira placed her palms together.

He indicated that they should follow him inside a square single-storeyed house that had seen better days, and they obliged. Shukara looked untroubled, but Tamira knew her well enough by now to recognise that she was alert for danger.

The house was lightly cluttered but clean, consisting of a single room with a rough-finished table occupying the centre. The east and west-facing walls each had a narrow window hacked out to let in daylight. Light poured in through the west-facing window as the sun neared the horizon.

Tamira detected faint odours of spices and mint over a musty clay smell. Each area of the room had been set aside for a purpose, pots and bowls piled up near a cooking pit dug beneath a small chimney. Neatly folded blankets marked the sleeping area.

A man stood within, north Arakan rather than Kavari, and certainly no ranger. He carried a teh pot from the cooking pit to the table, limping heavily and leaning on a stout stick. A dusky weathered face was set amidst a thick black beard and shoulder-length black hair. His left eye was covered by a brown leather eyepatch and a pale scar cut angrily through his face from brow to lips.

He sat clumsily, gesturing for his guests to join him as he filled four cups with teh. "Be welcome in my home."

They sat, Jassan next to the stranger, Shukara and Tamira sitting across from them. "I am Adjatay," their host introduced himself, hand on heart.

"Shukara, and Tamira," the mage replied, failing to copy Tamira's palm-to-palm response, her right hand beneath the table. "I had hoped to discuss our journey." Shukara looked at Jassan, her tone asking what her words did not: why had he brought them to this house?

The ranger sipped his teh, but Shukara's remained untouched. Tamira was in no hurry to drink hers, disliking mint, but some traditions were ironclad, hospitality among them. She compromised by raising the cup briefly to her lips.

Jassan ran a finger down his cup. "Adjatay is a friend. He can assist in planning our journey."

She raised an eyebrow. "How so? Forgive the observation, but it looks beyond him."

The ranger took a breath. "Adjatay knows the Black Citadel, he was–"

His head arched back, as did Adjatay's. Both men began to choke, their hands trembling but unable to move.

"An assassin?" Shukara guessed, placing her right hand on

the table, her stave gripped tightly. Tamira had watched her mix various reagents into water in the inn, drinking it before they left. If the ranger had betrayed them, it would not end well for him or his friend. "Explain yourself, Jassan."

He sucked in a breath, the invisible hold on the ranger lessening slightly. "He's an outcast from the Black Rose, believed dead. He can't accompany us, but he can still help."

She looked at Adjatay. "No one leaves the Black Rose alive. But a cripple did, and lives within a ten-day of their stronghold?"

Adjatay jerked a nod. "I was a master of the sect. I fell out with Grandmaster Linus three years ago," he rasped, Shukara's projected will still invisibly clamped around his throat. "I fled, and my brother and sister assassins pursued me across the desert. They caught me, cut my face, broke my legs, and left me to die."

"I was part of a water-scouting party," Jassan said. "We found him by chance and carried him back to our camp."

Shukara looked from face to face, judging the veracity of their tale. She sipped some teh and Tamira followed suit, finding it too heavy with mint as expected.

Both men slumped with a gasp as Shukara released her hold on them. Jassan rubbed his throat. "A mage ... where from?"

"Tokombu," she answered, watching Adjatay carefully. Gauging his reaction, Tamira suspected. If he was exiled from the Black Rose three years ago, he would not know of the assassin raid on Tokombu. His demeanour didn't change.

Tamira recalled her own exile. "How can you afford this house, to eat, to live?" His blue djellaba wasn't new, but it was well-mended.

"A cousin of Jassan's owns the house. I carve figurines from stone and rely on Jassan and his kin to sell them here and on their travels," he said, nodding to stone chippings on the table. "I never venture far from this house, and my former brethren have no interest in the village itself."

Jassan grinned. "Not that they would recognise you now, anyway." He looked at Shukara. "He had a shaved head and chin when they left him for dead."

"I harbour the Black Rose no loyalty," Adjatay assured

Shukara. "I'll aid any who oppose them."

Shukara regarded him. "How do you know *I* oppose them? Suppose I have business in the Black Citadel?"

"The questions you asked me earlier were not those that would be asked by a petitioner or one invited," Jassan said, "but rather those I'd expect from someone wanting to reach there without attracting undue attention."

Adjatay sipped teh. "That is why he came to me. One does not simply ride to the Black Citadel and knock on the door, or hope to find a side entrance conveniently unlocked."

Jassan nodded. "And I won't get paid if we die."

"Speak on." Shukara clasped her hands attentively.

"Patrols ensure no one travels the Black Trail unnoticed, and vultures feast on those unable to provide satisfactory answers if questioned. A small village and caravanserai sit next to the oasis near the citadel, the villagers dealing with traders. None enter the Black Citadel uninvited."

"I can be persuasive," she said.

Adjatay looked unimpressed. "The sect has dealt with magi before."

"I got us inside Mask's Kasbah Baraq," Tamira said. "And we saw off three of the Magi of Hrek afterwards, including a magister."

The former assassin regarded her with interest for the first time. "No mean feat, but the Black Rose have spent a thousand years entering places thought impregnable, reaching those believed unassailable, and have accordingly removed those vulnerabilities from the Black Citadel." His expression turned thoughtful. "But there may be a way…"

*

The former assassin proved a boon, providing many useful details that stitched together several partial ideas into a plan with a chance of success. Night had fallen, and he had promised to sketch a layout of the citadel tomorrow. He clearly hated the Grandmaster and hungered to see the assassins pay, but Shukara couldn't look past the truth that he had been one of them. Jassan's motive was simple; she had offered him a ruby in exchange for his services.

Adjatay had left the house for some air, leaving Shukara and Jassan to finalise a few details. Tamira had slipped out of the house earlier when no one was looking. Finally done for the night, Shukara left too, watching Adjatay.

"A beautiful night," he said without turning. "You use scented oils," he said, explaining how he knew she was there.

"It is," she agreed. Countless stars twinkled above, scattered across the black canopy overhead. She recognised many constellations from her home to the south, but others were unfamiliar.

"I look up at the stars most clear nights, but it's your companion I watch tonight." He pointed down into the lower village, and movement caught Shukara's eye. Tamira was running from roof to roof, a dark shadow returning to them.

"She moves well," he said with a cripple's envy. "There's room for improvement, but she has good balance and instincts. She would have thrived in the Black Citadel."

She might have thrived with her family had it not been for the Black Citadel. "Would you consider training her?" She had too much potential to return to thievery and an early death in the slums of Mask.

He chuckled. "It would take years to teach her how a body works, how to kill, how to pick locks and leave no trace of her passage."

"I promised to aid her revenge, but your former associates are by no means the last of those who wronged her. She is young; agree to train her in your arts upon our return."

"*If* you return. How you plan to overcome a stronghold of assassins is beyond me."

"We'll return." Tamira had silently joined them, breathing hard and coated in a sheen of perspiration.

Adjatay studied her. "It would take me two years to teach you what I know, and you would need to study herb and plantlore with a local apothecary to master poisons and antidotes. And after that, you would need to return to Mask or a similar city to better learn the secrets and weaknesses of the human body from healers, and have weapons constructed and know how to use them."

Tamira looked at him and nodded. "Two years."

"I will pay you," Shukara said, thinking of the two gems

remaining to her. She could spare one, perhaps even loot valuables from the citadel. *If we live.*

Adjatay nodded slowly. "Very well, but not for money. There is a sword hanging in the Grandmaster's rooms, a trophy. It has a golden hilt and a slim, curved blade of excellent iron."

"A sword?"

He nodded. "It was once wielded by Verak, Captain of Mask's Royal Guards. I defeated him in a duel and took it from his body in remembrance."

*

Tamira's chest tightened, her head suddenly light. "You were one of the assassins who raided the palace? Killed my … king?"

"Another killed King Xarius. I was tasked to kill the oldest princess." He grimaced. "An ill night, being sent after children. Verak killed Princess Xaria as we cornered him, to keep her from our hands. He challenged me, I accepted and killed him." Adjatay's face turned reflective. "He saved me from staining my hands with a child's blood and gave me an honest fight. What shred of honour I gained from that night I owe to him. For the Grandmaster, the sword is a pretty trophy. For me it is a reminder of a brave man called Verak and of my old life as Karib, a Master of the Black Rose."

"We will find it," Shukara promised, giving Tamira a warning look. Tamira held her tongue.

Adjatay – Karib – looked satisfied. "And if by some small chance you return, I will train Tamira."

Tamira forced herself to smile at the man who had once hunted her through the Royal Palace. "I will learn everything you can teach me," she promised. "And use your lessons well against my enemies." *All of them.*

Chapter Twenty

The caravan's departure from Pashbur was a riot of organised chaos as Koyo's thousand camels left the village's northern pastures in a steady stream to be loaded up with cargo: mostly salt transported to Pashbur from across the province. A further thousand camels joined them, either hired by Koyo or owned by smaller traders wanting to join the caravan for protection.

Even accounting for the provision of food and water for the three-month journey, the camel pullers were paid a pittance, but Jassan revealed that they made their money bringing along goods of their own for sale. Some even owned their own camels and were permitted to include them in the file they led. Most of the camel owners in the caravan had started off as camel pullers gradually increasing their herd, and now employing pullers of their own. Some had been hired to carry Koyo's goods; others, carrying their own cargo, paid Koyo to join the caravan.

Up to forty camels were roped together into a file, a camel puller leading each file, and the train was four files wide. The leading elements of the huge caravan had already left Pashbur, heading for the trail.

"I'm glad you followed my advice to arrive early," Jassan said in greeting. "The rear of a caravan is always last to reach water." The ranger nodded his approval at their djellabas, similar cotton robes being worn by almost everyone to protect them from the sun. It was early morning but already oppressively hot.

"You've arranged our passage?" Shukara asked.

Jassan nodded. "Yes. I bought four camels with the money you gave me and paid for our inclusion in the caravan." He pointed to a group of camels being loaded with salt. "I bought enough salt blocks to load on them to make a credible cargo."

Tamira frowned. "There won't be much room to sit."

Jassan laughed. "There won't be any room to sit on them. I've hired two camels for you to ride while we're with the caravan, but after we leave it we will walk for most of the Black Trail. You can take turns to ride the fourth animal, which will carry the hay."

"Hay?" She had assumed they would ride all the way to the Black Citadel. A three day walk in the baking sun did not appeal.

"Hay for the camels, or do you think they eat rocks? Unlike us, they can go days without water and feed, but both water and vegetation will be scarce in the desert. We'll eat mostly dates, rice and dried meat."

"We may not be fit for an eight day walk back to Pashbur," Shukara said.

"The salt's just to give us a plausible reason to travel to the Black Citadel. We can ride back," he assured her. Tamira noted that neither mentioned the strong possibility that there might not be a return journey.

Jassan produced two long blue cotton scarves which he wrapped around their heads, fashioning them into a turban like the one he wore. "This is a shesh." He pointed to the loose end wrapped around their shoulders. "Wrap that around your face if it gets windy, otherwise you'll get a mouthful of sand."

"What of our camel puller?" Shukara asked as she adjusted her shesh.

"He is called Sulen ban Lan. I've travelled with him before, a good man," Jassan assured her. "When we leave the caravan at the Black Trail, I'll lead our camels."

Villagers gathered to watch the caravan's preparations, kin to many travelling with it. At least eight months would pass before the caravan returned. Three months there, two months to rest the camels, and three months back. If they returned. Some never did.

A camel puller shouted over to Jassan who waved back. "That's Sulen."

Tamira and Shukara were introduced to Sulen ban Lan, a thin man with a straggly beard. Despite being Maskan, he wore a Kavari shesh; almost everyone attached to the caravan did. Thirty-eight camels sat strung together in a line near him, laden with goods, fodder and water skins.

Tamira studied the beasts dubiously. She had been warned to treat them with caution, and the bad-tempered glare one shot her convinced her that it was advice worth following.

Shukara mounted her camel without assistance, clearly no stranger to the odorous beasts. Tamira looked at her own mount with trepidation. She had fearlessly climbed walls and towers, leaping from rooftop to rooftop; surely a beast of burden offered no challenge, she told herself.

She sensed amusement from Shukara, Jassan and Sulen as she struggled to get up onto the saddle, an embroidered cushion tied to a wooden frame. She took hold of the front and rear saddle horns and hopped up, scrambling onto the cushion and swinging her left leg over the other side. "Easy," she grinned, ignoring the camel's throaty grumbling.

"Well done," Shukara said dryly. They had been given camels near the front of the file, Tamira's mount behind Shukara's.

Sulen walked to the front of his file of camels and gently used a stick to encourage it to rise. One by one he and Jassan got the camels to their feet. They looked a ragged line of beasts, but Tamira knew them to be hardy creatures. Jassan had impressed on her that a very thin line separated life and death in the desert, and to mistreat or neglect their camels was a sure way to cross it. For camel pullers, their charges were more than a livelihood; they were life itself.

"Hold onto the pommel and brace yourself," Jassan warned Tamira as he prepared to stand the beast.

"Worried I might fall off?" she asked scornfully as she took hold of the front saddle horn.

Jassan just grinned and shook his head. "Upupupupup," he said to the camel with one hand on its harness, encouraging it to rise.

The camel grumbled – and Tamira found herself flung forward as it rose back-first. She cried out and tensed her arms, holding tightly to the pommel. The camel's front legs then stood, and Tamira took a calming breath. Jassan chuckled as he moved down the line.

"It's a beast from the Underworld!" she called after him.

"It's a she," he called back. "And if you sit that way, you

won't be able to sit tomorrow or for days after," he said, pointing to Tamira's legs dangling on either side of the camel. "Straighten one leg out and rest your foot near the camel's neck, curling your other leg round the pommel."

Sulen returned to the front of the line and took hold of the rope, leading the camels forward on foot. Tamira found her camel's swaying motion disorientating at first, almost like being back on the boat, but she forced herself to relax. After a while she leaned forward and tentatively patted her camel's head, its hair short but coarse. The camel's head jerked up in surprise, but she didn't seem to mind the attention.

They left Pashbur behind, passing between two towering rocks called the Kavari Gate. The caravan stretched ahead into the distance, its head disappearing into the sun-blasted desert.

An eight-day journey across the Kavari waited, with death at its end. Perhaps her own.

*

Five days passed. Tamira had thought Mask's long summers had prepared her for the desert, but she had learned differently. Her respect for the desert-dwelling Kavari increased tenfold. At least in Mask there was shade to be found. In the desert there was no escape from the sun, nothing but baked sand and rocks as far as the eye could see, a parched furnace beneath a cloudless blue sky.

The only respite came at sunset, the desert cooling fast. Jassan claimed that in winter, desert nights turned truly cold, something Tamira had trouble believing.

Shukara looked back. "Are you coping?" The mage bore the heat stoically, tough and indomitable.

"I can manage," Tamira insisted. She struggled to imagine the sheer size of the desert. They had travelled across it for five days, five days of nothing in any direction. And they had crossed but a fraction of it.

It had changed, however. The hard, rocky ground had turned to sand, the larger dunes stretching up a hundred meters. Tamira occasionally walked to stretch her legs. Wading through the sand proved a chore, and she wondered how the camel pullers could endure weeks or months of it.

Tonight would be her last with the caravan. Sometime tomorrow they would reach the point where the trail broke in two, one path continuing south, the other leading west. The Black Trail.

The Black Trail would in theory decrease the caravan's journey by several days, Rhemi's oasis ideally located for travellers to water their camels and refill their skins. But the Black Rose did not welcome caravans of such size, and so almost all were forced to travel south for several more days before turning west.

A small part of Tamira wanted to stay with the caravan, to brave the desert and see what waited on the far side. She knew this was partly fear whispering in her ear, a dread that churned her belly whenever she thought of the looming confrontation with the Black Rose. But the desert called to her too. She found peace among the dunes, surrounded by sand and sky and the shared purpose of her fellow travellers. At night, she stared up at the stars and moons, so bright but so far.

Windblown sand grazed her cheeks, a sudden gust catching her by surprise. Tamira wrapped the loose end of her shesh around her face and hunched low. Aside from running out of water, sandstorms were a caravan's greatest fear. Bandits could be fought off, tribesmen could be bartered with, but there was nothing to be done against a storm of sand and wind except hunker down and pray not to be buried before it passed. Jassan's advice was to shelter beside a camel.

The caravan stopped before dusk, its camels tended to first. Their burdens were removed, and they were examined for illness or injury before being fed and watered.

While the camels were being attended to, the cooks set up fires and cooked rice in large cauldrons. Tents were raised, and rangers returned from scouting out the trail ahead.

Tamira had noticed Jassan turning increasingly restless as the days passed. "What ails you?"

"I rarely stay with a caravan for so long. I prefer to range ahead to check wells, scout for bandits and negotiate our passage with any nearby clans. To be tethered to the caravan itself is tedious."

"It's only been five days," she teased.

He smiled. "I often scout for days at a time, usually with a band of fellow rangers, but sometimes on my own."

"We'll be leaving the caravan tomorrow."

His smile faded. "I know."

Tamira left him to his thoughts and helped Sulen tend to the camels. She was learning that they provided more than transportation. Lacking wood or brush for the fires, camel dung was dry enough to be an effective substitute. She had not been surprised to see Sulen milk the females, but she had laughed that first night on seeing him collect their urine, learning later that it was used to clean hair and treat sores.

Tamira, Jassan, Shukara and Sulen sat around their fire, joined by a cook and two caravan guards. The sky burned red and orange to the west, the sands turning into a shifting sea of crimson. The first stars were already visible in the east.

Shukara had said little since entering the desert, a tall brooding presence. Preparing to face the Black Rose, Tamira hoped.

They ate rice, dates and sipped their rationed water. The ration was always a topic of debate. Too much, and they would be dead before reaching the next well or oasis. Too little to replace what they sweated out, and they would be stricken or dead even faster.

Tamira always looked forward to the evening meal, enjoying the camaraderie from those who shared their fire. The caravan was a nomadic village, and each night caravaners visited a different fire to trade stories.

Few women were present in the caravan, and Shukara and Tamira never strayed from their own fire. Jassan always stayed with them, perhaps feeling protective. If his presence deterred any unwelcome attention, all the better. Shukara's magick would at best draw unwelcome attention to them, and at worst might see them driven from the caravan to die in the desert.

Jassan was a fine storyteller, sometimes provoking laughter, other times chilling his audience with tales of horror. Last night he had spoken of the fall of Mask's last king, not knowing the dead king's daughter listened, her tears hidden by the night. Adjatay must have shared some details, enough for Jassan to tell of Verak's last stand.

Adjatay. The former assassin was an open wound, an unanswered question. He was among those she wanted to kill but would fail to do so without his training. Could she really endure two years learning from one of her family's killers?

Restless, Tamira slipped away from the fire, returning to the tent she shared with Shukara. She yearned for a steam tent, but water was too scarce to replace what they would sweat out. In the desert, she had discovered, bathing was done with dry sand, and camel urine for the hair.

Tamira gathered her blankets and returned to the fire. She curled up and closed her eyes, letting the stories and quiet conversations wash over her.

*

The next day started like those previous, the caravaners rising early to break their fast, pack up their tents and reload the camels. The rule of thumb seemed to be that if the camel grumbled, it could carry more; the moment it ceased grumbling, the caravaners stopped loading it.

"The Black Trail is a short distance ahead," Tamira heard Jassan tell Shukara. While he and Sulen untied the four rearmost camels, Tamira used her reins to command hers to lie down. This was her sixth day in the saddle, and she had learned enough to control the animal and sense her moods.

After briefly wishing Sulen a safe journey across the desert, Jassan led Shukara and Tamira away from the caravan without comment or ceremony.

Tamira watched the caravan proceed south, part of her still wishing they were travelling with it. But the Black Trail lay to the west, a three-day journey to the Black Rose stronghold where either death or vengeance waited.

Perhaps both.

Chapter Twenty-One

Weary legs carried Shukara ever closer to the Black Citadel. The sand was mostly gone after the first half-day, reduced to a thin layer covering the rocky trail. She had thought two years of hard travel had toughened her feet against blisters but was learning otherwise. Jassan showed no sign of fatigue; either he was tougher than she thought, or he hid it better.

Regardless, the ranger marched on at a steady pace, a curved sword sheathed by his side, and a bow made from horn, wood and hide strapped to his back. A quiver of black-feathered arrows hung from his belt.

It was Tamira who gave Shukara cause for concern. The girl had insisted on walking for the first day, even when her heat-sapped strength clearly flagged. She had insisted on walking the second day, too, until exhaustion finally drove her into the saddle.

On the third morning Shukara had insisted Tamira ride from the outset, and she hadn't argued. The princess-turned-thief would need her strength if their plan were to succeed.

Rocky hills had loomed ahead when they stopped at the end of the second day. Now nearing the end of the third, those hills rose to their left.

"Are we being watched?" Shukara asked.

Jassan nodded. "Ever since we reached the hills. Before, I'd wager. The Black Rose don't welcome guests and at best tolerate traders."

"Have you seen them?" Not so much as a pebble had tumbled downhill.

"I glimpsed one. Whoever it was, I think they were testing me to see if I noticed them." He glanced at her. "Don't worry, I pretended I didn't."

Their food and water almost exhausted, Shukara knew they must reach Rhemi soon.

Jassan rounded the last bend, slowing. "There." He pointed ahead.

Shukara joined him and followed his gaze down the long, gradual slope leading to the plateau beyond, mostly flat except for a lone mountain peak. It was what lay before the mountain that quickened her heart – an oasis of lush vegetation surrounding a large pool of water, fed by an underground spring. Water, blessed water!

The Oasis of Rhemi. *But where then is the village? The citadel?* She squinted, discerning a small sand-coloured village squatting at the foot of the peak, a much smaller sibling to Pashbur. "Rhemi?" she asked.

Jassan nodded. "Yes. We've arrived. Nearly."

She frowned. "Where is the Black Citadel?" The floor plan sketched by Adjatay was of a large fortress of multiple levels, but nothing in the small village qualified. He hadn't bothered to describe the citadel's outer appearance, simply saying they would know it when they saw it.

"It's there," Jassan assured her.

"All I see is the mountain," she snapped, too tired and thirsty for games.

"It *is* the mountain."

Shukara stared at it. She cast a spell, one that bent the air before her to magnify the distant peak. Sure enough, narrow windows had been carved out of the mountain, a massive iron gate visible at the foot. *They hollowed it out...*

She took a breath, staring at the stronghold of her enemy, a mountain filled with trained killers. But she had travelled too far, for too long, to succumb to despair. "What are you waiting for, Jassan? Take us to Rhemi."

*

Tamira leaned back, eyes closed as the sweat tent left her soaked in perspiration. She barely remembered the last day of the journey, feeling a slight sense of shame that the desert had beaten her. Jassan had scoffed at that, pointing out that if she lived, *she* had won.

"Feeling better?" Shukara asked. They were the only two in the tent, scraping off their dirt.

"Much." The village – Rhemi? – had no inns or taverns, only a caravanserai for visiting traders. They had arrived just before dusk, Tamira having been carried into a room to rest while their camels were led into stalls for food and water.

She had awoken the next morning, her strength further restored by a meal of goat, rice and milk. Neither the caravanserai nor the village had a bathhouse, but sweat tents made from stretched hide were available near the oasis, a welcome bathing alternative to itchy sand and sour milk. *And to wash my hair in water that hasn't been pissed from a camel…*

"If you need another day to recover, we can wait. But to linger in Rhemi will rouse suspicion," Shukara said.

"I'm fine," she insisted. "We can proceed as planned."

Shukara nodded. "Good."

Tamira scraped herself clean with sticks while Shukara poured more water onto the bucket of hot coals, further heating the tent. Bathing in the precious spring water was forbidden due to fear of drought, sweat tents the only alternative. Jugs of tepid water were provided to wash off the sweat.

Feeling truly clean for the first time in days, Tamira pulled on her shendyt and tunic, the odorous cotton of her djellaba stiff with dust, sand and stale sweat. Village women washed clothing in large tubs near the spring, and Tamira handed one her djellaba and a coin. The cleaned djellaba would be left to dry in the sun.

Shukara left the tent, wearing her shendyt and nothing else, ignoring the stares she attracted as she walked down to the oasis, arranging for her own djellaba to be cleaned. The washerwomen silently watched the tall mage standing unself-consciously half-naked, letting the sun dry her glistening skin. Goatherders watering their herds stared at her. Tamira had heard southerners regarded public nudity differently from those in northern Araka, but hadn't quite believed it.

Tamira walked through the long grass and vegetation surrounding the water, wondering how such an idyllic place could be home to merciless killers.

"Hey! Not there," a villager called out in warning.

Bile rose from her gut as she looked ahead, realising why everyone else was staying well away from that part of the oasis. Roses grew wild and unfettered, made distinctive by their infamous black petals.

Tamira backed away, knowing the assassins of the Black Citadel would brook no interference with those flowers.

She turned to find Shukara pulling her tunic on, unaffected by the attention she had attracted. "Come, let us find Jassan."

*

They sat in the caravanserai's common room. Unlike Pashbur's perpetually busy caravanserai, Rhemi's was almost deserted, few traders braving the Black Trail. The villagers were a subdued people, so used to living in fear of the assassins that they didn't even seem to know they were afraid.

The common room consisted of unadorned clay walls, small wooden tables and worn cushions stuffed with camel hair. Shukara supposed that given the lack of both custom and competition, there was no reason for the owner to spend coin on improvements.

Refreshed by the sweat tent, Shukara had changed into her orange djellaba. Tamira's blue djellaba had dried quickly in the sun and she had changed back into it. Their façade depended on her dressing like a Kavari, even if her dusky skin clearly marked her otherwise.

Jassan joined them. "I've agreed a price for our salt."

"A good price?" Tamira teased. "Did you haggle, 'husband'?"

"The merchant assured me I've robbed the food from his children's mouths," the ranger said happily. "They get few visitors here, and the Black Rose insist on the lion's share of salt brought in by the regular traders."

Shukara frowned. "If our salt is sold, we must act tonight. To delay will attract suspicion, now that we no longer have reason to be here."

Jassan eyed her. "After your appearance this morning, the men of Rhemi are unlikely to protest you lingering here a day or two."

Shukara ignored his comment. These northerners were odd. Men and women shared the same sweat tent where she came from, and young women didn't cover their upper body until they were betrothed.

Tamira started to laugh, but fell silent. "Black Rose," she muttered, eyes cast down.

Sure enough, three men in black robes entered the caravanserai, straight swords belted to their waists. Assassins of the Black Rose.

"Names and business in Rhemi," they demanded of Shukara and her companions.

"I am Naeem, a salt trader," Jassan lied. "This is my wife, Tamra." Tamira was barely old enough for marriage but her skin was too light to pass her off as the Kavari's daughter.

"And you, woman?" the lead assassin demanded of Shukara.

"I am Shuka, a traveller," she answered, head low. "Master Naeem takes me to my betrothed in Hawla to the west."

The assassins lost interest in them and spoke briefly with the caravanserai-keeper who nodded so much it was a wonder his head didn't fall off. He poured them water and all three sat at a table, paying no mind to the other patrons.

Shukara allowed herself to relax. The caravanserai-keeper walked over carrying three clay cups and a pot of teh, placing a cup before each of them. He poured teh into each cup.

Shukara sipped hers, disappointed at the lack of mint. It did include a sweet flavour she didn't recognise. "We'll enter the citadel tonight, lest our presence attract any ... any further..." Her head started to slowly spin.

Tamira frowned. "What's wrong?"

Nausea seized Shukara, her body increasingly numb. *The teh...* "Drugged," she managed to gasp out before darkness took her.

*

Shukara awoke in darkness. Drugged. Had they known she was a magicker? Drugging her seemed a precaution too far for three assassins seizing an unarmed woman. But how could they have known? Betrayal?

"Is anyone there? Where am I?" she asked, allowing fearful confusion into her voice. She took stock of her condition, relieved to find that the assassins had not harmed or abused her. Her captors were noted for their professional ruthlessness. They killed and tortured, but for coin or information, not pleasure.

"In the Black Citadel," a disembodied voice answered from above. She was in a cell, accessible only through a barred grate in the ceiling. The cell stank of stale human waste, and she felt rock beneath her feet.

"Why?" If the fear in her voice wasn't entirely feigned, all the better. *Tamira, Jassan ... where are you?*

"You know why, mage."

Betrayed indeed. Adjatay? "Mage? I'm no mage!" Her denial sounded weak even to her. She was unsurprised to find both her stave and reagent bag missing.

The voice laughed. "Few women are as tall as you, and our sketch of you is accurate. Besides, we found your reagents and wytchwood stick. The wytchwood, we burned."

"Sketch?"

"Mask's Magi of Hrek warned our agent in that city of your coming and passed us your likeness. It seems you displeased the magi there, and they want you dealt with. Your coming here presented an elegant solution."

Erasi, gods rot you. The Magi knew the Eye were involved in Cirimon's death, and Erasi or her fellow brokers had traded Shukara for their own survival. Perhaps her solution to the Bloody Lotus problem had been one step too far. That she had travelled to the Black Citadel was indeed an elegant solution for the Eye, the Magi and the Black Rose. "Convenient for you all."

"Indeed," the voice agreed. "If only everyone we're contracted to kill would be so considerate as to come to us. The Kavari man and the Maskan girl with you?"

"A merchant and his wife hired to bring me here." The question gave her hope the pair were still free. But even if they were, what good could they do? *Take her back to Pashbur, Jassan. Tamira, convince Adjatay to train you, and return here one day to avenge me.* She suspected the assassins would let them leave, the Eye of Mask apparently omitting any mention of Tamira.

"The Grandmaster will question you himself to learn why you came here with violent intent. Every truth, every secret will be scoured from you. But we are not needlessly cruel.

Give it to her." The last was said to someone else. A water skin was dropped into her cell.

Shukara grabbed the skin and gulped the water down, tepid liquid soothing her cracked throat, a not-unfamiliar flavour to it.

"We wouldn't want a dry throat to prevent you answering the Grandmaster's questions."

"A thoughtful gesture." The water tasted bitter and sulphuric. *Henya root, red lotus, powdered mashur weed. And firethorn seed...*

Hope stirred.

*

Tamira watched in consternation as Shukara slumped to the earthen floor and quickly deduced the teh to be responsible. Neither she nor Jassan seemed affected, so she amended her deduction; the drug had been placed in Shukara's cup, perhaps to ensure she got the full dose.

"She has fainted," Tamira shouted. Knowing scant heartbeats remained until the assassins reached them, she reached under the mage's robe and pulled free her wytchwood stave, snapping it in two. Hoping the table concealed her actions, she opened the dhaemonhide pouch and grabbed a handful of reagents before dropping the smaller piece of wytchwood inside it.

The assassins reached the table, and two seized the fallen mage while the third pulled free his sword, daring the ranger or thief to intervene. Thoughts of resistance flickered through Tamira's mind, but she remained still. Jassan didn't react either and Shukara was carried away. The third assassin picked up the reagent pouch.

"Sit still. We'll be questioned when they return, but if our story holds we may be able to save her," Jassan whispered.

Tamira jerked a nod, stuffing the pilfered reagents and the remaining piece of wytchwood inside a cushion beneath the table. Now four inches long, she hoped it was still usable.

Chapter Twenty-Two

Night fell. The assassins questioned Tamira and Jassan hard in the caravanserai, but they stuck to the agreed narrative and left their questioners no reason to doubt they were salt traders who had agreed to let Shukara travel with them.

Tamira had feigned shock on being told their companion was really a mage. No, she had not suspected anything. No, she had not seen her cast spells. Though she had caught her husband staring at the woman … had Shuka bewitched him? She was from Mask originally (yes, the city itself), her husband a Kavari salt trader. Their first visit to Rhemi? Yes; he was new to the trade, having used Tamira's dowry to buy his camels.

Another assassin was summoned, one who questioned Tamira exhaustively about Mask. She answered each question easily, satisfying the assassins that she was a native of that city.

Tamira had feared they might be killed anyway, but perhaps the Black Citadel's twisted code of honour stayed the assassins' blades. Tamira's voiced jealousy that the mage may have bewitched her husband helped convince the assassins that she was nothing more than a foolish girl.

They would soon learn otherwise. *If we can enter the citadel.* She had memorised the floor plan drawn by Adjatay and remembered his suggested means of entry, but the possibility remained that the assassins had removed that vulnerability.

Time dragged by in the common room, but she and Jassan knew that to leave too soon would have drawn attention, so they sat and waited for dusk. When the sun finally set, Tamira retrieved the reagents and wytchwood fragment from the cushion and they retired to their room. Jassan finally judged the hour late enough that most would be asleep, and he slipped outside. Tamira changed into her shendyt and tunic, and she too crept silently out of the caravanserai.

No moons shone tonight, but henya root mixed in their

water enhanced their vision. Darkness would be their ally this night. *I should have stayed with the caravan.*

"Ready?" Jassan asked.

Tamira's hands trembled and she tasted vomit. "Yes."

They headed down to the oasis, the soft crunch of stones beneath their sandals the only indication of their passage. The Black Citadel was mostly dark, but a few lights shone from narrow windows carved out from within. Tamira knew from Adjatay that the citadel never truly slept, a small army of slaves working day and night to maintain it and tend to the assassins' every need.

Tamira snuck over to where the black roses grew, a thorn pricking her thumb as she snatched one up. She looked around, struck by the absurd notion that the assassins might have some unnatural means of knowing when someone interfered with their prized flowers. Nothing happened, and she stuck the rose into her waxed leather pouch.

The oasis waters were still and black as obsidian. Tamira left her sandals by the water. Jassan followed her example, also removing the string from his bow, wrapping it in leather.

Tamira stared into the opaque water. "I hope Adjatay was right about this." *Karib. The man sent to kill me.* If he was wrong, he might unknowingly complete that five-year-old contract to end the Xarian Dynasty.

"Yes." They both began inhaling deeply, stretching their lungs to their limits and holding briefly before exhaling. This they did ten times.

Now. Tamira waded into the water, gasping sharply at the bite of its unexpected chill. She braced herself and swam out to where it lapped against the mountain stronghold, taking a deep breath before slipping under the water.

She swam down, fighting against the air in her lungs to go deeper. Even Shukara's sight potion failed to penetrate the blackness, so Tamira relied on touch, feeling the side of the mountain. Adjatay had been clear; swim to where the water met the mountain and then to the middle. *And down.*

Her hands pushed against rock, so she let half the air out of her lungs to go deeper. Time was running out but just as she considered going up for air, she felt a gap. She returned to the surface, caught the waiting Jassan's attention, and took another deep breath before sinking below the water again. She swam down and pulled herself into the gap, praying that it was indeed the passage Adjatay had spoken of and not a natural opening in the mountain.

Tamira kicked her feet hard, fighting her body's screaming desire to breath in as her lungs burned. She swam on desperately, knowing that to turn back was suicide. By rights she should have drowned by now, but she had put more than henya root in their water. Knowing they would need to swim, Shukara had told her of venna moss, a reagent she had prepared to help them last slightly longer without air.

Tamira had grabbed some from Shukara's pouch when she collapsed and mixed it into their drinking water with the henya root.

Her lungs spasmed, blasting out the air remaining in them, but she clamped her mouth shut, fighting the frantic need to inhale, her body starting to convulse. Suddenly the rock overhead ended, and she kicked herself upward, her head emerging from the water. She knelt, sucking in lungful after lungful of blessed air, her throat and lungs burning. When she had recovered enough to stand, she did so, the water ending at her thighs.

Moments later Jassan's head exploded from the water, likewise gasping for air.

Once she had gotten her breath back, Tamira took stock of their surroundings. The chamber was in darkness, but she sensed it was wide. A faint light was visible ahead, so she waded towards it. She bumped into rock and, knowing she had reached the end of the channel, hauled herself out of the water.

"I nearly drowned," Jassan complained as he followed her. "First time I've nearly been killed by too *much* water."

"Adjatay did warn us it was a long swim. He said the assassins train for years to swim the passage without drowning," she reminded him, grateful for Shukara's mysterious moss.

The assassins' forebears had been a tribe once, seizing the oasis and guarding access to it jealously while hollowing the mountain into a stronghold.

They had turned silent killing into an art, and in time into their profession. The Black Citadel was (almost) impregnable but the lack of water inside made it vulnerable to siege, so a channel had been carved out to the oasis to create a well of sorts inside the mountain, deep enough under the water that it would remain unseen. It was known only to the assassins.

Kavari and Maskans had both independently besieged the Black Citadel over the centuries, believing the assassins could only store so much water inside their stronghold. They never knew that water flowed inside the mountain from the slave-carved channel. Legends persisted that the assassins drank each other's blood, legends the Black Rose were happy to encourage.

They inspired more legends by using the channel to sneak assassins outside the citadel, killers who emerged like ghosts from the water to wreak havoc on the besieging enemy before disappearing once more into the spring. In the end, losses and frustration drove every enemy away from Rhemi. But Adjatay had betrayed the Black Rose's secret to Tamira and her companions who now used it against them.

A single torch burned from a holder nailed into the rock wall down the corridor, enough to provide light without risking any of it escaping through the underwater passage to reveal the secret entrance.

"What now?" Jassan asked as he restrung his bow and removed the protective leather from his arrow quiver. He quietly removed his sword from its sheath and laid it on the ground.

Tamira wondered when she had become the leader. "We wait for someone to come, deal with them and steal their clothes," she decided. Shukara had kept this part of the plan mostly to herself, but it probably involved striding through the mountain obliterating every assassin in sight. That was unfortunately beyond their ability.

"Adjatay said the assassins send slaves outside to fetch water from the oasis lest the villagers suspect the well, so I doubt anyone will come here," Jassan said.

"During the day, he said. He also said the slaves gather water from here at night, as the Grandmaster prefers the gates locked after dark. Sending slaves to the oasis at night would mean an escort to prevent them fleeing, and they'd be vulnerable to ambush."

Jassan nodded, taking up a position near the corner of the wall. "Then let us hope someone gets thirsty soon."

Their wait was brief. A scuffling sound announced someone approaching.

Jassan motioned Tamira to stay quiet and out of the way. She leaned against the wall, feeling nauseous once again.

The light dimmed for an instant as whoever came for water passed the torch. Jassan pulled out a hunting knife, silently leaving his sword on the ground.

Someone entered the chamber – two someones! – and Jassan sprang out to confront them, his hesitation lasting barely a heartbeat. His knife took the biggest target in the throat, a gout of blood splashing over Tamira.

The second person shrieked and fled back down the corridor. Jassan dropped the knife and snatched up his bow, pulling free an arrow and notching it in one smooth practiced motion.

He aimed down the corridor for a moment and loosed. His expression told Tamira he had aimed true.

Tamira forced herself to look at the first body while Jassan dragged the second back into the well chamber. The first was a man well into his middle years, his dark weathered face mapped with scars and a bent nose.

Jassan released the second body and joined Tamira at the first. "Adjatay told me once that the citadel guards are assassins past their prime, too old or arthritic to move as they once did, but still ferocious fighters."

"Why was he down here?"

"Escorting that slave." Jassan pointed at the second, smaller body, a girl not much older than Tamira. And still alive, she realised.

Jassan knelt next to the stunned slave. "I shot you with a fowling blunt," he said to her, holding up an arrow ending in a round iron ball rather than a pointed tip. "Tell me why you were sent down here, or I'll use this." He showed the terrified slave his knife, his voice coldly merciless.

"Water ... for the prisoner," she said.

"Prisoner? A tall black woman?" Tamira asked sharply.

The slave shrugged her ignorance.

"You were to take it to the cells?" Jassan asked.

The girl nodded.

"Would he have accompanied you?" He pointed to the dead guard.

The girl shook his head. "He was guarding the entrance to this chamber."

A look of regret passed Jassan's face. "That's all we need. Be at peace." The girl's neck made a horrible cracking sound as he broke it.

"Why? She helped us!" Tamira cried out.

"What would you have had me do with her? Tie her up? With what rope? Leave her here and hope she sat quietly until we were done?"

Tamira stared down at the dead girl.

"Had they known she talked, they would have killed her anyway," Jassan said, perhaps to convince himself as much as Tamira. "This is what vengeance looks like, girl. Prepare yourself for more."

She took a breath. "They sent a guard to help draw water?"

Jassan shook his head. "To keep an eye on the slave, lest she decide to try and swim out of here."

"Oh."

"Take her clothes, I'll take his."

The dead guard's robe was luckily dark, concealing its former wearer's blood. Assassins wore black, guards grey, and slaves brown. In the citadel, at least. According to Adjatay, the assassins used colours fitting for the environment when executing a contract: differing shades of grey for night work, and shades of brown when in the desert.

Tamira steeled herself and removed the dead girl's brown robe, her skin crawling as she pulled it over her own clothing.

"The cell guards will be expecting that water," Jassan said, filling the empty skin.

"Give it to me," Tamira said, struck by inspiration. When he did so, she ground up some reagents, including a firethorn seed, and mixed them into the water. She looked up at Jassan. "They'll think this is simple water."

His grin mirrored her own, hard and vicious. "And instead…?"

She shrugged. "No idea. But if I can slip Shukara her wytchwood, then she can handle the guards." One plan discussed in Pashbur but ultimately discarded had been for

Tamira to leave Shukara and Jassan by the well and sneak further inside alone, sketching symbols in chalk near the entrance hall. Shukara's spell – which she remained tight-lipped about – would do something to the symbols. Tamira still remembered them and possessed a fragment of chalk.

"Then let's go."

"Wait here," Tamira said. "If the guard's post is found empty the alarm will be raised. I'll find Shukara."

"What if anyone comes here for water?"

"If they do, deal with them."

"'Deal with them,'" the ranger muttered.

Tamira left him standing at the corridor's entrance while she walked to the cells. If she recalled the citadel map correctly, the dungeon was one level up from the well chamber.

She forced herself to walk slowly and keep her head down, playing the meek slave. Her heart skipped a beat as an assassin passed her, but he didn't give her a second look.

On seeing the mountain stronghold, she had imagined it to be filled with narrow passages and cramped chambers, but the Black Rose had never stopped expanding. The corridors were narrow but the chambers she passed were wide with high ceilings, the brown walls sanded smooth and hung with tapestries. Given their bloody trade, Tamira half-expected to find the walls decorated with weapons, but found none. She conceded such décor would be unwise with so many slaves roaming the halls.

Many of the corridors were tight, deliberately so, she suspected. Any army that got inside would find itself having to fight through a series of bottlenecks.

Tamira reached the dungeon, forcing herself to take a breath. The smell reminded her of the Poor Quarter: shit, piss and unwashed bodies. She walked inside, keeping her head low. What she did see made her shiver. The main chamber was dark, the only light coming from two candles on the table at the end of the room. The walls were solid rock, but a series of barred grilles were spread along the floor. The cells, she decided. And Shukara was likely trapped inside one.

Two guards sat at the table while a third stood over a cell, looking down. Tamira had harboured the faint hope that the guards would pass the hours with a flagon of wine or spirits and she'd find them in a stupor, but both looked alert and sober. Unsurprising, in hindsight. The Black Rose took pride in their discipline. A cup and dice sat on the table, but no other distractions.

Tamira walked up to the guards, wondering if she should speak. She remained silent and held out the water skin. Shukara's wytchwood fragment was hidden up her sleeve.

The guard standing over one of the cells spoke. "If only everyone we are contracted to kill would be so considerate to come to us," he said. Tamira froze in panic. *A trap!* "The Kavari man and the Maskan girl with you?" the guard asked, and Tamira realised that he wasn't talking to her, but to the prisoner in the cell; the reference to herself and Jassan confirmed Shukara's presence.

"The Grandmaster will question you himself, to learn why you came here with violent intent. Every truth, every secret will be scoured from you. But we are not needlessly cruel." The guard shot Tamira an impatient look. "Give it to her."

Tamira walked to the cell and knelt, dropping the water skin between the bars. Enough henya root remained in her body to let her discern a figure below. Shukara. She released the stave fragment too, knowing the mage would see it when the henya root in the water skin took effect.

Tamira stood, hoping that Shukara would recall the earlier plan and assume that Tamira did too.

The guard watched Shukara drink from the skin. Thick muscles covered his arms and his black hair was tied back. Unlike the other two guards, he was clean-shaven and not unattractive. "We wouldn't want a dry throat to stop you answering the Grandmaster's questions."

"A thoughtful gesture," Shukara called up.

"Have you no other task to attend to, slave?" one of the other guards demanded, noticing Tamira's continued presence.

She bobbed her head. "Yes, Master. I've to take chalk to the entrance hall." She spoke loud enough for Shukara to hear.

"Then begone." A flicker of curiosity passed over the guard's face, but he evidently decided that he didn't care why someone wanted chalk in the middle of the night.

Laughter bubbled up from the cell. "Best run, girl."

Chapter Twenty-Three

The entrance hall was the result of centuries of excavation. A vast hollowed-out chamber stretched up through three levels, a dozen pillars remaining to support the upper floors overhead. Separating the hall from the main gate was a narrow tunnel maybe ten metres long.

The open hall struck Tamira as an odd decision until she looked up and back. The ground floor tunnels narrowed, the two levels above with balconies looking down into the hall, and the ceiling – the fourth level's floor – had murder holes cut into the rock.

An enemy succeeding in breaching the gate and fighting through the bottlenecked tunnel would enter the hall – and find themselves trapped. Oil and rocks would fall through the murder holes, and archers on the second and third levels would rain down arrows from the balconies. The invaders would then face either a battle through the bottlenecked and no doubt fiercely held tunnels, or a chaotic retreat through the gate tunnel leading outside.

Tamira backtracked a little and found a large, empty library. Unlike the narrow low-ceilinged corridors, the rooms tended to be wide with high ceilings, perhaps to spare the inhabitants from feeling too enclosed.

The library shelves were cut into the walls, filled with tomes and bound scrolls. Stone tables and stools were carved out in the middle of the room, worn after centuries of use. Like most chambers in the citadel, iron sconces held candles, albeit only one in three were lit at this late hour. A large caged candle sat in the middle of the stone table. Adjatay had said the citadel never truly slept, and Tamira saw the proof of it. Keeping the library lit at night seemed a waste of candles, but perhaps those in charge wanted no risk of fire from late-night visitors bringing their own candles too close to the dry papyrus.

The risk of fire seemed to be one of the foremost

considerations of the Black Rose. No fabric or papyrus was to be found near any candles, and every room contained at least one bucket of sand. Sensible; a blaze inside the mountain would quickly fill the passages and chambers with lethal smoke.

Shukara had not told her what the symbols would do, nor did she know how long the mage would wait before incanting her spell. This would all be for naught if a slave or assassin cleaned off the chalk before the spell was cast.

The rock floor was smooth and held the chalk well. Tamira drew a large circle with a four-foot diameter. The glyphs she drew inside the circle meant nothing to her, but Shukara had insisted she memorise each exactly.

The last glyph completed, she pulled a red woollen rug over the circle, careful not to smudge the chalk. If anyone entered the library, her work would remain undiscovered. She remembered Shukara's last words to her, telling her to run. To the guards it would have sounded like mockery, a slave being warned not to be lazy; Tamira knew she was being warned not to be there when the spell was cast.

*

Shukara sat on the rock floor, waiting. Thanks to the henya root Tamira had put in her water, she was able to see the wytchwood fragment the thief had dropped into the cell with the water skin. Only half of her stave, remained but it should be enough. *Gods bless you, Tamira.* She made no move to retrieve it lest her movement draw a guard's attention, savouring the anticipation.

She had waited two years for this day; she could wait a little longer. If she acted too soon, she risked casting her spell before the glyphs were complete, or before Tamira had time to escape. Too late, and the guards would take her to the Grandmaster. They *would* meet, but on Shukara's terms, not his.

Judging enough time had passed for Tamira to have drawn the glyphs (assuming she remembered them correctly), Shukara rose quietly to her feet and picked up the remaining half of her stave. She gripped it tightly and focused her thoughts, adjusting to its changed size and reorganised matrices.

Feeling whole once more, she began the enchantment. Three elements were needed: A firethorn seed to change her body's chemistry sufficiently for this specific spell, wytchwood to act as the spell's matrix, and the glyphs to both direct and constrain the spell's result. She raised her arms and worked through the intricacies of the spell, knowing that it would drain her. Words incomprehensible even to her escaped her lips as she seized reality and bent its rules.

"*Bhuvamet*," she whispered, triggering the conjuration. *Run, Tamira*, she thought as a dizzying nausea washed over her.

*

"What are you doing in here?" the guard demanded. Three men had caught Tamira trying to leave the library. Two were grey-robed guards, old, grizzled and armed with curved swords, but the youngest man wore only a knife on his belt. His black robe marked him as an assassin.

"C…cleaning," Tamira stammered.

"With what?" Her lack of tools had not escaped the leader's notice.

Tamira swallowed, feeling sick. "I left the brush inside," she said, head down.

"Show us," he insisted, as she feared he would.

Running was a choice, but one quickly discarded. Her only hope was that Shukara's spell would do *something* to distract attention from her. Preferably without killing her.

Immediately on re-entering the library she sensed something was wrong. The air felt heavy and held a previously absent whiff of sulphur. She looked over at the rug she had pulled over her handiwork and saw wisps of smoke rise from the wool. *The glyphs … they're burning through…*

Shukara had cast her spell.

The space above the rug rippled, reminding Tamira of air shimmering in the heat. Something pressed all around her, hurting her ears.

All three men felt it too, Tamira forgotten. "What is happening?" one asked. A charred circle became visible on the rug as the chalked symbols burned through.

Tamira cried out as the air buckled and ripped in two, leaving a smouldering black *thing* in the centre of the chalk circle. She gagged as a sickening wave of sulphur rolled off it, and stared in appalled fascination at Shukara's handiwork. *Gods, you Called a dhaemon!*

The dhaemon – it could be nothing else – stood perhaps nine feet tall, roughly man-shaped but with oddly twisted legs ending in bony claws. Muscles rippled across its otherwise lean torso, legs and all four arms. It stood unclothed and bore no evidence of gender. Four ebony spikes jutted out from its head and its slitted eyes burned crimson.

The dhaemon's disorientation passed, and it took in its surroundings before staring balefully at the four people standing appalled before it. A crackling rumble issued from its black-fanged mouth as it threw back its head. Laughter, Tamira numbly realised. *What have you done, mage?*

One arm reached over its back and pulled free a massive obsidian blade, cruel-edged and wickedly honed. Tamira figured a strong man could wield it two-handed, but the dhaemon held it effortlessly in one.

"Sound the alarm," the eldest guard told the assassin as he and his other companion drew their swords. The black-clad man nodded and ran out of the library, doubtless glad to not have to face the summoned horror with only a dagger.

Tamira stumbled back a few steps, watching as the two guards faced off against the dhaemon, swords readied.

The dhaemon leapt at them, its roar like an avalanche of stone, black blade raised. One guard darted in and aimed a silent slash at the creature's leg, intending to cripple it–

–only to explode in a gout of blood and gore as the hell-blade whipped down, cleaving him in two. The remaining guard backed off a step, appalled at the dhaemon's speed. Tamira edged towards the door while the creature taunted the guard with a hellish grin and a chuckle like grinding stone.

The guard's face was grey, his death assured. Tamira fled the library, leaving him to face it alone.

*

A bell started tolling, its deep tone echoing through the mountain's halls and tunnels. Jassan listened, uncertain whether the raised alarm signalled Tamira's success or failure.

Indecision briefly rooted him. Should he stay and wait for Tamira to re-join him, or visit the dungeon himself? *A look cannot hurt.* He left the guard post, confident the alarm would explain his roaming the citadel with a bow.

The passage was deserted, unsurprising as it was the lowest level of the citadel. Jassan climbed the steps leading up to the next level, hoping that the alarm had drawn away the guards. The tunnels down here were low and dark, sparsely lit by an occasional torch attached to the walls.

Jassan suppressed the urge to laugh at the absurdity of his situation. Quite what he was doing skulking around the stronghold of an infamous sect of killers in a bid to rescue a mage seemed suddenly beyond him. *But if we succeed, it could give my people a future.*

He smelled the dungeon before he reached it, a stench of human waste that lingered in the cramped passage. Years of experience allowed him to use fear to sharpen his senses rather than make him slow and clumsy, and he took a breath before entering the dungeon.

Three guards stood within, arguing with one another. "–kill her, and maybe it goes, too," one said.

Another opened his mouth to answer but was interrupted by the third who spied Jassan. "What are you doing here? Can you not hear the bell?"

A familiar calm settled over Jassan, the calm of a ranger accustomed to having Death by his shoulder for weeks at a time. He notched an arrow to his bow and drew it back before releasing, the third guard staring down at the arrow sprouting from his chest.

Jassan wasted no time in self-congratulation, already notching a second arrow to his bow as the guard's knees buckled. The remaining two wasted no time either, running at Jassan with blades drawn.

His second arrow leapt into the second guard's throat,

heartbeats before he reached the ranger, Jassan deflecting the dying man's sword with his bow before clubbing him to the ground.

Jassan dropped the bow, his curved sword hissing free from its leather scabbard in time to parry the last guard's blade.

Ranger and guard traded blows, the clash of iron on iron echoing around the dungeon. The guard sought to overwhelm Jassan with a flurry of high and low blows, his right foot lashing up in a bid to knock him off-balance.

Jassan skipped back, giving his opponent a hard grin. Once mediocre with a blade, he had since been tutored by one of the Black Rose's finest swordsmen.

A further exchange of blows saw the guard driven back, sweat slicking his grey hair and angular face. His right foot fell through a metal grill on the floor, an entrance to a cell. As Jassan intended. The guard lost balance, his face showing surprise, followed by a grimace of pain as Jassan drove his sword into his chest.

"Shukara?"

"Down here," a voice said from one of the cells.

Sighing in relief, Jassan leaned over the grate. "Give me a moment and I'll get you out of there."

"Do not hurry yourself," was her dry reply.

He found a key lying on the table and used it to unlock the padlock securing the grille, throwing down a rope to allow Shukara up. "Don't say I've not earned my fee!"

Chapter Twenty-Four

Tamira ran through the corridors towards the dungeon. The rapid tolling of a bell echoed through the tunnels and halls of the Black Citadel, shattering the peace. There was no more need for stealth – the alarm had roused every assassin and guard in the citadel, and all rushed to answer it. None would wonder why a slave was running in the opposite direction.

The Black Rose were many things but complacent they were not. They might not know why the alarm had been raised, but they armed themselves and went to face the threat without hesitation. Several carrying swords rushed past. Knowing what they faced, Tamira almost pitied them.

Shukara's mad plan was now clear to her; create a distraction near the citadel entrance to draw the bulk of the Black Rose there, and use the confusion to reach the Grandmaster's chambers. But that meant freeing Shukara before either the defenders killed the dhaemon and went looking for the intruder who had summoned it, or the dhaemon killed the defenders and went looking for more victims.

Neither prospect appealed.

Tamira entered the dungeon and saw a guard leaning over Shukara's now-open cell, lowering a rope. Her heart clenched in fear, her hope that the guards would have all left to answer the alarm dashed. Then she smiled in recognition. "Jassan."

The ranger looked over, relief etched on his face. "When I heard the bell, I thought maybe you'd been caught so I came here." Three guards lay dead on the ground.

"The bell's part of her plan," Tamira told him as he pulled the mage out of the cell.

"You both have my thanks." Shukara looked dishevelled, her long hair dirty and tangled. She looked at Tamira. "You did well putting reagents in my water and returning my stave." She cocked her head, listening. "My spell evidently worked."

Jassan retrieved his arrows from the dead guards. "Spell? What did you do?"

Tamira shook her head. "She summoned a dhaemon."

Jassan's mouth opened. "A *dhaemon*?"

"Lacking an army, *Bhuvamet* was the best I could do," Shukara said, untroubled by their consternation.

"That thing has a name?" Tamira shuddered.

Shukara frowned. "You saw it? I told you to run."

"Can we discuss this later?" Jassan interrupted, looking warily at the exit. "Let's return to the well and swim out of here before your friend goes exploring."

"Leave? Our task is not yet finished," Shukara said. "Reagents?"

Tamira handed her all that remained, and the mage began grinding some up and mixing them into a cup of water on the table. She drank some of it down. From what she had told Tamira, care had to be taken when mixing different reagents to ensure one did not interfere with another.

"You're mad," Jassan told her. "If we go out there, we'll be caught between the assassins and your damned dhaemon!"

Shukara poured a little water into the dice cup and stirred in some reagent dust. "Tamira drew the summoning glyphs near the citadel gates, so it and most of the assassins will be there. According to Adjatay, the Grandmaster's chambers are up and to the rear, one of the most defensible places in the citadel. He is likely coordinating the defence from there." She lifted the dice cup and held it against her right eye.

"Even if the dhaemon keeps the assassins busy long enough … *if* … we'll still face a Grandmaster Assassin. Who'll not be alone."

Shukara removed the dice cup from her eye, blinking away water. "It gets some of the reagents into my blood quicker than ingestion," she explained on noticing Tamira's baffled look.

"Get her back in her cell! Can you not hear the alarm? The Grandmaster will question her after the threat has–" The guard – the talkative one Tamira remembered from her earlier visit to the dungeon – spotted the bodies.

He wrenched free his sword and lunged forwards before Jassan had time to draw his own weapon. Tamira watched helplessly as the blade whipped towards Shukara.

An invisible force seized the guard and hurled him brutally against the wall. Tamira heard bones shatter and the man slumped limply to the ground.

*

Shukara felt the reagents take effect, altering her sufficiently to cast the spells she would need, her training allowing her to withstand the intoxicating side-effect of the lotus. She stood over the broken guard, looking down in satisfaction at this latest in a long line of men who had underestimated her. Noting he still lived, she drew air together into her left hand, feeling it solidify. The 'handle' formed, she extended it into a blade and cut his throat. She stood, letting the 'blade' dissipate back into air once more.

Power electrified her blood like an intoxicant, power to end her two-year quest for vengeance. "I am going after the Grandmaster," she told the ranger and thief. "You may come, or you may leave."

Jassan looked uncertain. "If we meet your dhaemon, you can control it, yes?"

"No," she said regretfully. "Had I been present during the summoning then yes, I could have bound it to my will. As it is, the only limit I placed was the duration of the spell. After one hour, it will return to the Underworld." Unless the assassins succeeded in killing it. She hoped not; it had taken her years to glean a dhaemon's name and she would rather not have to find a replacement.

"I'll come," Jassan finally decided. Men hated looking weaker than women. It seemed the ranger would rather risk injury to his body than to his pride.

"I'm coming too," Tamira said. "I owe the Grandmaster a debt and need to find that sword Adjatay wants." She shrugged with the bold inexperience of youth. "I've already survived one meeting with the dhaemon. If I see it again, I'll run."

Jassan looked down at her. "What if it runs faster than you?"

She hid her fear behind an impudent grin. "I don't need to run faster than *it*."

He shook his head. "And if we meet assassins on the way?"

"We'll deal with them," Shukara promised. The Black Rose had crossed the Magi of Tokombu. Tonight, they would learn the depth of that mistake.

Magicker, thief and ranger left the dungeon, worn winding stairs taking them up to the gate level. At first, they encountered only cowering slaves, but Shukara knew that would not last. Jassan claimed to remember Adjatay's plan of the citadel, so Shukara let him lead, bow in hand. The bell had ceased tolling, but echoes of the battle and the passage of those rushing to join it whispered though the tunnels of the citadel.

*

Jassan peeked round a corner and motioned for the others to stop. Notching an arrow to his bow, he turned the corner and let loose, drawing a second arrow the moment the first left his bow. That too he notched and loosed, pulling free a third before he realised there was no need. He returned the arrow to his quiver and drew his sword. Killing wounded enemies was distasteful to him but better than risking them crawling off to alert their kin.

One of the two assassins still lived and Jassan finished him off with a sword-thrust to the chest. He felt little guilt, mercy anathema to the Black Rose. More deserving of his guilt was the slave girl he'd killed below.

Shukara seemed content to let him deal with the few stragglers encountered, conserving her power for the battles still to come. Barely more than a child, the best Tamira could offer was to stay out of the way. *We should have sent her back to the well.* But then the dhaemon might have found her.

Jassan thought heavily of the citadel's children and slaves, trapped in the mountain with a dhaemon. Had Shukara's single-minded quest for vengeance blinded her to the innocents she had imperilled?

He shook off his reservations, knowing any distraction would see him and his companions dead. They reached a winding stairwell that would take them closer to the man they had come to kill.

Three levels up, Jassan paused. "We'll need to get closer to the front of the citadel, climb up another two levels, and then head towards the rear. The Grandmaster's chambers are one level up from there."

Shukara nodded. "Lead on."

Muffled sounds from the battle still travelled the passages, louder now, and Jassan knew they weren't far from the assembly hall in the heart of the citadel. The dhaemon may have proved unstoppable in the narrow tunnels where the assassins could only face it one or two at a time, but it would have a tougher time in a large open space if that was where the Black Rose chose to make their stand.

Jassan led them down a long corridor at a brisk pace, arrow notched to his bow. He turned a corner into a large chamber and jerked to a halt, his blood going cold. Eight men and women were gathered within, pulling on leather armour and arming themselves with spears, swords, shields and bows.

His bow whooped as he pulled back and released the string, the arrow hissing through the air, his aim unerring. Years of training guided his hand down to his quiver even as a small voice whispered there were too many, too close.

Shukara stepped past him, her voice hard as a blacksmith's anvil. "Both of you, find cover." She ignored her own words and strode towards the group already advancing with weapons raised.

Stave held high, she walked on, not slowing her pace as the assassins closed in. The air surrounding her sparked into flame, a writhing cocoon of living fire that grew, fire that rolled over the foremost assassins in thick waves.

Shukara keened as she walked on, a silhouette amidst that growing inferno. Jassan grabbed Tamira as the heat became unbearable, dragging the stunned girl out of the room. "Run!" Screams followed them down the passage, rising above Shukara's otherworldly dirge.

Jassan and Tamira ducked into a side passage as the fire hungrily pursued, the only sanctuary from the mage's indiscriminate wrath. Every breath was a struggle as the fire devoured the air.

The screams proved mercifully brief and the heat died. Jassan risked returning to the chamber once the fire was gone. In its place lay eight charred husks, the room a scorched shell. Shukara stood in the centre, unharmed.

"You can enter now," she called back quietly. He hesitantly entered, the walls and floor black. Heat still clung to the floor and walls, reminding Jassan of a baker's oven. The sickly stench of cooked flesh made Tamira bend over and retch. Charred wood and blackened metal lay next to the corpses, all that remained of their weapons.

Two men carrying crossbows entered the room from the far side, drawn by the noise. The mage slew them with a rain of heat-twisted weapons snatched from the ground.

*

Shukara walked past the bodies, the bleeding as well as the burned. It was not often she had cause to employ so much magick in such a short span of time, and it took a toll on her, consuming much of the ingested reagents. But she was far from done.

She could hear the battle rage close by, the dhaemon having reached the main assembly hall. Stairs led both up and down but Tamira snuck into an adjacent room. She returned and motioned for Shukara and Jassan to join her.

"Keep low," the girl whispered as she led them to a balcony overlooking the hall. Shukara peered over the edge and saw what she had wrought.

The assembly hall floor was three levels below them, a vast semi-circle carved from inside the mountain. It was from this room that the Grandmaster habitually addressed his followers. Tonight, it was where they died.

The guards and assassins had drawn the dhaemon into the hall, no doubt hoping to use the wide, open space to manoeuvre and overwhelm it with numbers.

Judging by the number of fallen, that strategy was proving less successful than they had hoped. Archers in other balconies around the hall fired arrows and bolts into the dhaemon, but *Bhuvamet* still fought. Three of its arms hurled bodies, fallen weapons and debris at the archers while its fourth arm wielded its black sword against those on the ground.

A band of spearmen tried to fend off the dhaemon, but it

simply batted aside their weapons and struck them down. A swordsman darted in and slashed at the dhaemon's flank, causing it to roar in pain. It turned and snatched him up, tearing the hapless man in two.

Others formed a shield wall and tried to weather the storm of blows it rained down on them, but they were quickly overwhelmed. The assassins fought bravely, but they were trained specifically to assassinate quickly and quietly, and the normal tools of their trade proved useless against this otherworldly foe.

Darts, arrows and knives dipped in poison had no effect. An assassin wielding two scimitars boldly engaged the dhaemon on her own, acrobatically evading its black sword while striking blows with her own weapons.

For a time, she prevailed, but the dhaemon tossed its blade from hand to hand to deliver a storm of strikes from every angle, catching the assassin off-balance and cleaving her in two.

Still the assassins fought on, indoctrinated to defend their stronghold and knowing the dhaemon would hunt down everyone inside anyway. *Including their families.* Shukara put that thought aside. The children should be safe in the narrowest passages, those too small for the dhaemon to crawl through. *Bhuvamet* paused as if smelling something, and it looked balefully up at Shukara. This was the first time she had summoned the dhaemon without binding it to obey her, a fact the dhaemon was no doubt aware of.

Whether the fighters routed or fought to the last, the dhaemon would not be long in finishing this battle. Then it would roam the citadel hunting down every survivor until the spell expired.

Shukara swallowed down bile. "Let's go."

Chapter Twenty~Five

They encountered two more bands of assassins, and Tamira watched Shukara resolve those encounters with the same ruthless efficiency she had demonstrated earlier. One group was torched, the other smashed against the walls, and Jassan used his bow against the few she missed.

The mage walked fearlessly through the corridors with single-minded purpose. Tamira sheltered in her wake, knowing these fights were beyond her.

She had voiced the possibility that the Grandmaster might lead the fight against the dhaemon in person, but Jassan had advised such wasn't the assassins' way. They valued success and efficiency over displays of heroism. Grandmaster Linus would remain safe in his chambers and direct the fight from there.

Two guards stood outside those chambers, a man and woman, whom Shukara smashed against the wall almost absently, smearing blood and brain against the wall. She had travelled Araka to avenge the attack on Tokombu; the man behind that assault waited beyond the wooden doors before them. The same man who had sent his assassins to kill Tamira's family.

"The doors might be–" Jassan began.

Shukara shattered them into kindling with a twist of her hand.

"Locked," he finished. He readied his bow, his quiver almost empty. Tamira hoped he knew how to use the sword hanging from his left hip. She rested a hand on her own dagger.

The trio entered Grandmaster Linus's chambers. Adjatay had described them, a series of several rooms including a bedchamber, a study and an audience room. The antechamber they entered was large with a high ceiling. Trophies of every description decorated the walls, from tapestries to weapons to animal heads, to gold and jewels. None were bought or gifted. All had been paid for in blood, trophies from the sect's battles and killings. Verak's sword and the Bone King's staff would be here if anywhere in the Black Citadel.

The floor was bare stone, comfort not a consideration. All the seats inside were bone-frames covered in a rigid leather hide.

The large round table in the centre was one of the few signs of opulence present; thick and polished cedar with a menagerie of lions, giraffes, elephants and antelope carved across it. Shukara's pouch lay on top. Also within the room stood a massive basalt statue of a man, its features lost to age and weather. A trophy from some far-away land, she supposed, brought to Rhemi, broken up and then reassembled in the antechamber.

Two men and a woman stood within, startled fear etched on their faces as the three travellers from Pashbur entered. That fear vanished when they saw who they faced. *They thought we were the dhaemon.*

One of the men wore leather armour over his black robe, young, dark and bearded. The woman was north Arakan, her dusky face lined with age and framed with long grey-white hair. She wore a thick white robe and carried a tall wooden staff.

The second man was north Arakan too, younger than the robed woman but with a harsh, weathered face. His scarlet robe was plain except for a rose embroidered on the breast in black thread. *The Robes of the Grandmaster. Linus himself.* Finally face to face with the Black Rose leader, Tamira felt the urge to turn and run. A fanatic's eyes stared at the three intruders, eyes belonging to a man who had proven himself the most murderously ruthless of a sect whose livelihood was death.

The man who sent his killers against her family.

The younger assassin raised his crossbow, Jassan loosing his arrow before he could fire. Shukara didn't react, her attention entirely on the white-robed woman. She had travelled for two years to kill Grandmaster Linus, but he might have been absent for all the notice she paid him.

"The woman is a magicker," Shukara warned. "You must deal with the assassin, Jassan."

Tamira saw Jassan's face ashen, and no wonder. They had counted on Shukara crushing the Black Rose leader. Instead she faced an old mage, fresh and armed with a full staff of wytchwood instead of a broken fragment. Tamira suspected that, unlike warriors, magi kept improving with age.

"I assume you are the one I have to thank for unleashing a dhaemon in my home," Linus said, his voice deep and assured, his anger leashed.

"Payment for the murder done by your people in *my* home," Shukara said, eyes never wavering from the, thus-far, silent mage. "Did you think Tokombu would let that pass unanswered?"

Linus watched her, his face a mask. Only the fire in his eyes betrayed his rage. Most of his followers were dead, and even if he survived tonight, the Black Rose was done as a power. "Not one soul in Tokombu will survive when I make them answer for this."

"You've seen what one magicker can do. My people will not be caught unawares again. Or will your companion help?" Shukara asked. Dilated eyes never wavered from the mage.

"Magister Bildren is a guest in the Black Citadel, an emissary from Mask," Linus said. Tamira watched how his eyes took in every detail of Shukara, Jassan and herself. He might seem happy to talk, but he was doubtless assessing their strengths and weaknesses.

"From the Kasbah Arcana, I assume," Shukara said. "I met some of your colleagues recently."

Bildren spoke for the first time, her voice soft and raspy. "Really?"

"Yes. Magister Cirimon and two lesser magi." She smiled unpleasantly. "Briefly."

Bildren nodded slightly, her mouth tightening. She patted Shukara's dhaemonhide pouch on the table. "Some interesting reagents in there. I was about to leave here to attend to your dhaemon, but I suppose I can delay long enough to deal with you."

"Stay away from me," Shukara whispered to Tamira as she prepared to face Bildren. Jassan loosed an arrow at Linus, which the assassin avoided with ease. The ranger dropped his bow and drew his sword, sweat gleaming on his black face. Linus shrugged off his robe, revealing a shendyt underneath, his bare torso lean, muscled and showing few scars. Either he fought rarely, or he fought very well. Jassan was about to discover which.

Tamira leaned against the wall, heart pounding as her companions prepared to fight. Determined to be of some use, she ran her eyes along the trophies on the wall, hunting for Verak's sword and the Bone King's staff.

*

Shukara gripped her wytchwood stave, fearing she was outmatched. Bildren was decades older, undoubtedly a more practiced magicker, and bearing a whole wytchwood staff rather than a twice-hacked fragment.

Shukara's advantages were few but perhaps crucial. Bildren was a more experienced magicker but how often did she practice her arts in combat? Was her mind still dextrous, could she still cast offensive spells with little thought while maintaining a defence?

But Bildren had advantages beyond her experience. Had Shukara caught her unawares, she could have overcome Bildren easily, but the Maskan magicker had just consumed reagents in preparation for battle with a dhaemon. Shukara's best hope was to keep Bildren on the defensive and employ a variety of spells in the hopes of finding a weakness.

She hurled a fist of solid air at Bildren, but it dissipated back into gas. Dismayed, she realised defensive wards were woven into Bildren's robe, freeing the Maskan from having to maintain them herself.

Shukara drew heat from the air around Bildren to try and freeze her, and then sent the heat back at her. She lashed Bildren with fire, hurled items and even the dead assassin at her.

Bildren's wards countered everything. Shukara had barely a heartbeat's warning before Bildren struck back, and then she was on the defensive.

Desperately, Shukara countered every spell thrown at her, surviving fire, air, and raw energy. Bildren tried to crush her, to rip her apart. She barely survived, and only due to the Maskan magicker being slower. Bildren was powerful but evidently out of practice fighting another magicker.

Knowing raw magick couldn't defeat Bildren's wards, Shukara looked for something else. The strain of consuming so many reagents, of employing so much magick in such a short space of time, was taking a toll on her mind and body. She needed to end the fight quickly.

Her eyes caught a possible solution. She threw a flurry of blows at Bildren, deliberately misdirecting every third one. *Not quite enough.*

The fight intensified. Beyond mere fire and air, both magi bent and twisted reality itself against the other. Even as she did so, Shukara sent slices of air away from Bildren. *Almost...*

*

Tamira stood, the gold-handled sword of Verak warm in her sweaty palm. It had been her father's sword when he was a prince, gifted by tradition to Captain Verak upon his coronation. There was no wytchwood staff in sight, so she anxiously watched Jassan duel Linus. She had tried to watch Shukara fight the older mage, but it had been like staring at the sun. The air itself twisted and took flame around them, the mountain trembling.

Unfortunately, Jassan was faring poorly against Linus, bleeding from several wounds. Tamira had picked up Jassan's bow and notched an arrow, thinking to kill Linus, but she lacked the strength to even draw back the string.

"You fight well, Kavari," Linus said. He seemed genuinely impressed that the ranger had lasted so long against him.

Both men sweated freely, though Jassan's was mingled with blood. "I was taught by Karib."

Linus faltered a step. "Karib? He died years ago."

Jassan took advantage of the assassin's surprise to seize the offensive. After a few parried lunges, however, the assassin countered to regain the initiative.

"A party of rangers, myself among them, found Karib wounded in the desert. He still lives and sends you his regards," Jassan said, breathing heavily.

"He taught you quite well." Linus drew more blood from Jassan's arm with a vicious slash. Tamira knew little of swordsmanship, but the assassin's footwork looked excellent.

There was a rumble of stone.

*

Shukara barely fended off a spell intended to reduce her to a dry husk. Another spell struck, working to age her a decade for every passing heartbeat. She snapped off a counter-spell to thwart it. Her plan needed a few more strikes to be delivered, but to divide her concentration would prove fatal as the duel neared its end.

A desperate inspiration struck her. Bildren's robe was surely warded against entropy such as the spell she had just sent against Shukara, but...

She copied Bildren's spell and flung it back, but at her wytchwood staff rather than against the magicker herself.

Bildren's onslaught ceased. An apprentice magicker's connection with their staff started early, with the staff's matrix itself mirroring the thoughts of the magicker. It grew with them, their thoughts winding through it to employ magick.

Bildren's staff was suddenly aged, and her mind struggled to find the changed matrices within. She would soon adjust, after which she could restore the staff and resume her assault against an almost drained Shukara, but until then...

Knowing she had won a few moments respite, Shukara threw four more blade-thin air bursts at the towering statue. And one final burst behind it.

The statue exploded from its plinth, a shower of rock toppling down on Bildren. Her wards protected her from the rocks themselves, but not the crushing weight.

When the dust cleared, Shukara saw the old magicker was half-buried under the rubble, her staff several feet away. Shukara took a steadying breath, shaking from the effort of so much magick so soon.

The others... Jassan was stumbling back, desperately fending off the assassin's sustained assault, defeat inevitable.

Tamira stood nearby, a sword in her hand, but helpless to help. She was clever enough to know that dashing in would do no good.

Shukara had enough left within for one last spell, and she struck Linus with a bone-shattering blast of solid air. Satisfied the assassin was dead or dying, she turned her attention back to Bildren.

"Clever," Bildren managed, coughing up blood.

Shukara nodded. "You fought well, elder. Better you had not intervened in my feud with the Black Rose."

"Feud … was with us, too."

She frowned. "You – the Kasbah Arcana – hired the assassins to steal the Bone King's staff? Why? I won't find it here, will I?" She sighed. "I thought my task was done, but it looks like I must visit the Kasbah Arcana. *Bhuvamet* will enjoy it there," she lied spitefully. A kasbah full of magi was beyond her even with a dhaemon.

Bildren drew strength from somewhere, perhaps desperation. "Forget your petty vengeance. A shadow lies over the world, growing in strength. Need yellow … lotus."

Yellow lotus was a powerful narcotic to all, but held prophetic properties to magick-sensitives – if one succeeded in distilling glimpses of possible futures from narcotic-fuelled nonsense. "Tell me."

But Bildren had lost consciousness.

I'll return home and report to the new High Magister, Shukara decided. If Tokombu was still her home. Two years in the wilderness had changed her. *I'm just weary.* Let the High Magister decide if it was worthwhile going to war with Mask for an old staff only a dead man could use.

*

Tamira stood over the broken Grandmaster of the Black Rose, Verak's sword in her hand.

Linus was grey-faced, clearly in a lot pain and perhaps dying. "Karib always admired that sword and the man he killed to get it." A glint of malice showed in Linus's dark eyes. "That's why I made him surrender it to me."

Tamira nodded. "He'll teach me your skills in exchange for

195

this sword. But first, I want you to know why I'm here."

Linus barked a laugh. "In truth, I barely noticed you."

"Karib is not the only one living you believed dead," she told him quietly. Jassan was out of earshot, his wounds being tended to by Shukara. "Five years ago, you were paid to kill the King of Mask and all his family."

A spasm of pain crossed his face. "And?"

She spread her arms. "And Xaria lived, standing before you."

Linus's eyes widened. "Karib swore you were dead, slain by the man who wielded that sword."

"I escaped through a secret passage while Captain Verak killed a slave in my place." Tamira's face came unbidden to mind. A gentle soul who had counted herself fortunate to serve a princess.

"But … *Karib* led my people to your palace, tried to kill you and *did* kill the man who saved you," Linus protested as Tamira aimed the blade at his throat.

"Don't worry," she assured him. "Karib will live only so long as he is of use to me. Then he'll join you in the Underworld."

Despite his obvious pain, Linus managed a chuckle of wry delight. "Good girl." His laugh ended in a choking spurt of blood as she slid the sword through his throat.

"Is your business here done?" Shukara joined her, looking down at the corpse and the black rose Tamira had dropped on his chest.

Tamira nodded. "Yours?"

Shukara glanced over at the half-buried mage. "For now."

Chapter Twenty-Six

A day passed. *Bhuvamet*'s rampage had lasted only an hour, but that proved long enough for the dhaemon to destroy the fighting strength of the Black Rose, and no small number of innocents besides. The cowed remnant left the Black Citadel without protest, carrying their wounded out of the front gate. What welcome awaited them in the village was of no concern to Shukara.

The Black Citadel, once feared stronghold of the Black Rose, had been reduced to a corpse-strewn tomb. Shukara, Tamira and Jassan occupied a few bedchambers, and feasted on the copious supplies found in the kitchen in one of the lower levels.

A day of rest had seen Shukara mostly recovered from her duel with Bildren, and Jassan's wounds were thus far free from infection.

The ranger had been acting furtively since their victory, climbing up to the top-most level of the citadel and launching a flaming arrow high into the air. Since then he had taken to looking out of the narrow east-facing windows, as if waiting for something. Or someone.

No trace of the Bone King's staff had been found in the Black Citadel, neither alongside Linus's other trophies, nor in Bildren's room. Shukara suspected that it had been sent to Mask, either to the Kasbah Arcana or the High Temple of Hrek.

Bildren still lived, in the infirmary, her body broken beyond repair. Jassan and Tamira wanted her dead and were bemused at Shukara's refusal simply to kill her. But Shukara knew that Bildren was powerless without her staff and she wanted to question the magicker. Why send a score of assassins across a continent to attack Tokombu? The southern magi were no threat to Mask, and the Black Rose's fee for such a venture would have beggared a small kingdom. *So why?*

Meanwhile, she searched Bildren's room, the magicker's reagents now in Shukara's pouch with her own. Her gorge rose on finding a desiccated head locked in a small chest, horror turning to cold rage upon recognising it. Wisps of hair jutted from the leathered chin, remnants of a once-lustrous beard; High Magister Dhoul, late master of Tokombu's magi.

The magi had assumed at the time that the assassins had removed Dhoul's head to prove to their client that they had completed the contract, and Bildren's possession of it confirmed her involvement. *But why keep it?* Some tribes kept pieces of their vanquished foes as trophies, but Bildren was no savage.

The eyelids opened, revealing milky orbs that were once eyes. Taut leathered skin stretched as Dhoul's mouth opened, his lips long-since rotted away. A dry whisper escaped from that narrow slash of a mouth. "Who is there?"

Gods, no! Shukara stared at Dhoul. The full horror of his murder was now laid bare. A magicker – Bildren? – had been among the assassins, preserving the head upon its removal. Killing Dhoul hadn't been enough, hadn't even been the goal. The Kasbah Arcana had wanted to question the High Magister, and had kept him at their mercy since his death. For two years Dhoul's soul had been trapped within his head, subject to unspeakable torment while Bildren and her colleagues ripped free every secret they desired from him.

She'll wish she'd been crushed to death, she'll beg me for mercy before I'm done, Shukara promised herself. *Or perhaps I'll do to her what she did to Magister Dhoul and return her thusly to Tokombu.*

"Is someone there? I thought I heard..." Dhoul managed sibilantly through dead lips.

Shukara fought for calm. Anger ill-became a magicker, she had been taught. The consequences were often ... regrettable. "Master Dhoul, it is I, Shukara," she said gently.

"Shukara?" Blind eyes stared through her. "Uhurela's apprentice?"

Shukara thought of Uhurela, stern but patient with her sulky young apprentice. She had succumbed to swamp fever sixteen months into their journey north, Shukara helpless to save her. "Yes, Master. Twenty of us left Tokombu to avenge you and the others killed by the Black Rose, but I'm the last one left. Who … did this to you? Bildren?"

"Yes, Bildren. She wanted information. No matter what I told her – and I told her everything – still she wanted more."

"I'll free you, Master," Shukara promised quietly. "And then I'll deal with Bildren."

"No, you must not," Dhoul said, face twisting in alarm.

"I've already bested her," Shukara assured him. "She lies dying."

"…Misunderstand. More at stake … *world* at stake. Talk to her … *listen* to her."

Shukara took a calming breath. "Yes, Master."

"First, give me peace."

Shukara swallowed. "Of course." She mixed together some reagents with water and drank the potion down, letting it do its work before pulling out her stave. "I'm ready, Master."

A hiss passed Dhoul's mouth. "Death will be … welcome. I thank you, Shukara. And am sorry for what will come."

"Join your ancestors, Master Dhoul, and be at peace." Fire enveloped the head, consuming its leathered skin and charring the skull beneath. Still it burned, hotter and hotter until nothing remained but blackened bone and ash. Shukara left the room, her rage unquenched, the infirmary her destination.

"I know what you did." Shukara stared at the old magicker dying in a bed.

Bildren grimaced, broken ribs pressing down on her lungs. "You found High Magister Dhoul."

"What remained of him. He's at peace now."

Hard dark eyes fixed on Shukara's own, seeking not forgiveness but understanding. "It was necessary. Even Dhoul came to understand that in time."

"He bid me hear you out," Shukara said reluctantly.

"Will you?" There was fear in the old woman's voice, not of death but of failure.

"Yes." The word tasted bitter to Shukara. Doing so offered legitimacy to what Bildren had done to Dhoul, perhaps even vindication. But she would honour the dead High Magister's wishes. Death would come for Bildren regardless, and whether it came silently or heralded by screams ultimately made no difference. *If the gods are just, let them make her answer for her sins.*

Her lip curled. *If.*

"We'll need yellow lotus," Bildren said.

"I have it. But first tell me why your people sent the Black Rose to Tokombu, why you killed Dhoul and did … *that* … to him. The magi of the Kasbah Arcana already have monopoly over the Art in Mask. Do you seek to extend it across all of Araka?"

Bildren croaked out a laugh. "The Cult of Hrek rests its heel over the Kasbah Arcana, ready to stamp down should our loyalty ever be in doubt, should their fear of us ever outweigh our usefulness. Some of my colleagues may dream of becoming the centre of Arakan magick, but myself and others have more pressing concerns." She glanced at a clay cup with entreating eyes.

Shukara poured her some water and passed the cup over.

"Thank you. Shortly after the last king of Mask was slain, the Archpriest of Hrek bade the magi delve into the future for possible threats. His control over Mask was still tenuous, and he feared it would prove brief.

"With every mage in the city not under our protection slain and the magisters fearing the Cult turning on us, those of us with an affinity for prophecy turned to the yellow lotus, eager to demonstrate our value."

Shukara held prophecy in poor regard. Yellow lotus was necessary to enter the required trance, but it was also a powerful intoxicant and as such distilling glimpses of the future from lotus-inspired nonsense was a fool's errand. The visions could have myriad meanings and were only ever clear in hindsight. And sometimes not even then. "What did you learn?"

"Lotus was consumed in dangerous quantities, ruining a few magi. But enough of us succeeded in piercing the mist obscuring time's path to see ahead."

"But you see only possible futures, nothing is fixed," Shukara said.

"Yes. The Archpriest wanted to know of possible threats to his rule, but what we found was worse, far worse. The further one looks ahead, the more time diverges into multiple paths.

And almost every path we saw led to the world's end."

Shukara crossed her arms, feeling a chill despite the day's warmth. "All of us who study magick know that everything will end one day. Entropy will not be denied."

"The ending we saw comes sooner, far sooner. Humanity will be gone within a score of centuries at most."

"Two thousand years ... so I can continue my preparations to return home without fear of interruption," Shukara said dryly.

Bildren scowled. "The world's fate will be decided by degrees; actions taken or not taken today, a year from now, two years, one hundred. We assured the Archpriest his rule was secure—"

Shukara thought of Tamira's quest to avenge her family. "And is it?"

"For now. Some of us saw him in the Xarian Arena, slain by a young lioness with black petalled fur in front of thousands, the Cult helpless to do naught but garland the lion with gold and allow her to leave. As you say, prophecy can often be senseless."

Shukara smiled privately. The lion was once the sigil of Mask's royal family. "Continue."

"We turned again to the lotus, delving into the future in search of paths that might save the world. We've kept this dread revelation from the Cult, even from most of our own."

"The world's ended before. Relics from a time before our own have been found."

"Will you wager that humanity will crawl once more from the ashes to rise again? Those few of us in the Kasbah Arcana who know of this dread future will not. We sought solutions."

"Did you find any?"

Bildren jerked a nod. "Perhaps. We tried to guide our visions towards saviours and threats. Sometimes the world ends in a thousand years, two thousand. We dreamed of the coming horror being pricked by a black rose and shying back, of gods reawakening and gods dying. And we dreamed of a dead man walking the land once more, making a pact with Death."

"The Bone King," Shukara said, chilled at the thought.

"A powerful foe. We planned to destroy him. Our visions suggested the Black Rose were crucial, so I came here and told all to Grandmaster Linus. He agreed to send his people to Tokombu to recover the Bone King's staff, and to aid us find and destroy him."

"The Black Rose do – did – not strike me as altruistic."

"Better; they are pragmatic. They live in this world too. We have the staff and learned much from Dhoul. His knowledge helped us narrow down the Bone King's likely location, and Linus promised to send an expedition there with me." Wounded eyes accused Shukara. "The world survives in scant few of the futures we beheld, and with the Black Rose gone, you may have just closed those paths forever."

It wasn't every day Shukara was told she may just have helped end the world. A guilty thrill went through her; who didn't dream of leaving their mark on the world, to *matter*. And whose vanity could not help but be flattered by the revelation that they had helped write the world's ending?

Shukara put aside the warring guilt and dark delight, rising above it, but it was hard to feel much guilt for something that wouldn't come to pass until her bones were dust. "Why not approach us openly," she said, determined Bildren own her own share of the responsibility. "My colleagues live in this world just as much as the Black Rose. If you felt you could trust killers-for-hire, why not fellow magi?"

"We're still beholden to the Cult of Hrek who would regard that as betrayal if they learned of it," Bildren reminded her. "And we could not risk you refusing us and hiding the Bone King's staff."

"It's only a staff."

Bildren snorted. "A staff of wytchwood prepared by the most dangerous necromancer ever to walk the world. How did it get to Tokombu? Was it found by one of your forebears or did the Bone King entrust it to them? Are the magi there beholden to him? All questions we had, sowing doubts enough to send the Black Rose rather than risk trusting you."

"Justifying the torture of Master Dhoul's soul for two years." Shukara managed to keep her anger at bay.

"Yes." Bildren's voice held no apology. "And we learned much from him, secrets known only to one wearing the mantle of High Magister. In time Dhoul accepted why we acted as we did, and cooperated with us when the stakes were made known to him. I would have freed him once I was satisfied there was nothing further to learn from him."

"And now?" Shukara spoke quietly. What had been a quest for vengeance with no stake beyond the lives of herself and her companions had become something greater.

Bildren's breathing had become laboured. "My journal contains everything I've learned about the Bone King, about the threat to us all. Responsibility … is yours. Take yellow lotus with me, and we will dream of the future one last … time."

"You can show me?"

Bildren managed a nod, her face grey. Death stalked the Black Citadel for her, drawing ever nearer. Shukara quickly mixed yellow lotus seeds into Bildren's cup and lifted it to the dying magicker's lips, pouring it down her throat. Shukara drank the remaining half.

The lotus soon took effect, Bildren's pupils dilating. Shukara fought off the intoxicating effects that threatened to muddle her mind, and quested out to her enemy. She had never taken yellow lotus before, relying on Bildren's skill to bend the rules governing time, to see where one path became many, a tree of infinite branches.

Darkness and nausea wracked Shukara, flickering images and dreams prowling her thoughts. She knew these were born of the drug. Bildren was an anchor in her mind, pressing on with the reckless confidence of one dying regardless.

It begins. Shukara knew the thought was not her own. Darkness fell over her mind, dreams and memories expunged from the space she and Bildren stared into, expectant. *A possible future comes.* They would see what Shukara's wrath had begat now that the Black Rose had died before it could become the world's unlikely saviour.

Chapter Twenty-Seven

A city appeared, a city like no other Shukara had ever seen before. Rectangular towers of glass and metal rose to impossible heights from streets of stone. The sun glinted off … things … made from polished metal that sat in the oddly smooth streets. They were all over the place, not moving, an eclectic mix of sizes and colours – reds, whites, blues and blacks – resting on thick black wheels.

What marvel is this place? I've known nowhere like it. And then, impossibly, Shukara realised she *did* know this city. A weathered black pyramid loomed over the heart of the city, surrounded by crumbling houses of red mud. The High Temple of Hrek. None of the metal and glass edifices were built near it, the Old Quarter kept much like now.

This is Mask. The Royal Palace was visible, as was the now-crumbling Xarian Arena, relics from the past perhaps preserved for posterity. The River Tyre flowed past a harbour hosting titanic ships made from iron. *This is the future.*

It is the end, another voice corrected. Bildren.

Our descendants have built impossible marvels. What end is this?

Then where are they? Bildren asked.

Sure enough, there were no people. Anywhere.

Except one. *Look.*

No, you look.

Disembodied, Shukara watched him, a Keramese man with short white hair running through the streets as if hunted. He wore an odd garment that covered each leg like sleeves, and a thin, short tunic of sorts. Black leather covered his feet, like sandals but made from a single piece of leather rather than a collection of straps.

She sensed that the man had once been chained, but those chains were now gone, broken, and he despaired of their loss even as he revelled in the freedom. The man flickered, and for a moment she saw him dressed in a leather kilt and linen tunic, sandaled and wielding a sword and shield, his white hair curled. Laughing and spitting in a god's eye. *A man untethered from time.*

The city fell away. *Time is short, and you've seen enough of the world's end. Now we must search for our hope and despair, allies and enemies.* Shukara's head started to spin, a side-effect of the drug. Intoxication compromised the lucidity of the visions.

A pride of lions led by a cruel male with a thick red mane ran up a mountain covered in black roses, pricked and slashed by thorns. The lions bled and died, including a cub that evaded the roses only to die from a gold-capped tooth dropping from her father's mouth.

A tree of wytchwood grew tall, its shadow falling over the mountain, the black roses withering to dust. Camels reached the mountain, tough and hardy, and blue flowers bloomed in place of the roses.

The gold-capped fang fell from the motionless lion cub's side, a drop of blood watering the ground. A single black rose grew upwards from where the blood landed, larger than its predecessors.

A red-furred fox ran through lush green lands, hunters in pursuit. They snared it and the lands turned arid. The animal was caged, beaten and made to fight other beasts. Stronger it grew and fiercer, a fang of obsidian growing in its mouth.

The rose grew around a black pyramid and golden merchant's scales, its thorns pricking both, blood dripping onto its petals until finally they turned red. Only then did it release its hold.

A white-feathered eagle stood tethered to the ground, wounded and cornered by enemies. An hour glass sat beside him, filled with blood rather than sand, Shukara somehow knowing that the eagle was meant to die before it emptied. But instead the eagle cried out and spread his wings, talons flashing. The hour glass emptied and cracked, never-ending blood flowing as the eagle laughed and cried as it slaughtered its enemies.

A corpse awoke, looking down at the black rose, the wytchwood tree, the camel, red fox and white eagle. The eagle grew older and died, chains piercing its wings and dragging it into a pit. Years beyond count passed, and the corpse reached for the chains, pulling the eagle up from the pit to fly once more...

Shukara gasped, her eyes snapping open. She felt drunk, an unwelcome effect of the yellow lotus, but at least she still lived. Bildren's eyes stared up unblinking.

A kinder death than she deserved. But a necessary one to pass her mantle to Shukara. The visions they shared lay heavy on her, little making sense.

Prophecy was a fool's game, and Shukara wondered if Bildren had fallen prey to its trickster's wiles, led to errant assumptions.

Fate makes fools of us all. She would return to Tokombu. Let the world tend to itself for now.

*

A caravan of Kavari approached Rhemi, ten camels led by a score of men. *Traders?* Tamira thought not, as she watched their approach from a narrow citadel window. The heat shimmered the air, leaving them oddly ethereal. *Maybe Jassan knows them...?*

A dark suspicion crowded her mind. *That wily bastard!* She left the window and ran to find Shukara, heading first for the library. The mage had been oddly subdued since the death of Bildren, distracted by something she refused to discuss.

Tamira wondered if the mage could ever be content, or if her restless nature fated her to become a rootless vagabond, chasing one cause after another until Death finally caught up with her.

Tamira reached the library, finding Shukara reading within, squinting over a hard-bound journal by candlelight. Scrolls lay on the stone table, and Tamira saw maps sketched on them. A hint of sulphur seemed to linger in the air, or perhaps Tamira imagined it. Scorched glyphs remained on the floor, marking the dhaemon's entrance into this world.

"A caravan of Kavari have arrived," Tamira said, looking away from the burned floor.

Shukara looked up, blinking in surprise at her. *She didn't even notice me enter.* "What of it? The citadel gate is closed."

"Kavari rarely come here, but twenty appear three days after the Black Citadel falls?"

"Jassan," Shukara said, realisation dawning.

Tamira nodded. "Yes."

They reached the citadel gate before the ranger and did not have to wait long for his arrival. "Is there something you wish to tell us?" Shukara asked, a flicker of guilt passing over Jassan's face on seeing them.

He feigned nonchalance. "You came here to confront the Black Rose. Now that they're gone, what about their citadel?"

"You're claiming it for your clan," Tamira guessed.

"Yes." He shrugged defiantly. "Someone will, why not my people? For centuries caravans have had to avoid the Oasis of Rhemi, prohibited by the Black Rose. With them gone, caravans will now be free to use the trail, saving days of travel."

"You were confident we would succeed?" Shukara asked.

"I wouldn't have accepted your contract had I not been fairly sure we would succeed," he said with a forced grin. "Before we left Pashbur I arranged for some of my kin to follow a few days behind. If I sent a signal, it meant the citadel had fallen. If I didn't, they were to assume me dead."

"I saw only twenty," Tamira said.

"Enough to hold this place until my clan can arrive in force." He watched Shukara warily. "If you have no objections?"

Shukara considered it for a moment. "I care not who holds this place," she answered. "My only condition is that I be allowed to stay for as long as I wish and that the library remains undisturbed."

Tamira saw his relieved smile. Had the mage taken umbrage at his presumption or wished to claim the Black Citadel for herself... "You'll always be welcome here. Both of you."

Shukara left without another word, heading back in the direction of the library. Tamira watched Jassan open the gate to let in his twenty clansmen and the camels bearing their supplies.

"What if the villagers object to you claiming this place?" she asked.

"Too late, we're here," he said bullishly. "They'll realise better a clan of Kavari than bandits. With our rangers leading caravans through here, Rhemi will prosper."

The ranger sounded enthused, and why not? He may have just made his clan rich, giving them an alternative to their nomadic camps and villages.

A thought occurred. "Will Adjatay be coming here?" The Black Citadel had been his home once. If so, she would be staying too, learning the assassin's trade from him.

"No, there's too many steps here for his bad leg. He'll stay in Pashbur."

Then that's where I'll go. "What of you?" She and Shukara had assumed the ranger would lead them back.

"I'll be returning to Pashbur in a few days," Jassan assured her. He turned to greet the blue-robed men entering the citadel. "Chief Meddur! Be welcome. I have teh waiting."

The eldest Kavari, a gaunt-faced man with a greying beard, looked around the vast entrance hall. "A fine prize. You have done well, Nephew. Our clan will sing your name around the campfires for many generations. Did the assassins give you much trouble?"

"Nothing my companions and I couldn't handle," Jassan answered with a self-deprecating grin.

Chief Meddur had the weathered face of a man whose responsibilities weighed him down, but he managed a faint smile. "Their stronghold is now ours. A place of safety for our people. A *home*."

Tamira felt a lump in her throat. *Home*. She wondered if *she* would ever call a place home again.

*

The Kavari settled quickly into the citadel, scrubbing away bloodstains staining the walls and floors, heralding a new beginning for the mountain stronghold. After the battle, Tamira had helped Shukara and Jassan carry the dead into the assembly hall. With the citadel now claimed by the Kavari, the rangers removed the bodies from the mountain, paying the wary villagers to build a pyre and burn them. The Kavari had looked upon the burnt and mangled remains of the assassins, thereafter treating Shukara with a careful courtesy.

Revenge rather than gold had motived Tamira's journey to Rhemi, but she had hoped to take her share of the gold from the citadel's treasury. Unfortunately, the vaults holding the wealth of the Black Rose still proved elusive, perhaps not even kept within the Black Citadel. Jassan's contract was considered paid, at least.

A few more days passed.

Tamira waited outside Rhemi's caravanserai, having awoken and broken her fast early. Jassan had spent the morning preparing three camels for the return journey to Pashbur, the sun peeking over the horizon by the time they were ready to leave.

"Your thoughts?" Shukara asked as Tamira stared along the Black Trail leading to the main caravan route. The few travellers who dared travel it had done so knowing their lives were forfeit if the Black Rose objected to their presence. That would change, Tamira knew, Jassan's clan eager to open the trail up to the vast caravans travelling to and from Pashbur.

"Nothing, just … remembering."

"Will you become a pupil to Adjatay?" The mage knew of the former assassin's involvement in the death of Tamira's family.

"Karib wanted to meet Princess Xaria," she said. "Once Tamira has learned all he can teach, he finally will."

Shukara smiled. "That will be an interesting encounter." She was staying behind in Rhemi for a while longer, claiming that she had not yet finished with the library.

Tamira looked up at the mage. "What will you do now?"

Shukara looked away, a frown creasing her sharp features. "I will return home and tell my people the Black Rose have paid for their crimes against us. After that…" She shrugged. "I'll see."

Jassan joined them, still pained by his bandaged wounds. "A caravan is due to pass near the Black Trail in a ten-day or so, Shukara. One of my kin will escort you there to meet it. If you're still planning to go south?"

Shukara faced him. "Yes. You've proven a stalwart companion, Jassan. May you have good health and prosperity."

Jassan smiled. "May your return home be swift and safe. And the next time you need a ranger to guide you to a den of assassins…"

"Find someone else?"

He laughed. "Just so!" The mage and ranger hugged briefly.

Shukara looked down at Tamira, a rare fond smile on her face. "We have had interesting times together. I hope you find what you need."

Tears welled in Tamira's eyes, a lump forming in her throat. "You saved me from the streets, helped me avenge my family and find the courage to choose who I might become."

They embraced. "Be a lioness," the mage whispered.

In good spirits, Tamira and Jassan began the long journey to Pashbur, the ranger leading the camels while Tamira walked alongside him. Assassins, a dhaemon and a mage had failed to stop them; Tamira felt confident the burning sun and pitiless desert would prove no more successful.

She turned back and raised her hand. Shukara raised her own briefly and then turned away. Tamira watched the tall mage walk towards the Black Citadel, finally disappearing from view.

Chapter Twenty-Eight

The sky burned crimson as it set over Lake Toko in the west. A lion coughed in the distance, audible over the constant din of crickets and other insects. A dung beetle collided with Shukara before falling to the ground, protected by its glossy black carapace.

She picked it up and held out her hand until it took flight again, careening out of control into the night.

The waters of Lake Toko turned gold against the sunset, a flock of flamingos glowing pink as they took flight. Animals drank from the lake, watchful for lurking predators on the prowl for easy prey.

Shukara forced her weary legs to keep moving, the soles of her feet blistered and sore as they chafed against worn leather sandals. She had paid for passage on a caravan heading west from Neirhu, but as the traders had no business in Tokombu she had walked the last half-day alone. Her destination waited ahead; Tokombu, City of Magi.

She found that 'city' was still an exaggeration, that there had been little change in her absence. A village, really, that had grown around the Collegiate. Fifteen months had passed since her departure from Rhemi and her return to Tokombu, part of that due to her lingering in Khemyatta to visit its famed library.

A herdsman led his goats back to the safety of Tokombu's palisade, giving her a guarded look. The palisade looked flimsy to her eyes, built to delay raiders just long enough for the villagers to flee inside the basalt college building. Not that any raiders were foolish enough to harass Tokombu, save for the Black Rose. *And they've paid for that transgression.*

The surrounding fields were blessed with fertility thanks to Mount Serah, a volcano north of Lake Toko. Early inhabitants had fled the area centuries before, during an eruption and never returned, believing it heralded the wrath of the gods. As such, the worldly magi had found the area perfect for their needs; a freshwater lake and good fertile land just begging to be tilled.

Mount Serah still belched smoke occasionally, but Tokombu's geomancers delved it often, assuring the magisters that, while a sea of molten magma raged beneath them, it lacked the pressure to cause an eruption.

The volcanic region had provided the magi with more than just fertile land. Erosion had exposed a wedge of once-flowing lava, basaltic rock now jutting out of the ground, dense enough to resist the erosion that had removed the softer ground once burying it. The first magi to settle in the area had claimed that cliff of black rock and used their arts to excavate chambers and passages, turning it into a centre of learning.

Shukara struggled to comprehend the quantity of reagents required by those early magi to quarry the dense, unyielding basalt. The Cult of Hrek had sacrificed countless slaves mining and transporting such rock to construct their pyramid in Mask, and as impressive as the Black Citadel was, the red mountain from which it had been excavated had consisted of softer material.

She approached the palisade, its gate manned by two guards. They wore no armour, only goat-skinned aprons around their waist and cow tails tied below their knees and around their upper arms. One of them wore a calfskin headband, signifying that he was married.

The tallest barred the gate with his long spear. "Tokombu is closed to travellers after dusk." He pointed to a caravanserai a short distance to the south. "You may stay there."

He was polite. Guards in Tokombu quickly learned not to judge people by their physical appearance. A frail elderly woman might well be a quick-tempered magicker of terrible power and little restraint.

Shukara took a breath. Part of her was tempted to acquiesce and spend the night in the caravanserai. She had been absent Tokombu for over three years, what would one more night matter?

But the patience that had seen her survive three years of

near-constant peril deserted her. "I am Shukara, a Magicker of the Collegiate. I must report to the Council of Magisters."

The guards regarded her doubtfully, not that she could blame them. All Tokomban magi had identifying tattoos inked onto the left side of their upper faces, but after the early mishaps of their journey north, the expedition had learned the value of anonymity. The tattoo ink had been magickally drawn from the skin, a painful experience. Furthermore, the rigors of the long journey south had reduced her appearance to little better than a beggar.

"Do you have proof of this?" the married guard asked, pointedly looking at the ink-free left side of her face.

Shukara showed them her wytchwood stave and clenched air together to tap both men on the head. But gently, in recognition of their courtesy. "I left three years ago with Magister Pauck's expedition. We were required to remove our tattoos."

Both guards bowed and stepped aside with alacrity. "Apologies, Magicker."

"Your vigilance does Tokombu credit," she said, walking through the cedarwood gate.

The village was like most others in the area, a collection of round buildings made from stone or wood, all roofed with thatch. Shukara took a breath, smelling smoke and cooking food as she walked through the village spreading out from the black cliff in a crescent.

Chickens and goats roamed freely. Deep-throated cattle lowed from the nearby pastures, and a gang of children ran past, laughing loudly as they played.

A young woman carried a basket on her head. She was wearing only a grass skirt and several beads. Only upon marrying would she cover herself fully, replacing the grass skirt with one made from thick cowhide, treated with charcoal and animal fat. As a magicker, such customs no longer applied to Shukara.

Many windows had been cut out from the cliff to allow air in and out of the college, and every night saw crystal-light or candlelight escape many of those windows, magickal study often running long after dusk. The entrance was illuminated by long, burning torches stabbed into the ground. Intended to impress, the entrance was no longer merely a doorway leading inside the cliff.

Generations of artistically gifted magi had worked on the cliff face immediately surrounding the entrance, turning it a hundred-metre high and fifty-metre wide rectangle of polished black rock, smooth obsidian. Chisels created from the air – unyielding as diamond and sharp enough to cut stone – were used to carve intricate designs and motifs into the rock. A massive bust of Tokombu's founder, High Magister Odephus, gazed down upon all who entered. Tall, thick pillars carved to imitate wytchwood staffs flanked the entrance, a tall, wide hole in the cliff.

As a newly arrived child she had gaped up at it, her resentment at being sent here briefly forgotten. Now she chiefly felt impatience, a burning desire to speak with High Magister Dhoul's successor and report her success. *And after that…?*

Was this insular community still her home?

Four guarded the torchlit collegiate entrance instead of the two spearmen that had been the tradition before the Black Rose raid. Two magi wearing grey apprentice robes and carrying wytchwood staffs stood with two spear-wielding guards. Having seen the deadly speed of the assassins, Shukara had no doubt the Black Rose would have found two bored apprentices little challenge, dispatching them before they knew they were under attack. But whatever helped the resident magi sleep better at night.

She vaguely recognised the apprentices by sight if not by name. The woman was aged maybe twenty, the man several years older. A vertical line inside a circle was tattooed in indigo ink upon the dark faces of both, confirming them as apprentices. Newly arrived initiates were marked with the circle to signify the beginning of their studies. On being judged ready to visit the wytchwood grove to craft their staff, the line was tattooed inside the circle, raising the initiate to apprentice. A star tattooed over the circle signified an apprentice raised to magicker.

"Identify yourself," the male apprentice demanded as if the safety of Tokombu rested on his thin shoulders. *Which it may do, gods help us.*

"I am Shukara, a Magicker of this collegiate," she said, showing her stave, the wytchwood easily recognisable to any magi.

Both apprentices squinted at her in the darkness, looking for her now-gone tattoos. Her skin was a few shades darker than the male apprentice's, but it wouldn't take long before they realised she was unmarked.

"She's carrying wytchwood but has no tattoos," the female apprentice said quietly, her staff held ready.

The male scrutinised her features. "No, but I recognise her. She left with Magister Pauck shortly after the attack."

Shukara took a step forwards, relieved at being recognised. "Indeed. The assassins paid others to ambush any who pursued them, so we removed our tattoos." She swallowed down a sudden lump in her throat. "None of the others survived. I wish to see the High Magister." *Whoever that might be*.

The male studied her, perhaps seeing the toll the quest had taken from her.

"Skiphu," the female called out.

A boy of maybe ten years appeared, wearing the grey tunic of an initiate. A blue circle stood out on almost-black skin, the ink still fresh and unfaded by the sun. "Khula ... I mean, Apprentice Khula?"

"Run to Magister Leera and tell her a survivor from Magister Dhoul's expedition has returned, called Shukara." Shukara guessed Leera was the designated duty magister of the night; the apprentice evidently preferred to let her decide whether Shukara's return justified disturbing the High Magister. "And Skiphu? Report to Magister Sata tomorrow morning after our duty here has finished and tell her you need reminding of the proper way to address those higher than yourself."

"Yes, Apprentice," the chagrined boy said as he ran off on his errand. Shukara smiled at Khula's self-important tone. Apprentices often had fragile egos that took offence at any imagined slight against their 'lofty' rank. She was embarrassed to admit she had once been much the same.

The apprentices seemed uncertain whether to keep her outside or permit her to enter, their indecision resulting in the former. Not that she minded. It was a pleasant night.

Skiphu returned a short time later, breathless from his run. "I've to take Shukara to the council chamber," he gasped. "The magisters will receive her there." Shukara noted Khula offered no chastisement for his neglecting to put any rank before *her* name.

Chapter Twenty-Nine

The council chamber looked smaller to Shukara's eyes than she remembered, a large black-stoned circular room with a ceiling maybe twenty feet high. Light came from a series of crystals plugged into sockets carved into the walls, crystals that required recharging from sunlight. As such they were regularly cycled with spares to ensure that the council chamber was never in darkness. Such crystals were used to light every corridor and communal room within the Collegiate. Many magi used them in their private rooms, but they shone perpetually until exhausting their stored sunlight, requiring thick, black cloth to cover them when darkness was desired. As such, some magi preferred to use candles.

Seven basalt podiums were positioned at the opposite end of the room from the door, matching the curve of the walls. Shukara's spirits dipped on recognising the man standing at the High Magister's podium; Errat, a fussy, sometimes petty, man noted for his administrative skills who favoured Tokombu remaining insular. He had been among the most vocal of those opposing retaliation against the Black Rose.

Three podiums were to the left and three to the right of Errat's, where the magisters would stand. So far only three of them were occupied, the remaining magisters still to arrive. There were no seats in the room, a legacy of High Magister Odephus. History reported him as a man of will and vision, often frustrated by the habit of magi to procrastinate. By keeping the chamber chair-free, he ensured that meetings would never last too long, a tradition that none of his successors had seen fit to end.

Each magister was responsible for a specific area of college life: the training of initiates and apprentices; the defence of Tokombu; ensuring that the collegiate was stocked with sufficient supplies such as food, clothing and reagents; tending to the wytchwood grove; maintaining and expanding the Collegiate and village; and maintaining diplomatic relations with neighbouring lands.

Leera, the fifth magister, took her place at a podium. Well into her middle-years, she oversaw Tokombu's diplomatic relations, appointing ambassadors when required. It was an open secret among the magi that she also acted as spymaster, maintaining a network of spies across the continent.

Errat cleared his throat. "As Magister Derid is visiting the ashfields of Karadhur to investigate firethorn yields, we will begin." A score of magi were gathered in the room, with more entering as word of Shukara's return spread throughout the Collegiate.

A stern look from Errat stilled the murmurs. He looked at Shukara standing in the centre of the room, his gaze no softer. "I am pleased at your return, Apprentice Shukara. Where is the rest of the expedition? Did Magister Pauck return?"

Shukara collected her thoughts, noting the tension in Errat's voice when he asked after Pauck. Formerly the magister in charge of Tokombu's defence, Pauck had resigned his position to lead the expedition assembling to pursue Dhoul's murderers. Many years before, he had been an apprentice to High Magister Dhoul, and it was no secret that Dhoul had groomed him as his successor.

"I regret to tell you that Magister Pauck and everyone else who left with him is dead. I am the last survivor." Pauck had died two months after leaving Tokombu, sacrificing himself to allow the others to escape an ambush. That ambush had convinced the survivors that the Black Rose had turned too many against them, that they would never catch the fleeing assassins, let alone reach the Black Citadel, if they continued following them directly.

"—so we travelled west before turning north again," Shukara said as she described the journey. Errat's eyes had betrayed his relieved pleasure at Pauck's death, one less rival for him to contend with. He would doubtless have been happier if Shukara had never returned either, letting the expedition go down in Tokomban history as a grand folly.

Magister Horus's stony face looked grim. He had been trained by Pauck, regarding him almost as a father. Shukara was relieved to see that he had taken Pauck's place as magister. There was no finer battle-magicker, and he would be conscientious in his duty to defend Tokombu.

"On announcing yourself, you claimed to be a magicker … Apprentice," Magister Sata said, her eyes hard. The initiates and apprentices were her responsibility, and none undertook their Trials until she judged them ready.

Shukara looked her in the eye. "Mistress Uhurela deemed me ready a year after we left Tokombu. She and two other magickers set my Trial and declared my apprenticeship at an end."

"I see no star tattooed on your face," Sata said. "In fact, I see no tattoos at all."

"Early on, we realised those hired by the Black Rose to oppose our journey identified us by our tattoos, so we reluctantly drew the ink from our faces." The tattoos were hard-earned; removing them had been like losing a piece of herself.

"Continue with your story," Errat said. "We will discuss your status afterwards."

That they might judge her elevation to full magicker void and demote her back to apprentice was something she had not considered. She jerked a nod, biting back a heated retort. After so long away with no one to answer to but herself, accepting the discipline of the Collegiate would be a difficult adjustment.

She continued with her report, her voice the only sound in the chamber. Having to relate the deaths of every colleague was painful, but a relief also to finally let the Collegiate know of their sacrifice.

"You single-handedly defeated a Maskan magicker, a magister no less?" Errat sounded incredulous. "And with a broken piece of wytchwood?"

Shukara dared him to outright call her a liar. "Yes," she said firmly, looking him in the eye.

"She tells the truth," Magister Leera said. A whisper rustled through the gathered magi. Magister Horus gave Shukara a slight nod of grudging respect. Shukara knew that Leera was using a spell to monitor her for minute physical changes that would betray a lie.

"But you found no sign of the Bone King's staff?" Errat

asked, perhaps eager to lessen Shukara's success.

"No," she admitted. "It was not in the Black Citadel. I suspect it is in Mask, either within Hrek's High Temple or the Kasbah Arcana."

Errat looked around and then back at Shukara. "You have done well in avenging the unprovoked attack on us. The world will know not to cross the Magi of Tokombu. A pity that such rash action cost us a further nineteen of our colleagues, Apprentice."

Anger stirred beneath her breast. "I am a Magicker, declared as such by three magi." She glanced at Leera, knowing the magister could verify the truth of her words.

"We doubt not that you tell the truth, *as you know it*, but it is highly irregular," Errat said. Sata nodded, doubtless eager to see Shukara back in an apprentice's robe.

Politics. Shukara had forgotten how pervasive intrigue could be in the Collegiate, and it appeared to have worsened under Errat's rule. The High Magister had opposed Pauck's decision to follow the assassins, and he doubtless feared that Shukara's successful return made him look weak, and that she would be courted by those factions opposing him. Disgust wearied her.

"Shukara has more than earned her star," Horus said, his voice deep and measured. He had only remained in Tokombu at Pauck's insistence, to be its protector, and there was clearly no love lost between him and Errat. A cold rage had burned in his eyes when Shukara revealed that death had only been the start of High Magister Dhoul's ordeal. A quiet applause had echoed round the room when she spoke of freeing him from his torment.

"Apprentices are *my* domain, Horus," Sata said sharply. "I propose Shukara remains an apprentice. There is more to being magi than traipsing across the world killing people."

Traipsing ... Shukara fought to keep her expression neutral. Sata seemed to regard Shukara as an insolent upstart in need of discipline, but if she made an enemy of the magister, Shukara might be wearing apprentice-grey until her hair turned the same colour.

The whispers from the watching magi had turned sharp and angry. Many if not all had apprentices themselves and rarely took well any interference from the magister in charge of training. In their eyes Sata was declaring that the three magi who had elevated Shukara from apprentice were in error, which they saw as a reflection on themselves. Magi reacted poorly to any interference in the instruction of their apprentices, most believing that the magister in charge of training should focus their attention on the initiates, overseeing apprentices only from a respectful distance.

Errat looked around, not blind to the ugly mood. "That would be a poor reward for a collegiate hero, Magister Sata," he said in a bid to placate the assembled magi. "My judgement is that Shukara should remain an apprentice *for now*, with her being promoted to magicker at the earliest opportunity." He spoke up over the rising din. "She must carve a new staff from the wytchwood grove, after all, and it will take some time and much practice for the matrices to grow within it. A magicker must be able to work magick, must they not? And for an apprentice of Shukara's undoubted ability, the trial will be a mere formality."

The other magi regarded those last words thoughtfully, and Shukara knew she would be robed as an apprentice before morning. She was fully able to work magick through her stave – for now – but it had matured as much as its diminished size would permit. There was no doubt she needed a new staff of wytchwood, and her magick would be greatly curtailed until she and it had adjusted to one another.

But to be an apprentice again. The prospect grated. Worse, she would be restricted to the Apprentice Library, unable to fully research the Bone King and whatever evil threatened the world. "I submit to the will of the High Magister," she said, knowing further argument was pointless. "However, I believe there is no need for me to attend classes or be apprenticed to a magicker. I request leave to train alone, solely to mature my new staff. And that I be Tested four months from now."

Murmurs of agreement rippled across the room that Errat could not fail to have heard. "Agreed, Shukara." Sata looked disgruntled at the thought of an apprentice training without supervision, but she offered no comment.

*

Four months passed slowly. It proved a difficult time for Shukara, and not just because of her demotion to apprentice. After three years living as a vagabond, often sleeping outside, she found life within the Collegiate stifling and claustrophobic. She had difficulty connecting with people, scarred by the deaths of her colleagues. Even her friendship with Tamira and Jassan had been born of necessity rather than a desire for company.

A nagging loneliness still troubled her despite being among so many people. Her status as an apprentice meant the magi remained distant, and the other apprentices were too young, too callow for her to bond with. And besides, her exploits made her a figure of awe among them. She suspected that was also why the magi were ill at ease in her company, knowing what she was capable of.

Tokombu was still recovering from the Black Rose attack, its numbers diminished. The Initiate Quarters were full, but it would take years for the Collegiate to replace those lost. As such, every magi had turned teacher, those formerly dedicated to pure research now tasked to educate the next generation of magi. Each magicker had several apprentices, and those apprentices nearing their Trial taught initiates.

Shukara had found herself before classes, teaching the basics of magick to initiates eager to learn. What *she* had learned was that the Collegiate had no resources to spare to allow magi to research lore on the Bone King, separating fact from myth. Tokombu had a web of agents spread across Araka, but they were tasked to look out for tangible threats in the here and now, not vague perils that might be generations in arriving. Shukara accepted that the duty inherited from Bildren would be hers alone.

She had kept her own counsel, focusing her efforts on maturing her new wytchwood staff, cut by her own hand from the grove. It was slow and frustrating work, spells her stave could manage with ease proving difficult with the staff. The matrices were growing slowly within it, but it was still unwieldy, like a wagon wheel turning stiffly.

She pulled off her grey robe for the last time, her mind and body still fatigued from the Trial. Magi wore what they wished, most opting for light woollen robes in winter and those of cotton in the summer. Shukara decided to wear her shendyt and tunic, a cooler option in the hot basalt halls of the Collegiate. At least the seasons were in their proper time now; they were reversed in the north.

Her cramped room in the Apprentice Quarters had remained as barren as the night she had been assigned to it, a place to sleep and nothing more. She had seen no reason to decorate the room, intending her stay there to be brief. Not that she had many belongings to fill her new room in the Magi Quarters.

The Trial had been difficult solely due to her being hobbled by the new staff's unfamiliarity. Most of the magi, apprentices and initiates had crowded into the Hall of Testing to watch, Errat and Sata among them. Errat had likely hoped that she would fail, forced to remain an apprentice. Shukara was certain if that had happened, Sata would insist she be treated like every other apprentice.

The final test was one of combat, against Magister Horus. No one expected an apprentice to defeat the collegiate's foremost battle-magicker, nor were they required to. All an apprentice must do to pass was withstand a measured assault for three minutes. It was a test of wits, composure and reflexes, to see if an apprentice could remain calm and adapt to different spells being hurled at them.

Errat and Sata expected her to fail; she saw it in their eyes. And ordinarily they would have been correct. With her new staff she was too slow, like a dancer trying to perform in water. They had expected her fail; they hadn't expected her to put aside her staff and face Horus with her old stave. And no one present had expected her to not only defend herself but to take the fight to the battle-magicker. The three minutes had ended in stalemate, Horus regarding her with even greater respect, sweat slicking his brow. For her part, Shukara knew she was still years from being able to match him in single combat.

Errat had been livid but made no effort to try to overturn the result. There were no rules that said one must use their staff. The magisters had never considered that an apprentice would possess more than one piece of wytchwood.

Shukara left her former room, walking the Collegiate's halls for the first time as an acknowledged magicker. She passed no small number of apprentices, the younger ones, without a master or mistress, trying to catch her attention.

Already Errat's opponents had sent her notes of congratulations, seeing her as a potential ally in their endless politicking against Errat and his followers.

But she had no time for such intrigues. With her face still stinging from the newly-tattooed star over the circle and line, she was free to make use of the Magi Library. She would learn what she could of the Bone King, of what might possibly end the world, all the while maturing her staff.

She had discussed her vision of the future with others, some interested, others dismissing it as an hallucination born of lotus. Shukara knew she could count on none of them for help. Most magi willing to brave the world outside of Tokombu had already done so a few years previously, their bones spread from here to Arrioch.

Horus had suggested that they spar regularly, an offer Shukara intended to take advantage of to further hone her combat magick. She wondered if he saw her as a possible successor. If so, he would be disappointed. Once she exhausted the library and matured her staff sufficiently, she would leave Tokombu. There was a world waiting beyond Lake Toko, lands beyond even the Darish Sea.

Every end had a beginning, even the world's. It was out there somewhere, perhaps in a rainforest where the air was almost as thick as water, or to the north where frozen water fell from the sky, and she had years yet to find it.

Chapter Thirty

Melodious woodwind music drifted through the halls and across the courtyard of Kasbah Tahmour, seat of Gheran, Quaid of Pashbur. Oil lamps lit up the kasbah, the light glittering off jewellery worn by the guests. A fortune in gold and gems clung to the fingers, necks and wrists of Khespha Province's nobles and merchant princes, guests of the quaid.

Tamira had to fight the thief in her not to ogle the wealth on display, keeping her eyes downward as she flitted from guest to guest with a jug of wine, topping up any cup that threatened to shame the quaid by being half-empty.

A delegation from Khaddh had reached Pashbur two days before, resting after their months-long journey. A kingdom small in size but rich in diamonds, Khaddh lay very far to the south, and for two of its princes to visit the Theocracy of Mask was a coup indeed. The princes would remain in Pashbur for a further four days before sailing north to the city of Mask, and gossip said the Padshah of Khespha had tasked his son the quaid to treat them like kings.

Quaid Gheran had risen to the occasion, inviting the province's rich and influential to honour the princes. Royalty hadn't travelled all this way on a whim; they had come to broker trade deals with Mask, and Padshah Thekti was mindful of the opportunity to enrich his lands and coffers. That meant making deals with the princes before they met the merchants living in the city of Mask.

Thekti wasn't the only one who saw an opportunity in the visit. Relations between the padshah and the Anir Clan had been strained ever since Jassan's people had seized the Black Citadel. In the two years since, Adjatay had kept an eye on Pashbur's rulers. More recently, he had tasked Tamira to keep an eye on them, spying on them as part of her training. The night's festivities offered a unique opportunity to snoop around.

Kasbah Tahmour's steward had been forced to hire more

servants for the night from among the locals, and Tamira had ensured that she was one of them. The long, orange servant's tunic she wore ensured that she could move around much of the kasbah's lower level unchallenged.

Quaid Gheran held court in the main hall, clad in a blue djellaba of syek. He was aged maybe thirty, his short black hair and beard neatly trimmed. His Kavari ancestors had tied themselves to Maskan nobility through marriage early on, but his desert heritage was still evidenced by his dark complexion.

An older man stood by his side, lighter skinned and grey-haired. Vizier Fatisoph, Gheran's chief advisor and his father's hand in Pashbur.

Tamira slipped out of the hall, carrying an empty jug as she headed to one of the kasbah's four towers. Her initial reconnaissance had revealed that the vizier's office was in the front-left tower, so that was her destination. Once, she would have believed Gheran's rooms were the best place to search for any clues as to the padshah's intentions towards Citadel Anir, but Adjatay had taught her different.

Gheran might make the decisions but he relied on Vizier Fatisoph to see them executed. And so, it was his office that Tamira planned to enter. The former assassin had taught her much in the two years she had lived in Pashbur, repayment for both Verak's sword and news that the Black Rose were done.

The kitchen bustled with activity as cooks roasted beef and mutton, jugs were refilled with water or wine, and servants brushed past one another in their haste to fetch freshly cooked food to ensure the quaid's tables were never bare. There was a well in a small room next to the kitchen and Tamira drew water from it to fill her empty jug.

She hugged the shadows, waiting until the kitchen supervisor looked particularly haggard. Then she approached him. "Master, I've to take water to the guards on the upper floor?"

"What? Yes, just go," he snapped, perspiration coating his face. Any mistakes in the kitchen were his responsibility, and given the eminence of the guests, would see him beaten and dismissed.

"I'll need a pass," Tamira pointed out.

The man handed her a carved ivory token, already distracted by the next servant waiting for instruction.

Knowing the quaid's tower and the vizier's tower would be the most zealously guarded, Tamira headed to the nearest of the remaining two, the bored-looking guard letting her past on seeing the ivory token permitting her up to the next level.

She left the tower and hurried through the corridor towards the vizier's tower, alert for the guards responsible for patrolling this level. Any guard stopping her might be satisfied by her possession of the pass token, but better to remain unobserved.

Tamira heard the guards before she saw them, the sound of sandals scuffling along the stone floor sending a measured spike of alarm through her that she was disciplined enough to let inform her actions without dictating them.

Two choices were immediately available to her; go back the way she had come and take the longer route to the vizier's tower, or find cover and hope that the guards missed her.

Deciding that there was too great a chance of encountering another patrol circling round from the opposite direction, she looked for somewhere to hide. There were two doors built into the inner corridor wall, but she knew both might be locked, and even if not, the rooms might be occupied.

There was a narrow window built into the outer wall, and she squeezed her way through it and lowered herself down, clinging to the ledge by her fingers. She hung there, praying that no one outside the kasbah was looking up, and that none of the guards decided to poke a head out for some air.

Tamira slightly tensed and relaxed her arm muscles to prevent cramp but kept otherwise still. Footsteps grew louder, more than one set, and she held her breath. The ledge seemed solid at least; no apparent cracks in the brickwork or mortar that might send her to her death.

The guards passed the window and the sounds of their passage quietened. Confident they would have reached the end of the corridor and turned the corner, Tamira pulled herself up and back through the window.

She reached the vizier's tower without incident and

climbed the steps to the top. Adjatay had trained her to be invisible, to leave no sign of her passage. There were no guards in the top level of the tower, the vizier relying on a padlock to secure his secrets.

Tamira knelt, pulling out two lockpicks. She inserted one into the padlock, patiently wiggling it around until it caught. She inserted the second lockpick while holding the first in position, hearing the satisfying click of the lock's release.

She entered the office, closing the door behind her. Once inside, she stood still, looking and listening. The tiled floor looked even, and she saw nothing to suggest that the room was trapped. She stepped lightly across the room towards the desk, memorising the layout. When she left, nothing must be out of place. *I must be like a spirit, or a fish who can swim without leaving ripples.*

Tamira was thoroughly methodical in her search of the office, knowing the vizier would be occupied for most of the evening standing by the quaid's side. She found no evidence of plots against Clan Anir, no deployment of soldiers to the former Black Citadel. That wasn't entirely a relief. Did it mean that the rulers of the province were not moving against the Anir, or had she just failed to find any evidence?

One letter caught her attention. It was from a Limat Nisan-Anir, confirming that the terms of his marriage to the padshah's daughter were agreeable, and that he had invited Quaid Meddur's nephew, Jassan, to Pashbur to address the padshah's concerns. Jassan's arrival was expected just before the next full moons. Limat looked forward to tying the clans of the Anir and Bhuul through marriage.

Why would a member of the Anir clan be marrying one of the padshah's daughters? The best answer she could come up with was that Padshah Thekti sought to gain some control over the former Black Citadel through marriage, but that would only work if he married his daughter to the chief's successor...

Limat Nisan-Anir. He was a Kavari merchant of the Anir Clan living in Pashbur, one of several contenders to become the new Chief of the Anir – and thus Quaid of Rhemi – when Quaid Meddur died. But there was at least one other considered more likely than he to succeed Meddur...

He writes that the padshah's concerns will soon be addressed... A chill shivered through Tamira as she realised the implications of the letter. Jassan was due to arrive within the next ten days judging by the date of the letter, and his death would greatly increase Limat's chances of succeeding Meddur. That complicated Tamira's plans somewhat, meaning she must act sooner than intended.

I've stayed here long enough. After satisfying herself that the room was exactly as she had found it, she snuck out of the room and re-secured the padlock. She returned to the festivities below, just one more servant among many.

*

Tamira's morning run took her outside the village, her breathing steady. Her duties in Kasbah Tahmour had not been discharged until the early hours of the morning, but running calmed her nerves. This day was two years coming.

For two years she had been pushed to her limits and beyond. Her muscles had been stretched and strengthened, she had learned how to move, how to balance, how to disappear. Adjatay had taught her how to use knives and how to kill with her bare hands and feet. She had learned how to fight and how to win a fight before it started. Poisons, potions, crossbows – all the tools of an assassin's trade.

Adjatay was a gifted artist and had sketched detailed plans of the tools she would need. It would be up to her to find artificers capable of crafting them when she left Pashbur.

She ran up the hill to Adjatay's house, her home these past two years. The locals had become accustomed to her, her run occasioning no comment.

"Tamira," Adjatay said as she entered the small house. "Did you find anything of interest last night?"

She heated water for Adjatay's teh. "I searched the vizier's office but found nothing to suggest the quaid is moving against the Anir. No large payments out of the ordinary to suggest assassins or mercenaries being hired, no orders deploying soldiers. However, the padshah has promised his daughter to Limat Nisan-Anir. I suspect Padshah Thekti seeks to tie strings to Quaid Meddur's successor, and believes Limat the best candidate to serve his interests."

Adjatay mulled that revelation over silently before grimacing in pain. His old wounds were always stiff in the morning. "You're aware of the implications for our friend?"

"Yes. Limat has invited Jassan here. I suspect he does not intend for him to leave."

"I agree." He looked at her. "I think you've learned all I have to teach you."

He had said as much to her a number of times over the past several ten-days. Tamira felt ambivalent; pride on one hand that her training was complete, and sadness on the other for the debt she had sworn to pay.

She passed him the cup of freshly brewed teh.

Shortly after, Adjatay collapsed, paralysed temporarily by a poison slipped into the teh. Tamira left him lying on the ground while she retrieved a cloth-wrapped item from his trunk, discarding the cloth and the scabbard. Adjatay – Karib – stared at her helplessly as she stood over him with Verak's sword in hand.

There was disapproval in his eyes. "You will kill me with that?" Even staring death in the eye, still he taught, still he tested her.

"No," she assured him. "I also slipped ewert powder into your teh, enough to stop your heart."

His head jerked in a nod of approval. "How will you leave?"

"By the door, which I will lock. I will then extend a long branch through the window and slide the key back inside. It will look as though you died alone, that your heart gave out."

"Good." He took a shuddering breath as the poison attacked his heart. "*Why?*"

Tamira showed him the sword. "We almost met seven years ago, but Captain Verak ensured otherwise." She took a breath. "Once upon a time, I was Princess Xaria."

"Ahh…" He half-smiled in remembrance of that long-ago day. "So, Verak bested me after all."

She nodded. Tamira and Adjatay had been student and teacher, but Xaria and Karib were enemies with unfinished business between them. She respected the maimed assassin, had even grown to grudgingly like him, but she had promised this to her dead family and to herself.

"May you best your enemies, Xaria, daughter of Xarius, as you have bested me," Karib managed. "Save Jassan if you can."

"I will. May you find peace, Karib of the Black Rose," she said gently. He spasmed one last time and went still.

Chapter Thirty-One

Early summer saw Jassan return to Pashbur, his first visit in almost two years. The desert had been restless with storms, making the journey north from the Black Citadal – renamed Citadel Anir – more unpleasant than usual. Caravan Master Bhutto had paid him upon reaching the caravanserai, and Jassan had wasted no time entering the common room and resting his legs. Teh washed away the dust coating his throat, and the lotus smoke left him mellow and content.

Clan Anir had prospered over the past two years, vast caravans now travelling the Black Trail to Rhemi for water and supplies, the trail now part of the Kavari Caravan Route. Most of the clan found the citadel too confined for comfort, their nomadic way of life too ingrained in their bones to call it home. They either lived in rootless camps on the edge of the desert, relying on wells or oases, or built homes on the outskirts of Rhemi. The village had grown considerably since the Anir claimed the oasis, the original inhabitants accepting Kavari rule and sharing in the wealth brought by visiting caravans.

Rhemi's success hadn't been met with universal approval, with many in Pashbur regarding it as unwanted competition despite the days and desert separating them. Whispers had reached the Anir that Thekti Thami-Bhuul, Padshah of Khespha Province, considered them potential rivals.

A company of mercenaries had attacked the citadel shortly after the Anir had claimed it, but they fared no better than any other force (save Jassan and his former companions) in trying to breach it. Padshah Thekti had sent a messenger bearing his congratulations to Chief Meddur, along with a patent of nobility appointing him Quaid of Rhemi. But many suspected that Thekti had hired the mercenaries himself in a bid to seize the oasis and mountain stronghold.

More recently there was talk of Thekti marrying one of his daughters to Meddur's heir. If the padshah couldn't seize

Rhemi for a son, then he would settle for a grandson inheriting it. But who exactly would succeed Meddur was an unanswered question. The clan's elders would decide the next chief, looking for qualities more relevant than paternity. Jassan's cousin Afetey was a good ranger but too introverted to succeed his father as chief.

Jassan's mood began to sour. Seizing Rhemi from the Black Rose had left many considering *him* to be the next Anir chief. All he could do was hope that his uncle would live a long life and that some other hero would emerge to capture the clan's admiration. He had reclaimed his life as a ranger, escorting caravans back and forth across the desert.

Limat, son of Nisan, was another possible successor and had many supporters. A few years before, the elders would never have picked a merchant over a ranger, but a new dawn had risen over a clan no longer tied so tightly to the desert.

Limat's invitation north had come as a surprise. Did he seek to persuade Jassan to support him to succeed Meddur? Jassan felt ambivalent; he had no taste to rule, but he had never liked Limat.

After finishing his teh and deciding that he had smoked enough lotus for one day, Jassan left the caravanserai. The late afternoon sun was proving pleasant rather than oppressive, and he took his time walking the path separating the caravanserai and village.

Papyrus fishing boats and broad dahabiyas sailed the river to his left, a heated argument carrying over the water as rival fishermen squabbled over fishing rights. Crew from a passing dahabiya shouted insults and encouragement, doubtless wagering on the likely victor should it turn to bloodshed. Spears and gutting knives were brandished by the feuding fishermen, and Jassan knew that the waters of the Tyre would soon turn red.

The guard towers of Pashbur stood tall. Many of the clay buildings were joined together, divided internally and spreading up the hill. Voices echoed down the narrow streets as Jassan headed towards Kasbah Bhuul.

The souk occupying the kasbah was busy as ever, stalls and villagers crowded into the shaded courtyard. Jassan smiled on seeing his cousin Jeka at her stall, haggling with a portly

Maskan over one of Adjatay's stone figurines.

He leaned against a wall, not wishing to cost Jeka and Adjatay a sale. Thinking of the crippled former assassin reminded him of Tamira, and he wondered how the girl was doing. She must be about fifteen by now.

The Maskan finally left, looking pleased with his purchase albeit less so at the amount of coin Jeka had wrested from him.

"Cousin," he called out as he navigated through the crowd to Jeka's stall. "You look well!" The two years had added some grey to her hair and lines to her face, but she looked as strong as ever.

"Jassan," she said, surprise in her tone. "If it isn't the Conqueror of the Black Citadel himself, deigning to walk among his humble kin. I'm surprised you remember me, stranger."

Embarrassment warmed his cheeks. "Enough of that! Anyway, it's Citadel Anir now. And your father bids me ask you when he can expect his daughter and grandchildren to join him there."

Jeka made a face. "We're quite settled here. I'm sure the great Quaid of Rhemi has enough demands on his time without grandchildren tripping his feet."

"I'm just the messenger," Jassan said. "Children well?"

"Well enough. Afeta is to marry Nimo in the autumn."

Gods... He still thought of Afeta as a small giggling child. "Nimo?"

"Youngest son of Mirus ban Nimollo, a baker."

The name told Jassan that the family was not Kavari. He didn't care, but his uncle might. "I hope they have a good life together," he said. "Just make sure they take stock of the politics. Few Maskans know you're the daughter of a Kavari clan chief, and fewer care, but the daughter of a quaid is different. The padshah's son rules here."

Jeka nodded. "I know. That is why Afeta and Nimo will travel to Rhemi after the wedding."

Relieved that his cousin was aware of new dangers arising from their clan's rising eminence, Jassan changed the subject. "Things look much the same around here. I'll call in on you after visiting Adjatay."

Jeka's expression sobered. "Gods, Jassan ... you don't – of

course you don't know." She took a breath. "Adjatay died eight days ago. I'm sorry."

A dizziness struck Jassan, followed by sadness at his friend's passing. "How? What happened?" Dark suspicions crowded his mind; not every Black Rose had been present within the Black Citadel when Shukara's dhaemon brought death and horror to them. Had one learned that Adjatay was, in truth, Karib?

"The healer believes his heart failed."

Jassan let out a sigh, relieved his friend's end had been peaceful. "How is Tamira?"

Jeka's mouth tightened at the mention of her name. Some regarded Tamira's apprenticeship with Adjatay to be a façade to cover a less proper relationship, not helped by the girl's indifferent stone-carving skills. Jassan had done what he could to dispel the unfounded suspicions, but he was reluctant to say too much given what the former assassin was truly teaching Tamira.

"She's well, or she was when she left."

"Left?"

Jeka nodded. "She left a few days after Adjatay's cremation, paying for passage on a dahabiya bound for Mask."

"I see." Another suspicion formed. "Adjatay's death … there was nothing odd about it?"

"Not that I know of. Tamira had returned to Adjatay's house after her morning run through the village, but found the door locked and no answer. She fetched Juko and myself, and we forced the door open, finding Adjatay dead. The healer reported no injuries or cause for suspicion."

"What will you do with Adjatay's house?"

"I'll see what Afetey wants to do with it. Sell it maybe, if he plans to join our father in Rhemi." She glanced at him. "What brought you to Pashbur anyway?"

"Limat Nisan-Anir sent a letter to Rhemi inviting me to visit regarding some matter too important to risk putting to parchment."

A startled look crossed her face. "The gods are truly playing a grim jest on you. He was found dead in his house yesterday."

He ran a hand across his bald pate. "Dead? How?"

"A scorpion crawled into his djellaba two nights ago and stung him while he dressed. He died yesterday morning."

"Was there anything suspicious about *his* death?" Perhaps Limat had summoned him to reveal a conspiracy against the Anir.

Jeka shook her head. "No, his house was locked. Just bad luck."

Bad luck for him and a wasted trip for me. "May I visit your house to wash?"

Jeka managed a smile and pulled out a large wooden key. "Go. Help yourself to teh, and I'll see you later."

Chapter Thirty-Two

Jassan navigated the short narrow streets lying between the buildings, disquieted by Jeka's revelations. Limat he mourned not at all, though he wondered what the merchant had wanted to discuss with him.

Adjatay, on the other hand, was a friend he would miss. At least he had lived long enough to see Grandmaster Linus killed, and had regained some purpose in his life by teaching Tamira.

Distracted by his thoughts and slowed by the lotus smoked earlier, Jassan realised too late that he was in trouble. Two men attacked him from an alley, one wielding a long knife, the other a curved sword. He turned to run but found a third man closing in behind him.

Even as his right hand flew down to the hilt of his sword hanging from his left hip, he knew he would be too late. Had he drawn it several heartbeats earlier and backed against a wall, he might have fended off the three thugs long enough for them to fear discovery and flee.

Instead he was moments from death, knowing even as his blade slid from its scabbard that the closest knifeman would be in striking range before he could fully draw it.

A shadow dropped down from above. Short, lithe and wrapped from head to foot in a dark robe and shesh, he landed on the closest knifeman. Both collapsed to the ground, but only the masked man rose, his knife freshly bloodied. Jassan's would-be killer feebly clutched his neck, blood pumping out.

The other two thugs attacked, outrage twisting scarred unshaven faces as their companion bled to death. Jassan met the swordsman, parrying each wild blow. Long hours of instruction from Adjatay kept him alive as he focused on defence, letting his opponent tire himself out.

Mindful of the greater fight and not wanting to catch a knife in the back if the third attacker prevailed, he circled round to ensure he could see the other fight. Knife fights were bloody affairs with few participants escaping wounds. Jassan recalled Adjatay's oft-said joke: *What do you call the fighter who dies half an hour after a knife fight?*

The victor.

Jassan's unknown saviour fought with slightly bent knees, never overreaching or losing balance. He fought left-handed, confounding an opponent used to fighting right-handed men. The thug lunged, only to find his forearm seized by the masked man's right hand while his left buried his blade in the thug's stomach.

Realising that he was now alone, the swordsman backed off, eyes wide with fear. He looked around for a possible avenue of escape, giving Jassan an opportunity to breach his guard. The last would-be killer collapsed as Jassan's blade took him in the abdomen.

"Wait–" Jassan started to say as the small man dispatched the two gut-wounded thugs without fuss. "I wanted to question one to learn who sent them," he remonstrated mildly, not wanting to sound ungrateful.

"I already know who sent them," a female voice said, muffled by the dark shesh wrapped around his – her – mouth. She started to unwrap the loose end covering her face.

"Tamira?" Jassan said stupidly as he recognised his rescuer. Inches taller than the least time he had seen her, the confident demeanour she had assumed two years previously was no longer a façade. A long cloth-wrapped object was strapped to her back.

"Jassan, well met." She cleaned her knife and sheathed it in a leather scabbard in the small of her back. Calm eyes appraised him. "Are you coming, or would you prefer to explain the bodies to the quaid's guards? I'm sure he'd love an excuse to lock you in his dungeon."

"Where to?"

"Jeka's house. That's where you were going, strolling as if you had an escort of guards." She shook her head. "Careless of you."

"How do you know I'm going to Jeka's house?" His head was spinning, not helped by his earlier lotus indulgence.

"I've been following you since you arrived and overheard

you talking to your cousin. I'll meet you there." Without a further word she disappeared up the wall, the meeting of cloth and clay making barely a whisper.

*

He soon reached Jeka's two-storey home. The wooden key and lock were as old as the village, Jeka and the previous owners having never seen any need to replace it with a newer lock and key of iron.

His hand jerked towards his sword as something landed next to him, but he relaxed on recognising Tamira. "Is the ground not good enough for you?"

"I wanted to make sure there were no more ambushes waiting ahead." Her mouth twitched. "And there's no dung on the roofs."

Jassan inserted the long, five-toothed wooden key into the lock and turned it, opening the door. Chickens and two goats were kept on the ground floor, feeding from strewn hay. Sacks of grain lay piled up against a wall. Jassan climbed worn stone steps up to the next floor where his cousin and her family lived, finding it empty as expected. Tamira followed silently, her eyes finding every corner.

Jassan boiled some water and made a small pot of teh, going easy on the mint. He vaguely recalled Tamira wasn't fond of the herb. When he joined her in the main room, she'd removed the loose robe, revealing a shendyt and tunic underneath. Still lithe, her limbs were now toned with muscle and unsoftened by fat.

They sat at a long cedar table whose wood was dry and cracked from age. Jassan placed two cups on the table and filled both with teh. There was already a bowl of dates waiting. "My thanks for your assistance. I was a dead man," he admitted, angry with himself for falling into the ambush so easily. Distracted by Jeka's news and the lotus, he supposed. Such carelessness in the desert would be tantamount to suicide.

"You're welcome." She sipped the teh. "Thank you for your hospitality." She had left the wrapped object on the table.

"Adjatay taught you well." Jassan paused. "I was sorry to hear of his death."

"It comes for us all," Tamira said. "You knew him longer, it is I who should offer condolences."

He shrugged uncomfortably. "You said you knew who sent those killers after me. Who wants me dead?"

"Limat Nisan-Anir hired them to kill you."

"Limat? But he's dead."

"He hired them before he died," Tamira said.

The lotus had mostly left him, but still his head felt dizzy. It was a tangled web and he scarcely knew where to begin. "Why does – did – he want me dead? How did you learn of it?"

Tamira sipped from her teh. "He wants you dead because you're the favourite to succeed Meddur as Chief of the Anir and Quaid of Rhemi. Padshah Thekti is happy to have Rhemi part of his province, but would rather have the quaid there tied to him by blood. He agreed to marry one of his daughters to Limat, but only if it looked likely Limat would succeed Meddur. As a show of good faith, Limat arranged your murder."

"Bastard." Jassan shook his head. "How did you learn of this?"

"I found a letter from Limat in the vizier's office," she said calmly, as if infiltrating the quaid's kasbah was a walk in the market.

"So, I'm in danger here." A more alarming worry occurred to him. "My uncle's daughter and her family live here, are they in danger?"

"I doubt it. And now that Limat is dead he won't be hiring any more assassins. I think you're safe enough, though I wouldn't linger here overlong. Thekti might have preferred Limat as quaid, but so long as he can marry a daughter to Meddur's successor, I think he'll be content."

"I've no wish to succeed my uncle," Jassan grumbled. He looked up. "It's convenient that Limat died."

Tamira took another sip of teh. "Very convenient," she answered blandly.

Jassan decided to let the matter rest there. "Jeka thinks you sailed north to Mask some days ago."

"I let everyone believe that. I even boarded the dahabiya but slipped overboard and swam to shore shortly after we left the dock. Soon Tamira will be little more than a memory here."

"There's crocodiles in the river," Jassan pointed out.

She raised both eyebrows. "I waited until we were close to the shore, and I swam very fast. I've been skulking about the village ever since, waiting for you to arrive and following you. With embarrassing ease."

Jassan ignored that last comment. "So now what?"

"With Adjatay dead, I've no reason to stay. I'll return to Mask and attend to my business there." She glanced at the cloth-wrapped object. "I also wanted to make sure you got that. Adjatay would have wanted it to go to you."

Jassan picked it up, curious as to what it might be. Not one of Tamira's carving efforts, he hoped. He unwrapped the cloth, his fingers brushing against hardened leather.

A sword. The scabbard was gently curved, and his heart quickened as the cloth fell away, revealing the glint of gold. Jassan ran fingers along the golden hilt, recognising it as the sword of Verak, taken by Adjatay from the body of the king's guard captain and later reclaimed from the Black Rose. The payment Adjatay had demanded in exchange for taking Tamira under his wing.

There was a soft sigh as he drew the blade from its black leather scabbard, Maskan iron gleaming silver. Jassan had never beheld a finer weapon. He would have to wrap the hilt in leather or forever fend off thieves and robbers, but once disguised it would replace his own age-worn blade.

"That was once the sword of Verak," Tamira said softly. "Before that it belonged to then-Prince Xarius of Mask, given to the man entrusted to protect him upon his coronation as king. It was a gift from a king, and now it is a gift from a friend."

Jassan nodded silently. He would be honoured to carry it.

Tamira rose and put her robe and shesh back on.

"Take care, Jassan of the Anir."

"Take care, Tamira. May the gods watch you kindly." He watched as she silently left Jeka's house.

Jassan ascended to the roof, gazing out across the village as

the sun dipped towards the horizon. The future might one day
see him bound to Citadel Anir by chains of responsibility and
shackles of duty but, for now, a world awaited. Caravans
recently arrived from the southern kingdoms would remain in
Pashbur for the next couple of months to rest and fatten up
their camels, all knowing that to leave now would see them
mid-desert at the height of summer. But there was other
employment a ranger might undertake, escorting smaller
caravans to Rhemi where he could await summer's end.

And then? His ambition to travel the Spice Route east was
still unrealised. He could return to Pashbur in time to sign up
with one of those great caravans.

And after that? His future for now was a blank canvas, as
trackless as the desert he knew so well. He was Kavari, and
he would live as he always had, as his ancestors had before
him; one sandaled step at a time.

Epilogue

Gojan sat in the shade and watched the girl step off the recently docked dahabiya onto Mask's stone quay. She dressed like a Kavari, wearing a blue djellaba and shesh, but she was too light-skinned to be from that tribe. No one followed her off, suggesting to the boy that she travelled alone. He shook his head. Mask was not kind to lone travellers, and she looked only a few years older than he.

She asked something of a dockworker unloading salt from the boat and paid him a coin removed from the hood hanging down her back.

His interest stirred at the sight of money, Gojan watched her leave the quay and walk towards the gates leading into the Merchant Quarter. He was torn between following her or waiting for a chance to snatch some blocks of salt.

Gojan decided to follow the girl. Maybe twelve years old, he had been a beggar for most of his life but had recently turned to stealing.

He followed her through a narrow souk leading to the main market square, decreasing the distance between them. The souks were crowded enough for him not to arouse suspicion.

Gojan took a breath and reached into her hood, snatching at the coins lying within and dropping them into a small pouch hanging from his throat. The girl span around, surprising him with her speed, but he ducked and tore off down the street.

She didn't cry out or call for help, but a glance behind told him she was in pursuit. Gojan turned a corner and scrambled up onto a low roof, running to its end before leaping onto another nearby.

He glanced back and felt his heartbeat stagger as he saw the girl still in pursuit and closing fast. She wouldn't follow him into the Poor Quarter, she couldn't be so foolish, surely?

On he ran and jumped, struggling to believe that the girl kept up so easily. He crossed into the Poor Quarter and lowered himself down into a shadowed alley. If he could just reach the street, she would attract beggars like flies to shit, letting him lose her in the crowd.

Three men stepped out of a doorway. Gojan felt a chill despite the late afternoon heat; he had entered the wrong alley. He turned, praying frantically to any god willing to listen that he could climb back up onto the roof before the they could reach him.

The girl leapt nimbly down in front of him and shook her head.

"Run!" he screamed at her. Did she not understand their peril? He looked over his shoulder and knew it was too late. They were caught.

The three men spread out, blocking the alley exit and close enough to Gojan and the girl to grab them should they try to climb.

Two of the men drew daggers, smiling unpleasantly.

The third looked the girl up and down in appreciation. "A fine gift you've brought us, little rat."

Hrek save me. He felt something warm and wet drip down his leg. "I've some coin," he pleaded. *Please let me go.*

"Hmm." The leader took Gojan's pouch but seemed more interested in the girl. Gojan was sure she must be as scared as him, but she didn't show it. Maybe she was too stupid to realise what was going on.

You should just have let me go, he thought. She would have survived a loss of coin, but she wouldn't survive the men in the alley. Unless they were slavers, in which case death would be a mercy for them both.

The girl stepped in front of the footpads. "That's my money."

The leader gave an ugly laugh and reached for her. "It's ours now, and so are–" He choked as a hand whipped into his throat and keeled over as a bare foot found his groin.

The girl – small and lithe – no longer looked quite so young. She watched the other two, alert but calm.

Gojan pressed against the wall as the robbers attacked her, faces twisted in rage. Their leader knelt on the ground, clutching his throat and abdomen.

The girl hopped to her right to avoid one blade while her hands snaked up to grab the knife arm of her second attacker.

She made an odd twisting motion and the man cried out, dropping his knife. Her left hand caught it mid-air and stabbed the man's thigh, blood spraying out at the same time as her right elbow slammed into the side of his nose.

As he was sent sprawling, the other attacker slashed at her wildly, but she slapped his hand away and buried her knife in his throat, releasing it as he fell.

Gojan stared at the carnage. The one bleeding heavily from his thigh lunged, grabbing the girl's throat with both hands from her right side. Unarmed but not visibly alarmed, she drew her right hand diagonally up in a fist before hammering it down into his groin.

He released his hold, face twisted in pain, and her right elbow slammed up into his chin. She pivoted back and faced him, stabbing rigid fingers into his throat.

He fell to the ground with a horrible wet choking sound, blood still leaking from his thigh.

The leader was no fool; still clutching his own throat, he took one look at his dead or dying men and turned, staggering down the alley.

Gojan's erstwhile victim picked up a dropped knife and weighed it a moment in her hand before throwing it at the fleeing man. He stumbled to the ground, the blade sticking out of his back. The woman walked over, pulled it free and drew it savagely across his throat.

*

Tamira wiped the blood from her hands on the dead man's orange robe and quickly searched all three corpses for whatever coin they carried. They had mistaken her for an easy victim, but she had taught them otherwise.

"Choose your victims more carefully in future," she told the terrified boy snivelling nearby. His pouch lay on the ground, so she picked it up. Preferring the pouch to her hood, she removed a coin and tossed it to the thief before tying the pouch around her neck. Besides, she planned to change into a kalasiris once back atop her ruined tower in the Poor Quarter.

She walked out of the alley, her long djellaba dirty from travel. To all outward appearances Mask had not changed in the two years since she had left, but she knew that the criminal underbelly would have new faces and new rules. She would need to learn them if she wished to survive.

Adjatay had taught her never to rely on just one place to hide in, so she intended to identify several more haunts in addition to her old one.

Tamira had felt no satisfaction, only a little sorrow at her mentor's death. But she put it behind her. Those merchant princes and Hrekist priests who paid the Black Rose to kill her family still lived, a situation she did not intend to allow to continue for long.

Her eyes had turned moist as the Red City of Mask appeared on the horizon, her first sight of it in two years. She had wondered briefly about Shukara upon stepping onto the quay. Had the mage returned to Tokombu? Did she still live? Tamira suspected she would never know.

Patience was a weapon, Adjatay had taught her. She would slip back into her old life as a thief, scrounging coin to pay for anatomy lessons from healers, buy herbs and reagents from apothecaries, and pay artificers to construct the tools and weapons detailed in Adjatay's plans. Fifteen years old, she would wait until her full growth was upon her before moving on her enemies. That gave her two or three years to learn their habits, to know them better than they knew themselves.

Tamira walked along the sun-baked streets of Mask, one pedestrian among many. The red-bricked spires of the former Royal Palace, her dispossessed home, towered over the Old Quarter.

For every year of her life save the past two, she had lived in the Red City, princess, beggar and thief. Now she returned an assassin. The rooftops would be her highway; forgotten cracks in the city, her home; the night, her domain; and murder, her currency. *I'm the last Black Rose, and my thorns are sharp indeed.*

The End

Acknowledgements

Last year saw the birth of my daughter, Sophie, a wonderful if challenging time. Firstly I'd like to thank my wife, Dana, who at times has done more than her share of the parental duties while I've been preparing this book, before and after it was accepted for publication.

Our parents have also gone above and beyond helping us, be it advice, babysitting, or transportation. So on behalf of Dana and me, I'd like to thank Christine, Shosh and Danny.

Others have helped us while adjusting to the new addition to our family, too many to mention here, but you have our thanks.

I'd also like to thank:

My family and friends for their continued support of my writing.

PR Pope for a book cover that captures the look of the setting.

The good people at Elsewhen Press for not only accepting my second novel for publication, but also for helping make it publishable.

David Craig, June 2019

Elsewhen Press

delivering outstanding new talents in speculative fiction

Visit the Elsewhen Press website at elsewhen.press for the latest
information on all of our titles, authors and events; to read our blog; find
out where to buy our books and ebooks; or to place an order.

Sign up for the Elsewhen Press InFlight Newsletter at
elsewhen.press/newsletter

Resurrection Men
The first book of the Sooty Feathers
David Craig

Glasgow 1893.
Wilton Hunt, a student, and Tam Foley, a laudanum-addicted pharmacist, are pursuing extra-curricular careers as body snatchers, or 'resurrection men', under cover of darkness. They exhume a girl's corpse, only for it to disappear while their backs are turned. Confused and in need of the money the body would have earnt them, they investigate the corpse's disappearance. They discover that bodies have started to turn up in the area with ripped-out throats and severe loss of blood, although not the one they lost. The police are being encouraged by powerful people to look the other way, and the deaths are going unreported by the press. As Hunt and Foley delve beneath the veneer of respectable society, they find themselves entangled in a dangerous underworld that is protected from scrutiny by the rich and powerful members of the elite but secretive Sooty Feathers Club.

Meanwhile, a mysterious circus arrives in the middle of the night, summoned to help avenge a betrayal two centuries old...

Resurrection Men is the first book in David Craig's *Sooty Feathers* series, a masterful gothic tale about a supernatural war for control of the Second City of the British Empire, and the struggle of flawed characters of uncertain virtue who try to avert it. It is set in a late 19th century Glasgow ruled by undead – from the private clubs, town houses and country manors of the privileged to the dung-choked wynds and overcrowded slums of the poor. Undead unrest, a fallen angel, and religious zealots intent on driving out the forces of evil, set the stage for a diabolical conflict of biblical proportions.

ISBN: 9781911409366 (epub, kindle) / ISBN: 9781911409267 (400pp paperback)
Visit bit.ly/ResurrectionMen

About David Craig

Aside from three months living on an oil tanker sailing back and forth between America and Africa, and two years living in a pub, David Craig grew up on the west coast of Scotland. He studied Software Engineering at university, but lost interest in the subject after (and admittedly prior to) graduation. He currently works as a resourcing administrator for a public service contact centre, and lives near Glasgow with his wife, daughter and two rabbits.

Being a published writer had been a life-long dream, and one that he was delighted to finally realise with his debut novel, *Resurrection Men*, the first in the *Sooty Feathers* series, published by Elsewhen Press in 2018. *Thorns of a Black Rose* is David's second novel published by Elsewhen Press.